Moses and the Dragonborn

Dianne Astle

Six World Publishing

Copyright © 2017 by **Dianne Astle**

All rights reserved. No part of this publication may be reproduced, distributed or transmitted in any form or by any means, without prior written permission.

Dianne Astle/Six Worlds Publishing
www.benthedragonborn.com

Publisher's Note: This is a work of fiction. Names, characters, places, and incidents are a product of the author's imagination. Locales and public names are sometimes used for atmospheric purposes. Any resemblance to actual people, living or dead, or to businesses, companies, events, institutions, or locales is completely coincidental.

Book Layout © 2014 BookDesignTemplates.com

Moses and the Dragonborn/ Dianne Astle. -- 1st ed.
ISBN 978-0-9921626-7-2

I dedicate this book in memory of my mother,
Viola Rabinovitz,
who taught me to stand up
for what I believe is right.

For to be free is not merely to cast off ones chains, but to live in a way that respects and enhances the freedom of others.

—NELSON MANDELA

CONTENTS

A DRAGON RIDE 9
WATCHERS JOURNAL YEAR 937 18
THE MOSES PROJECT 20
BE MY TRUE LOVE 26
THE WATCHER OF ZARGON 32
WATCHERS JOURNAL YEAR 937 39
"D" DAY ON EARTH 41
"D" DAY ON ZARGON 49
DAY ONE: FARNE 54
WATCHERS JOURNAL YEAR 937 60
THE SALT MINES 61
THE BREAKFAST OF CHAMPIONS 70
EMANCIPATION 74
WATCHERS JOURNAL YEAR 937 77
THE QUEST BEGINS 78
ZINC, THE DOWSER 81
TERMITE WORMS 84
WATCHERS JOURNAL Year 937 92
ZINC AND THE FORKED STICK 93
WATCHER'S JOURNAL YEAR 937 98
TOXIC CLOUDS 100
AN OCEAN CROSSING 105
WATCHER'S JOURNAL YEAR 937 110
UNWELCOME GUESTS 112
RE-GENESIS 118
FARLAND 124

NIGHTMARES WALK AT NIGHT	128
THE GREEN EYED DRAGON	133
TRIALS AND TRIBULATIONS	137
WATCHER'S JOURNAL YEAR 937	148
CATCHING FISH	149
HELLO TINY	158
SO WHERE IS THE KING?	161
SIGNS OF LIFE	167
A MOUSE LEADS THE WAY	170
CAPTURED	177
COLLARED	180
FAMILY REUNION	184
SLAVES	188
ZOEY	194
A VERY BAD DAY	197
SAMSON	201
A VERY VERY BAD DAY	205
TINY RETURNS	207
JEON	214
THE INVISIBLE HERO	217
SAMSON ESCAPES	224
THE KEY	227
JACHOO	231
THE RESCUE	234
PRISON BREAK	238
FIREHAVEN	244
A SECOND QUEST	248
BACK IN DANGER	253
THE ROOM OF PORTALS	257
A MIGHTY WIND	259

DAWNING OF A NEW WORLD	264
THE KING'S DECISION	269
RETURN TO ZARGON	272
RETURN TO EARTH	276

CHAPTER ONE

A DRAGON RIDE

With no moon in the sky and clouds obscuring the stars, it was the perfect night for flying without being seen. The greenish blue dragon and the dark skinned boy had waited for a cloudy night without rain, a rare occurrence on the west coast of Vancouver Island.

This was the first time the dragon had flown through the skies on Earth, and he was enjoying the flight every bit as much as his rider. Below them was the island where the two of them attended school. They'd been in the air for an hour and the dragon reluctantly made up his mind to return to the school.

"Yeah!" the boy yelled as the dragon did a nosedive toward the ocean. "This is better than a rollercoaster."

They skimmed over the waves until a grey whale breached nearby. The dragon arced around the whale before climbing toward the clouds.

"Hold on," the dragon called back, his words carried away by the wind. "I'll do another roll."

The dragon rolled to the left and soon they were flying upside down. The boy laughed. "Ben, that was so cool. Do it again."

"Once more, then we need to head back."

"So soon? Okay, but on the next moonless night I want to fly further up the coast."

"Denzel, we're not doing this again. We agreed that if I took you for a ride you would stop asking."

"That was before I knew how awesome it was," Denzel said. "I was meant to be a dragon rider."

The dragon did what dragons always do when they are angry: He breathed fire, which streaked out like lightening across the sky to light up the clouds around them.

"Cool! Do that again," Denzel yelled into the wind.

The dragon roared in response.

"Okay. Okay. You're right. I did promise, but I still hope we can do this again sometime."

Denzel knew that Ben was just as reluctant to return, even though every moment they were in the air increased the chance of getting caught by Miss Templeton.

They were racing away from the island when the unthinkable happened. There was a clap of thunder and a huge face appeared on the cloud in front of them. They knew the face well, but had never seen it angry before. Static electricity danced in the dinner-plate sized eyes that were staring straight at them. Ben's wings beat backwards as he desperately tried to keep himself from flying through Miss Templeton's face.

The huge mouth spoke. Lightening flashed with every word. Denzel and Ben did not hear actual words, they heard loud claps of thunder, but they knew what was said. Come see me! Come see me, right now! Then the face broke apart and disappeared.

When Ben turned and flew back towards the school there was smoke coming from his nostrils.

"Don't go back yet," Denzel coughed. "We can't get into any more trouble then we're already in. At the very least take the long way back to the school by flying across the Island and around the southern tip."

Ben erupted in a roar. Fire lit up the sky.

"I guess that's a no then?" Denzel asked.

The dragon remained silent, but there was still flame coming from his mouth.

"What! Are you mad at me?" Denzel asked.

Ben roared again.

"I guess, that would be a yes," Denzel said, "but let me remind you that you wanted to do this as much as I did. You weren't that hard to convince."

Ben remained silent.

"I guess you did say no the first time I asked," Denzel said.

Ben didn't speak, but more smoke and flames issued from his nostrils.

"I guess you said no more than once," Denzel said. "I'm sorry for getting you in trouble, but I'm glad we did this. It was so worth it even if we get a detention."

At the word detention, the amount of smoke and flame coming out of the dragon's snout increased.

"Don't worry," Denzel said. "I'll tell Miss Templeton it was all my fault."

The dragon never said a word, but the smoke decreased a little.

Ben landed in the same spot where they had taken off, behind the barn, out of sight of the residences and the large gray stone building known as the castle that served as a school for the students attending Fairhaven. Ben transformed and in place of the dragon stood a fifteen-year-old boy with wild brown hair and brilliant green eyes. Smoke continued to come out of Ben's nose and mouth even after his transformation back into a human.

Denzel and Ben silently turned and walked toward the castle. On the third floor, above the classrooms, they would find the Principal of Fairhaven; Earth's Watcher and the Guardian of the portals that linked Earth to other worlds.

Denzel remained uncharacteristically silent as he walked beside Ben. He thought of and discarded excuses they could give the Watcher to avoid the detention that was sure to come. He also thought of the school's secret purpose. It trained the Chosen and sent them to other worlds to do the work of the Guardian. Denzel envied Ben who had been off world twice. The first time, Ben had stopped a war between humans and mer on Lushaka and discovered he had a secret identity. The second time he'd been sent to Zargon to find his mother's family so they could teach him how to safely transform from human to dragon and back again. Without that training, Ben had been in danger of becoming something that was neither human nor dragon. Denzel wondered how long he would need to wait to be Chosen to go through one of the five portals to another world.

Denzel walked silently beside Ben past the recreational complex with its gym and swimming pool, the separate boys' and girls' dorms, and the guest and staff quarters. At three in the morning most everyone was asleep. No one saw them except for a fur-covered creature who stood approximately four and a half feet tall. Moses fell in behind them. When they arrived at the castle, Moses followed them as they climbed the stone steps leading to the large oak doors. They pushed open one of the two doors and walked down the dimly lit hallway past the classrooms to the staircase that led to Miss Templeton's office. Once they arrived on the third floor, they knocked softly on the door.

"Come in, boys," the voice on the other side said.

Ben and Denzel stepped through, and quickly closed the door behind them before Moses could follow them in.

Miss Templeton sat at her desk wearing a faded blue bathrobe. Her long gray hair hung down over her shoulders. Her narrow face was grim and lacked her usual warmth.

"Don't bother sitting down," she said. "I will hear no excuses. Ben, I told you not to transform and fly over this island. There are good reasons not to draw attention to the fact that we have a dragon living here. We do not want the citizens of this world asking about this school and our students. We don't want journalists drawn to this island because someone saw a dragon flying above it."

"It's not Ben's fault. I talked him into it," Denzel said. Ben looked at his friend with gratitude.

"I do not doubt that, Denzel Carter, but it's Ben's gift and he's responsible for the use of it. But don't worry; you will share Ben's punishment because you knew Ben was not supposed to fly. So the only thing that remains is to decide the amount of detention you will serve."

Ben and Denzel held their breath as they waited for the words that would come next.

"It is now January twenty-fifth. Your detention will last until June twenty-fifth, which coincidently is the last day of school. With exceptionally good behavior I'll make it April twenty-fifth."

"What?" Denzel burst out, his heart sinking at the thought of six months of cleaning the kitchen and washing pots and pans.

"You don't think the detention is fair?" Miss Templeton asked, anger flashing in her eyes.

"Uh…uh…," Denzel began.

"What about you, Ben Taylor? Do you think it's fair?"

"It's fair," Ben replied quickly. "We're sorry for disobeying your direct order and it won't happen again."

Denzel stared at his friend in astonishment. Why wasn't he standing up for them? Then it struck him that Miss Templeton had the power to expel them from Fairhaven. Maybe Ben believed there was a chance that could happen. Actually Ben wouldn't be, there would be a problem with letting a dragonborn loose on the world.

Miss Templeton looked at Denzel. "What about you?" She spoke quietly, but with steel in her voice.

"I'm sorry too," Denzel choked out, but did not say a word about not doing it again.

Miss Templeton's face softened. "I suppose since you're here, we may as well test you both again."

She picked up the medallion sitting on her desk.

Ben stepped toward Miss Templeton, who laid her medallion on his outstretched hand. The medallion opened up to reveal dials for the day, month, and year, but the dials did not spin around as they normally did. The three pointers went directly to the same spot they had gone to the last time Ben was tested.

Miss Templeton dropped the medallion with a sigh. "It looks like you are still scheduled to go to Farne on the first day of the fifth month this year. I was hoping there was a mistake. It's not a world I feel comfortable sending you to. Your turn, Denzel, let's see if the Guardian still thinks you're a good candidate to be a Chosen." Miss Templeton emphasized the words 'good candidate' making it clear she had her doubts.

Denzel held his breath as Miss Templeton placed her medallion on his shaking hand. He didn't know what he would do if the dials refused to move. The only good news was the heartbreak would only last as long as it took Miss Templeton to wipe his memory clean.

As the needles started to spin, he released his breath and grinned. When they stopped, one needle pointed to the first day, another to the fifth month, while the last one pointed to the current year.

"Awesome. I'm going with Ben to Farne," Denzel said, punching the air with his fist.

"Not so fast," Miss Templeton said. "You could be going to a different world on the same day."

The principal closed her hand around the medallion and then laid it on Denzel's palm again. The medallion opened up for a second time, but this time it was changed. The dials with days, months and years were gone, and in their place was a single compass with six points on the circle. The dial went around and around before coming to a stop.

Denzel looked expectantly at Miss Templeton, waiting for her to tell him what it meant. She frowned as she stared at the dial.

"Apparently, you are going to the same world as Ben. You will be among the first Chosen that world has had in almost one thousand years, ever since their war to end all wars. For a long time they didn't even have a Watcher. Then a dragonborn who failed to make the transformation was sent."

"I heard about the Watcher of Farne when I was on Zargon. Zachery Zaltzburg is his name and he is the brother of an ancestor of mine," Ben said. "If he had stayed on Zargon he would have had a terrible life. The dragonborn are nasty to those who fail to make the transformation."

"I doubt his life on Farne has been much better," Miss Templeton said. "There is very little alive on that world."

"So he's your grandfather's brother?" Denzel asked.

"More like my grandfather's great-grandfathers great-grandfather's brother," Ben said.

"What!" Denzel exclaimed.

"Watchers live a long time," Miss Templeton told him. "I myself have been alive for close to a thousand years."

A look of shock appeared on Denzel's face, while Ben thought of Mack, the boy who had been his roommate for a short time last fall, but was now the Watcher of Zargon. Mack had been a strange boy, who knew Ben's secret without being told. He knew Ben was dragonborn and had tricked Miss Templeton so he could go through the portal with Ben.

"I wonder," Miss Templeton continued, "if Zachery knows that three Chosen are coming from Earth? After centuries of no arrivals he may have given up hope."

At those words the door burst open and Moses barged in. "Four," he said. "Moses go too."

"Hello Moses, I wondered how long you would stand outside my door listening to our conversation. Has no one told you that it is impolite to eavesdrop?" Miss Templeton asked sternly.

"I go where Allie go," Moses said, ignoring Miss Templeton's question.

"Yes Moses, but you are from Zargon." Miss Templeton frowned at the creature she had named Moses less than three months ago. "I wasn't counting the Zargonians."

"Zargon not good to brownies. Earth be Moses home now. I be given own name here," Moses said.

"I'm not sure you can choose your own world." Miss Templeton put the pendant she'd been holding back down on the desk. "The rules dictate that the Chosen return to their home world when a quest is over. Their home world is the world they were born on. The only exception to that rule is Ben's mother, who now calls Earth home because I requested special permission so she can live with her husband and Ben."

"Moses need special permission. Earth Moses home. I stay Allie," Moses said stubbornly.

"We'll see, but I wouldn't count on it." Miss Templeton words were accompanied by a shake of her head. "I plan to send you back to Zargon when you return from Farne. If the wrong eyes see you here, there will be too many questions asked about who and what you are."

"I be more careful," Moses promised.

"So who all is going to Farne?" Denzel asked.

"There is a larger group than normal going. From Earth it is you, Ben, and Allison."

"And Moses. Moses from Earth."

Miss Templeton frowned at the brownie. "From Zargon, the Guardian has chosen Moses, and Ben's uncle Zinc. I doubt there will be more Chosen selected, but can't say for sure there won't be."

"So the Guardian is sending an old man to look after us?" Denzel asked.

Ben rolled his eyes. "My uncle Zinc is the same age we are, and trust me, we'll be looking after him."

"The Guardian had a good reason for choosing Zinc and you would be wise to remember that, Benjamin," Miss Templeton said. "I myself would feel better if a graduate was going, rather than four students and a brownie. However, as always, I will trust the Guardian and send those who've been chosen."

"How are we going to find time to research Farne when we have to report to the kitchen every day for detention?" Denzel asked.

A faint smile crossed Miss Templeton face. "When you're not peeling potatoes and washing pots and pans, I expect you to read every book you can find pertaining to Farne. To help you do that, I'll give you weekends free of detention. The information you'll find will mostly be from the time before the war, as no one has come or gone from Earth to Farne since then. For now, I suggest you get some sleep in the few short hours that remain. Your detention starts tomorrow and you will need to be up an hour earlier than normal."

CHAPTER TWO

WATCHERS JOURNAL, YEAR 937

Another day is over. It was the same as every other day on this blighted world. Nothing happened. Nothing ever happens. I'm a Watcher with no Chosen to train and no portals to guard. How many years have passed since the last Chosen came to Farne? Better to ask how many centuries. It's no wonder that I'm half mad. Maybe more than half. No wonder I let the demon out of Sheol just to have someone to talk to. I knew it was a mistake even before I did it, and yet I might do it again, if things continue on the way they have.

At least, if I let another demon out, it won't be able to find a way off this world. There is only one gateway left. If one gateway on its own worked, I would use it to escape, and the Guardian could find someone else to be alone on this world.

The moment I stepped through the gateway, I would likely turn into a pile of ash and blow away in the wind. Zargonians do not normally live eight hundred and fifty-seven years, but what good is an exceptionally long life when there has been so little joy in it?

What a fool I am to write these things down, but what does it matter? By the time you read it, whoever you are, I will be dead.

If you are the next Watcher, then maybe my words will help you as you struggle with unremitting boredom and utter loneliness.

When you write in this journal, I hope there is more to say than I have recorded year after year. For hundreds of years the only thing I have ever written are the words: Today was just the same as yesterday. Nothing happened.

But today—was not the same as every other day. On this day, I confessed my sin as a Watcher to you, whoever you are. Tomorrow, I will probably tear this page out of the journal and you will wonder what was written on it.

CHAPTER THREE

THE MOSES PROJECT

Moses sat on a tree branch and looked through a third-story window into the dorm room with its two beds. He wanted to talk with his friend Allison, but couldn't do it as long as her roommate was there.

Moses could hear Crystal through the open window going on and on about her favorite subject — boys.

"Trevor is still interested in being your boyfriend, you know," Crystal said.

"Yes, I know. He's told me several times and so have you." Allison's voice betrayed her exasperation.

Crystal ignored it. "I don't know why you would choose Ben over Trevor. Ben's such a dork. I don't know what he did, but he's had detention almost every day for over two weeks along with that friend of his. They must have done something really stupid, but no one I ask knows what they did."

Allison frowned. "Ben is not my boyfriend. We are just very good friends."

Moses smiled. He didn't want Allison to have a boyfriend.

"And he's not a dork. There's more to Ben than you know."

Moses could tell Allison about Ben and Denzel's detention if her roommate would only leave.

"Trevor's so cool and he's really crazy about you. I really, really think you need to give him another chance."

Allison rolled her eyes. "Don't you ever give up?"

"No, not when people I care about are making a huge mistake."

"Fine, I'll give Trevor another chance. At least long enough for you to make a play for Daniel," Allison said. "I'll do it if you promise to let it drop, if it doesn't work out."

"Great. We can sit with Trevor and Daniel for breakfast tomorrow," Crystal squealed.

"And we'll be double dating by supper time," Allison added dryly.

"Awesome-" Crystal began. She was about to say more, but Allison smacked her with a pillow.

Crystal picked up her own pillow and was about to smack Allison when Moses darted in and made a face at her behind Allison's back.

"Eeek!" Crystal screamed dropping her pillow. "There's…there's something out there."

"What?" Allison asked. Moses grinned and quickly slipped around to the other side of the tree. Allison would now know that he was outside the window waiting for her. She would tell her roommate to go away so they could talk.

"Did you see it?" Crystal asked, her voice high-pitched.

Allison stared out the window. "What exactly did you see?"

"A face. Kinda human, but more like an ugly ape. Didn't you see it?"

Moses stopped grinning. "Moses not ugly ape. Moses be brownie, you stupid girl," he whispered.

"I saw something," Allison said, "but I can't say what it was. But I'm sure that whatever it is shouldn't be hanging around outside our window. In fact, if there is something out there it should go away right now." Allison stressed the words 'go away right now' as she glared out the window with a disapproving look on her face.

Moses sat back and waited. He kept whispering, "Go, go, go now," as if he could telepathically plant the idea into Crystal's brain that she had somewhere else to be. Finally, when Allison's back was turned he moved close to the window again, and when Crystal saw him, he crossed his eyes and showed all of his teeth.

"Yikes!" Crystal hollered. "It's back again."

Moses drew back under a canopy of leaves. Behind Crystal's back, Allison glared out the window, wagged her finger, and emphatically shook her head. Moses knew he was in trouble with his friend. Allison would likely give him another lecture on how important it was that his presence on earth be kept secret.

"It's the same thing I saw before, except this time it was threatening me. It showed all its teeth. I don't know what it is, or why it's looking into our window, but I don't like it. We need to make sure that Miss Templeton knows so something can be done. It's not safe to let it hang around our school."

"I'll be seeing Miss Templeton tomorrow," Allison said. "I'll be sure to tell her you believe there's something outside our third story window making faces at you." There was a skeptical tone in Allison's voice that made Moses chuckle.

"Wait," Crystal said. "She won't believe it. She'll think I'm a ditz. Please don't say anything to her."

"That's probably for the best," Allison said.

"I just hope whatever it is, goes away."

"Me too." Allison said loudly as she stared out the window with a look that made Moses' heart sink. There was no point in trying to talk to her tonight. Allison was in no mood to listen to anything he had to say.

"Not ugly," Moses muttered quietly. Then more loudly, "Moses be handsome brownie."

"Did you hear that?" Crystal asked.

"I can't say that I did," Allison said.

"It sounds like talking outside the window, but I'm sure whatever that was can't talk."

"No it can't," Allison said and walked over to the window and slammed it shut. She then closed the blinds so that Moses could no longer look in.

Moses ground his teeth and clenched his hands. He thought briefly about banging on the window and telling Allison he was sorry, but decided it might be wiser to talk to Ben instead. Moses climbed down the tree and hid behind it watching for students. When he made sure it was clear, he left the safety of the tree and ran as quickly as he could to hide in a bush behind the boy's dorm. There was no convenient tree growing outside Ben and Denzel's window, but their room was on the backside of the building where it was unlikely anyone would be walking at night. He waited until there were no students returning from the castle before running around to the other side of the building. A light was on in the boy's room so he threw a small rock at the window. It opened and a rope was thrown down. Moses climbed the rope, careful to keep from crossing in front of the window below Ben and Denzel's room. When Moses climbed through the window he discovered that only Denzel was there.

"Where Ben?" Moses asked.

"In the castle," Denzel said. "Miss Templeton is letting him look at the diary of past Watchers to see if there is anything to be learned about Farne that can help us."

"Why you not with Ben?"

"Ben and I haven't been getting along so well since I talked him into taking me for a dragon ride."

"Dragonborn need transform. Should not be forbidden."

Denzel smiled at Moses, "I always did like you. And it's not just because you happen to have the same name as my favorite uncle."

"What?" Moses frowned. "Someone else name Moses? Moses be my name."

"Lots of people have had the name Moses; just like lots of people have the name Ben."

"Oh…" Moses said, disappointed.

"You share a name with some great people who were important in the fight against slavery."

"There be slaves on Earth? There be brownies here?"

"There are no brownies on Earth but you. Nowadays, a slave can look like any student at Fairhaven, but people used to think anyone with dark skin should be a slave. My ancestors were brought to North America to work as slaves."

"Carters still slaves?"

"None that I know of. Slavery has been banned in the United States."

"How 'bout Canada?"

"It's banned here too. My parents are part of something called 'The Moses Project.'"

"What be Moses Project?"

"My parents and some of their friends work together to help people who are still slaves. People think slavery has ended, but there are millions of slaves around the world. My parents want to put an end to slavery wherever it exists."

"Denzel's parents good. Why name Moses Project?"

"Moses was the name of an ancient liberator of slaves. Would you like me to read you the story of how a man named Moses led slaves to freedom?"

"Moses listen." Moses sat down on Ben's bed, pulled his feet up, crossed his ankles, and leaned his elbows on his knees. Denzel pulled out the bible his father had given him from the bedside table and read the story of Moses and the children of Israel.

"Moses love story. Read again."

"Not tonight, but come back and I'll tell you another story of a famous person named Moses who helped free slaves."

"Brownies be slaves. Brownies need promised land. Earth good place. I stay here. Maybe other brownies come. Earth be their promised land."

CHAPTER FOUR

BE MY TRUE LOVE

The next morning, Ben got his toast and rolled oats and sat across from Denzel. He left an empty seat beside him for Allison.

"I beat Allie for a change," he said to Denzel. "She's usually here by now."

"She's already here," Denzel grimaced.

Ben stared at his friend, puzzled. Denzel nodded his head to the right where Allison was sitting beside Crystal across from her former boyfriend. Ben's heart sank as he watched Allison laughing at something Trevor said.

Ben's friend, Mack, who was now the Watcher of Zargon, had predicted that Allison would break up with Trevor before Christmas and she had, but Mack hadn't foreseen that the breakup would be short lived.

Ben felt dragonfire come to life in his stomach. He stood quickly and walked over to the cold-water dispenser. He filled a glass and took a drink. When the glass was empty he filled it again.

Ben was on his way back to the table when he heard Allison laugh. He stopped where he was and looked toward her. Her eyes met his and she sent him a warm and inviting smile. Trevor Robson's eyes followed her gaze and he scowled at Ben. Then he turned to his friends and said something that made them all look at Ben and laugh.

All except for Allison, who turned and frowned at Trevor. Once again, the heat of dragonfire rose up from deep within Ben. Wisps of smoke were already coming from his nose. To hide the smoke and cool the fire Ben took a drink of cold water as he continued walking towards Denzel. When he put the glass down the water was hot and steam rose from it.

Ben sat down with his back toward Allison. Every once in a while he heard laughter from behind him. He couldn't get over the feeling they were laughing at him. Dragonfire pushed to the surface once more. He forced the fire down and ate quickly. As soon as his food was gone Ben left. When he was out of sight and no one was around he released the dragonfire, scorching the concrete wall in front of him.

At lunchtime Allison made a point of coming up to where Ben stood in line.

"Why don't you come and sit with me?" Allison put her hand on Ben's arm.

"Are you going to sit with Trevor?" Ben asked.

Allison gave a brief nod.

"I won't sit with you then," Ben said.

"Why not?"

Ben didn't reply right away. They had reached the food and he filled his plate before speaking. "Trevor doesn't like me and I think he's a class "A" jerk. It's better that I stay away from him. I'd rather not risk doing this to him." Ben held up a burnt french-fry in his hand.

Allison gave Ben and the french-fry a look of disgust. "Suit yourself." She turned and went back to where she'd been standing in line with Crystal. As Ben watched Allison walk away he made up his mind to talk to her about the way he felt.

Later that day, Ben went to the section of the library forbidden to any student who did not know the true purpose of the school. In this section were books about the off-world experiences of the Chosen who had gone through portals to one of the other five worlds. There were also shelves of books that told the story of Chosen who had come to earth from other worlds to do the work of the Guardian. Not every story was in the library, but a quest was written up when it was thought to be unique, so students could read about the experiences of others before they went through the portal themselves. Graduates came back to the school to do research if they were going to a world they had never been to before.

Ben found Allison with a book in her hand, in the stacks dedicated to the world of Farne. He stood for a moment and watched her read. She showed no sign of being aware of his presence until he cleared his throat.

Allison looked up and smiled. "Hi Ben, have you come to do research for our trip?"

"Yeah, sure." Ben picked up a book, although doing research was the furthest thing from his mind.

"Allison…" he began and then stopped, unsure of what to say next.

She looked up from the book she was reading. "Yes?" Allison said when the silence stretched on.

Ben could feel his heart beating and his ears getting red. Earlier he'd come up with some clever things to say, but none of them seemed right for this moment in time. He desperately cast about for something to say, but nothing was coming to him. "Have you learned anything new?" he finally asked.

"The Watcher on Earth at the time of Farne's great war added an addendum to an encyclopedia which says that a Chosen from Earth at the time never returned," Allison said. "Contact with the Watcher of that world was lost. Earth's Watcher, Toshihiro Suzuki, was expecting the Chosen to return that day. When Suzuki asked the Guardian about it, the Guardian said the school on Farne was no more. The Watcher was dead and the Chosen were all dead. The Guardian told Suzuki the world of Farne would be in mourning until the time of Re-genesis."

"I wonder what the Guardian meant by that?" Ben asked. "Do you have any idea?"

"No, but I imagine it has something to do with the renewal of life."

"Allison…" Ben began, and then paused.

Allison stopped reading and looked at Ben. "Yes?" she said when he remained silent.

"Allison, I…" Ben started again. The words that he wanted to say would not come. He was afraid. Once they were out, they couldn't be taken back. If he asked Allison to be his girlfriend everything was going to change. For a long time he hadn't been able to talk to her at all. He had felt so shy around this girl he liked. He was afraid of losing the easy friendship they enjoyed following the time they spent together on Zargon.

"Yes?" Allison prompted. "Look Ben, I know you have something to say. Just say it."

"What is it with you and Trevor? Is he your boyfriend again or what?" Ben finally blurted out.

"Maybe," Allison replied.

"But he's not right for you!" Ben said more loudly than he intended. He didn't want other people listening in on their conversation.

"I think I'm the best judge of that," Allison sounded annoyed.

"Allison…I…I…" Ben started. It was so hard to get his words out.

This time Allison did not wait for him to finish speaking. "Whether or not Trevor is my boyfriend is my business."

"He's not the one. I…I…I… love you," Ben said and threw his arms around Allison and drew her close for a kiss.

Ben had never kissed a girl before and was unsure of how it was done. His kiss was awkward. Not only that, but he was kissing a girl who did not wish to be kissed in the aisle of a library where he didn't want to be seen by others.

The kiss did not turn out the way Ben hoped. Allison braced her hands against his chest and pushed back. Ben was shocked at her reaction and let go of her. Allison fell back, hit the bookshelf, and ended up sitting on the floor. Books fell off the shelf and hit her on the head. Ben tried to help her up, but Allison yelled, "Go away and leave me alone," just as another book fell off the shelf and struck her on the shoulder.

Ben did what he was told. He ran out of the library, down the steps and out of the castle. Instead of going back to his dorm room he went to the barn and saddled his favorite horse. He liked to ride when there were things on his mind he wanted to think about. Ben thought about the kiss, about how soft and wonderful Allison's lips felt and about the jolt of electricity that ran through him when their lips touched. And he thought of how he and Allison would never have the same easy friendship again. He was sorry about the loss of their friendship, but not enough to regret that their lips had touched.

In the following weeks, Ben did as Allison asked and left her alone. Well, as alone as possible when they were in all the same classes in a very small school. Anytime Allison looked in his direction, his ears turned red. He was afraid she was comparing his kiss to a kiss from Trevor; afraid she had told her friends and they were all laughing at him. Part of him regretted kissing Allison, and another part wished he could go back in time and do it all over again.

"What's with you and Allison?" Denzel asked one day.

"She thinks I'm a jerk," Ben said.

"Well, yeah, you are, but she's always been your friend anyway." Denzel gave Ben a little punch on the arm. "What did you do?"

"Nothing, really."

"Come on, Ben. Tell me what happened. I'm your friend."

"Okay, I tried to kiss her."

"So what's the problem?"

"She didn't want to be kissed."

"Ben, buddy, that's brutal. My heart bleeds for you, but I gotta tell you, you were a jerk. Never kiss a girl unless you're sure she wants to be kissed and you're sure that she wants you to be the one to kiss her."

"Yeah, I know. At least we were friends before. Now we're nothing."

"Okay. This is going to make our trip to Farne extra interesting. You're not going to be able to avoid talking to each other when we go through the portal."

Ben punched Denzel in the arm. "We'll just have to use you as our go-between."

"Not a chance," Denzel said, punching Ben's arm in return.

CHAPTER FIVE

THE WATCHER OF ZARGON

Mack sat with his elbows on the desk, his head resting on his clasped hands. He opened his green eyes and looked at the door. In a moment there was going to be a knock on it. Mack's weary eyes had been a pale blue less than three months ago on his home world of Earth. He had come to Zargon uninvited just when this world's Watcher was dying. With no other suitable candidate, Morton chose Mack to be his successor. In the short period of time since then Mack had been transformed from a frightened child who didn't understand why he was so different from everyone else, into one of the Guardian's Six Watchers.

He had always been an unusual child who'd known people's secrets without being told. Mack's uncanny ability to just know had made him distinctly unpopular with his mother's many boyfriends. He felt a twinge of regret when he thought of his mother. He would likely never see her again. Watchers did not often leave the world placed in their care.

Since coming to this world Mack had been given power, as well as the memories and accumulated knowledge acquired by every previous Watcher that had been Zargon's link to the Guardian of the Six Worlds. There were days when the power he'd been given and the knowledge of previous Watcher's did not seem like enough to guide the people of Zargon. The dragonborn were a challenging race. One of his greatest challenges stood just outside his door and was about to knock.

Mack sighed and said, "Come in," a fraction of a second before the knuckles rapped. The door flung open and Zinc Zaltzburg, Prince of Zargon strode in and flung himself in the chair across from Mack without waiting for an invitation. Zinc slouched in the chair and glared at Mack.

"What did you want to see me about this time?" Zinc asked, wisps of smoke coming forth from his mouth.

"Two things; the first is about Farne. Others have been chosen to go with you."

At first Zinc looked pleased, then a look of guarded suspicion settled onto his face. "Who's been chosen? Do I know them?"

"Most of them, except for Denzel Carter."

"What World is he from?"

"Earth. He's a friend of Ben Taylor, who's also going."

"Give me a break." Zinc slammed his open palm down on the desk. "Not Ben. He'll just get in my way."

"The Guardian has good reasons for choosing Ben. For one thing he has experience. It will be his third time off-world and it will be your first."

"Anyone else?"

"Allison Sims and the brownie who went to Earth to learn to be a healer are also going."

"Allison is a good choice; but a brownie?" Zinc asked with disdain. "Has a brownie ever been selected before?"

"No, this is the first time a brownie will go through a portal as a Chosen."

"I hardly think the brownie is a Chosen. Perhaps the Guardian was thinking of the brownie as a servant for me. As a Prince, I normally have servants who go with me when I travel. Yes, there's no doubt, the brownie is coming to be my servant."

"The brownie is not going to Farne to be your servant. Moses is a healer and is being trained by Allison. He has been in the very presence of the Guardian of the Six Worlds, which is more than you or any of the other Chosen on Zargon can say."

Zinc didn't say anything, but the scowl on his face and the smoke coming from his nostrils spoke volumes. Mack knew he didn't like the fact that a brownie and not a Prince had been with the Guardian in the place beyond time and space.

"Is there anyone else coming to help me rescue my father?" Zinc asked.

"I wouldn't think of the others as helping you. Those who go with you are your equals and you will need to put aside your differences and work in partnership with them. No one will be there to serve you, but you will have your best chance of success if you serve one another."

"Uh-huh," Zinc frowned as he flicked a piece of lint off the sleeve of his jacket.

"Yesterday, another person was chosen from Zargon."

"Good," Zinc said. "At least there will be one person I can work with."

Mack shook his head. "You'll need to be able to work with everyone."

"So who is the other person from Zargon?"

"Zoey Zanderson was chosen to go to Farne with you."

"What? This just keeps getting worse and worse. I can't imagine anyone less suited. Zoey is pig-headed and can't keep her opinions to herself. She doesn't think before she speaks. She doesn't know her proper place. She…"

"What do you mean she doesn't know her proper place?" Mack interrupted.

"She is from one of the least important clans and yet she dares to judge a Zaltzburg Prince." Zinc sat up straight and tall and glared at Mack.

"I understand that your teachers have had to intervene in disputes between yourself and Zoey more than once. Is that because you feel she doesn't know her place?"

Zinc stared at Mack in silence for a minute, before dropping his eyes and shaking his head. "She tells lies about me to the other Chosen."

"Why would she do that?"

Zinc pressed his lips together and stared at the door. Then he fidgeted in his chair and brushed more lint off his jacket. Mack waited in silence.

"Who knows why girls like her do anything," Zinc sneered. Then he sighed and spoke in a voice little louder than a whisper. "She calls me a traitor."

"She knows what you did then?" Mack said.

Zinc had a bleak look in his eyes and his face was grim as he wrapped his arms around himself to keep his hands from shaking. Moisture gathered in the corner of his eyes as he gave a brief nod.

"I see. You were never going to be able to keep it secret. What you need to do now is make sure people have something else to remember you for."

"They will remember me as the Prince who rescued his father and restored him to the throne," Zinc said, his voice getting louder with each word spoken. "I will…"

"I hope so," Mack interrupted. "But there is another matter to discuss. Your teachers continue to complain that you are not applying yourself. Just this morning the Physical Education teacher sent a note asking me to speak with you about your refusal to try rope climbing and rappelling down the side of the mountain in your human form. What's the problem? Are you afraid?"

"I'm not afraid of anything!" Smoke came from Zinc's mouth with each word spoken. "I just don't understand why you teach something so useless. It might be worthwhile on Earth, but if a dragonborn wants to go up or down a mountain we transform and fly."

Mack stared at the older boy and fought against a desire to wipe the sneer off his face. "On another world you could easily be in a situation where you are not able to transform because being seen doing so would cause your mission to fail," he finally said quietly.

"I can't imagine a situation like that and I'm not going to expend energy learning something that I'll never need."

"Alright, then it's time for you to leave Stonehaven since you clearly won't learn what we have to teach."

"I am learning what I need to. Besides, it's not your decision to make, I've been chosen by the Guardian." A smug smile appeared on Zinc's face.

"Yes, you've been chosen and I cannot alter that choice no matter how much I might wish to," Mack said wearily. "But as this world's Watcher and the Principal of Stonehaven, I can decide who will be a student here."

"You can't force a Prince of Zargon to leave this school," Zinc sneered.

"I can and I will," Mack said quietly.

"You have no power over me. I'm a dragonborn Prince and you're only an Earthling boy."

"Perhaps, but I've been given the gifts and power of a Watcher by the Guardian of the Six Worlds."

Mack's eyes flared with a brilliant green light. Zinc closed his eyes against the brightness.

"Since you are not willing to learn what we have to teach, you can leave this school and come back on the day of your departure," Mack said as the flare died down. "I will not have you here refusing to learn from Stonehaven's teachers."

"Where am I to go?" Zinc asked.

"That's up to you, but I imagine you might go live with your mother at her brother's house or with your sister, the Queen, or with a friend of the family."

"I don't like my half-sister, who will only be Queen for a short time. When I return from Farne my father will be the King again."

"Perhaps," Mack said.

"There are good reasons for me not to live with my mother and her brother," Zinc looked sideways at the door as if afraid of being overheard. "They want to replace Zanderella with me. If their scheme is successful, I will sit on the throne, but they will see me as their puppet. I don't want that and neither do you."

Mack looked at Zinc with approval for the first time. "Good," he said, "but you must still leave this school if you're not willing to apply yourself. Is there a friend or other family you can stay with?"

"No. My family is either angry with me for betraying my father, or wants to use me to take the throne away from Zanderella."

"I will find a place for you to go then. You need to be ready to leave here tomorrow at noon. If you want to be part of the team that rescues your father, then I expect you to return to Stonehaven on the first day of the fifth month."

"I don't want to leave! I refuse!" A great cloud of smoke issued from Zinc's mouth as he spoke. Smoke and anger go together for the dragonborn, but Mack also suspected that Zinc was trying to intimidate him with his ability to breathe fire.

"You have no choice, and do not doubt for a moment that I have the power to remove you from this school." Sparks crackled from Mack's fingertips and his eyes flared once again with a brilliant green light.

At first Zinc looked like he was going to call forth dragonfire and attack Mack, but then his shoulders slumped, and he unclenched his fists, and took a few deep breaths. "What can I do to change your mind? I want to stay at Stonehaven," Zinc finally said in a shaky voice.

"I will let you stay if you go to each of your teachers and apologize for your behavior and make a promise to learn every skill they are trying to teach you. I want you to become a model student. I also want you to do your best to get along with Zoey who has been chosen by the Guardian even though you consider her clan to be unimportant. I don't want to hear another word of complaint about your behavior from any of your teachers. If I do, you will be expelled."

Zinc sat in stunned silence and for a moment Mack thought he was going to refuse. Then Zinc gave a brief nod and without another word got up and left Mack's office, slamming the door shut on his way out.

When Zinc was gone, Mack sat back and closed his eyes. When he opened them again they had returned to their normal green, but looked wearier than they did before his encounter with Zinc. His left eyelid had a slight tic it didn't have before. He sat in his chair looking more like the frightened boy he had been when he came to Zargon, and thought about Zoey Zanderson's words when she had been told that the other person going to Farne from Zargon was Zinc. She almost refused outright, until Mack told her that it would greatly diminish her chances of being selected in the future, if she refused to answer a call simply because she disliked the other person chosen. In the end Zoey had assured Mack that she would find a way to work with Zinc.

Mack thought about his friend Ben Taylor and smiled. Ben had tried to help him with the rock climbing and rappelling lesson, but it had not gone well. Mack had been too frightened to climb high enough to rappel down. The teachers at Fairhaven had decided not to press him for they were certain he would never be selected by the Guardian to be a Chosen. None of them would have guessed he would soon be a Watcher on Zargon.

Ben was going to have his hands full with Zinc and Zoey along, both of them had a double dose of dragonborn arrogance, but Ben had been in difficult situations before. At least Allison and Denzel would be there for him. Mack wondered whether Ben had told Allison how he felt about her yet.

CHAPTER SIX

WATCHERS JOURNAL YEAR 937

I can't believe it. After all these years Chosen are coming to Farne. Not just one or two, but six are coming from two different worlds, including my home world of Zargon. One is a Zaltzburg, like me. I wonder if he will be half-mad. No, of course not. I wasn't born mad, was I? I don't think so.

My link with the Guardian is not as strong as it should be, so maybe I misunderstood the message, but I think one of the Chosen is a brownie.

I stopped expecting and hoping Chosen would come a long time ago. I even stopped listening for the Guardian's voice. For centuries all I ever heard was, "Peace, I am with you, do not be afraid." After a while those words hold no meaning. I even started to resent them. Words are cheap. It is action that counts.

You are shocked that I would dare to judge the Guardian. I tell you centuries of disappointment can do that to you.

I've learned to hate this world. It's been a long time since I've sent my mind out to find out what is happening on it. All I ever encountered was blight, death, and despair. If I had a second gateway I would have left a long time ago.

I wonder why the Chosen are coming? What can they do on this forsaken world? I don't really care, I'm just glad they are. And you know what? Once they're here, they're here forever. I'm not planning to help them get back to their own worlds.

You say the Guardian will replace me if I don't do the job a Watcher is supposed to do. I don't care; even death is better than continuing to live on this world alone.

I wonder what games they'll know? It doesn't matter, I can teach them.

What I fear most is that the only Chosen coming exist in my imagination.

CHAPTER SEVEN

"D" DAY ON EARTH

Ben lay awake in the dark thinking about what was going to happen in the morning. He desperately wanted to fall asleep, but his muscles stayed tense and ready for action. In the bed next to him Denzel was finally sound asleep. Denzel had kept him awake far into the night asking questions about what it was like to go through a portal. Ben silently cursed Denzel for his sleepless state. Perhaps, without all the questions he would have fallen asleep a long time ago.

"You close your eyes and walk towards a brick wall. When you open them again you are in another world and there is water beneath your feet," Ben had told Denzel for what seemed like a hundred times. "After that, every experience will be different."

Now that Denzel had finally fallen asleep, Ben lay awake, thinking about making this trip with Allison. They hadn't talked to one another since the day he tried to kiss her. Was she still mad at him? Would she talk to him when they went through the portal? Was there anything he could do to change the way she felt about him?

The sun was just starting to rise when Ben finally fell asleep. He woke up to Denzel shaking him awake. "You slept through the alarm. If you sleep any longer you'll miss breakfast."

Ben jumped out of bed, dressed in a hurry and went to the dining hall where he got some rolled oats and toast on a tray and stood looking around for Allison, but she had already come and gone.

After breakfast, Ben and Denzel went back to their room to get the backpacks they would take to Farne with them. As they returned to the castle, the people who knew they were going off world quietly wished them luck. When they got to Miss Templeton's office, Allison and Moses were already sitting in chairs across the desk from the Principal.

Miss Templeton held a teapot and on the desk were five cups and a plate of muffins. Ben and Denzel each took a chair from the stack against the wall. They sat on either side of the desk. Miss Templeton poured the tea and passed the muffins around. No one sat on the Principal's special metal chair with its Celtic knots that looked like it belonged in a throne room.

"Ben, you look tired. Didn't you sleep last night?" Miss Templeton asked.

Ben glanced at Allison as he shrugged his shoulders. She also appeared tired. He guessed that she too had trouble sleeping the night before. Allison looked up and their eyes met briefly, until she frowned and turned her eyes away. Miss Templeton looked from Ben to Allison with a puzzled expression on her face. Then her face cleared and she sat back and breathed a quiet "Oh dear."

"So is everyone ready to go through the portal today?" Miss Templeton asked looking intently from Allison to Ben and back again.

"Awesome! Can't wait!" Denzel jumped in.

"And you, Allison, are you ready?" Miss Templeton looked directly into Allison's eyes.

"Yes," Allison smiled. "I'm ready. It's great to know that this time I've been chosen, and it's not just because I touched someone at the wrong time."

"I think the events that transpired, when you went to Zargon, proved that what we thought was bad timing was actually perfect," Miss Templeton said.

Allison nodded her head in agreement.

"Moses be Chosen," the brownie said. "I go with Allie. I be happy."

Miss Templeton turned towards Ben. "And you, Ben, are you ready to go with the others?"

Ben looked at Miss Templeton and could see the concern on her face. "I'm ready," he mumbled.

"As I've already told you, Farne is a world of unknown dangers." Miss Templeton paused to take a sip of tea from her cup. "No Chosen has gone there since a war nearly destroyed that world more than a thousand years ago. I do not know what dangers you will face. If there is anything still living it may have been dramatically altered from what it was. You will need to depend on one another and upon the Chosen who are coming from Zargon if you hope to survive." Miss Templeton paused and stared at Ben and then Allison. "Your lives depend on the trust that you have for one another. If there is anything that will interfere with your working together, now is the time to speak of it."

Ben stared at Allison. She glanced at him and looked away.

"Don't worry, Miss Templeton," Allison said, "we will all do our best and I have no doubt we can work together to rescue Ben's grandfather."

"I hope so. Not every quest ends in success." Miss Templeton took another sip of tea. "The ones that fail often do so because the Chosen were not able to work as a team. It is not just about doing your best, but it is about helping those who go with you also do their best. You need to use your gifts for the good of all. Speaking of gifts, it is time for them to be given. Denzel will receive the standard three gifts. I'm not sure how many Ben and Allison will receive, as they already have gifts that were especially given by the Guardian in the place beyond time and space. I am unsure as to whether the same rules will apply to a brownie or whether he will be given any gifts at all. As you know, a brownie has never been selected as a Chosen before." Miss Templeton paused briefly and gave the brownie an uncertain look. Then she continued, "Allison would you like to go first?"

Allison stood and moved to the metal chair. As soon as she sat down light shone through the Celtic knots. The light grew in intensity and wrapped around her and appeared to flow right through her. The others watched in awe as the light shimmered and danced over and around the chair. The light flared twice, the last time so brightly everyone closed their eyes. When they opened them again they were astonished to see a rainbow of light shining around Allison.

"Oh my," Miss Templeton breathed. "That's extraordinary."

They sat in silence and stared as the multi-colored light shone from Allison as if through a prism. The light gradually diminished and then it disappeared into Allison and into the Celtic knots on the chair.

"I've never seen anything like that before." Miss Templeton jumped to her feet and walked over to Allison where she laid her hands on Allison's head.

Allison's skin began to change. Greenish-brown scales appeared everywhere her skin was exposed. A film covered her eyes. When she turned and looked at Ben her pupils were no longer round but were more like the eyes of a snake. A ridge grew all the way across her forehead directly above the eyes to provide even more protection.

"Now, what was that extraordinary second gift that caused the bright light and rainbow?" Miss Templeton murmured. She waited for something to be revealed. The only thing that happened was that Allison began to glow with all the colors of the rainbow. Light shone forth from her and it was beautiful.

"Wow!" Denzel said. "We have our own walking lantern."

"There is more to this gift than being your source of light Denzel, but I'm not sure what it is." Miss Templeton said as she waited for a revelation of what the second gift was. It didn't come.

"This is a gift I've never seen before. I doubt any of the Watchers have. I can't tell you what it is. Hopefully, you will know what to do with it when the time is right. I look forward to learning what this gift is, that caused you to shine with the Guardian's own light." Miss Templeton paused and then went on. "Allison, you will go from Earth with four gifts, which is, in itself, amazing. You will take with you the gift of healing and the gift of being able to discern the truth of who someone is and make it manifest for others to see. You may not need either of those two gifts, but they are permanently yours. You will also take with you the gift of armor and whatever the last gift is that made you shine so brightly."

Miss Templeton helped Allison up from the chair and then asked. "Who's next?"

Denzel and Moses both stepped forward, but Denzel was quicker. He sat in the special chair and the light came forth from the Celtic knots. The first gift given was the same gift that Allison had received. He was given the special armor and protection for his eyes. The second gift was strength. Muscles bulged all over his body. He legs and arms became thick and his chest barreled out. The third gift did not reveal itself to the human and brownie eyes watching, but Miss Templeton knew what it was. In her mind's eye she could see Denzel winning every race. "You will be strong and fast," she said.

"Cool! Really cool! I would love to keep these gifts when I come back." Denzel laid his left hand on the muscles in his right arm as he flexed them.

"Sorry Denzel," Miss Templeton said. "The only gifts that are permanent are the ones you are born with unless you meet the Guardian in the place beyond time and space."

Moses was the next one to sit in the chair. At first it seemed that the light was not going to respond. When it did, it flared as brightly as it had over Allison. Ben closed his eyes, but opened them in time to see the light break into the colors of the rainbow and dance happily over Moses' head.

Miss Templeton stared at Moses with a rapt look on her face. "My word," she said as she pushed her glasses further up her nose. "This is the most extraordinary day."

A finger of light went from Moses and touched the wall behind Miss Templeton's desk. The dancing came to a stop with the light pointing at the wall.

"Yes, I understand," Miss Templeton said to no one in particular and the light drew back from the wall and continued its dance over Moses. The light flared once more and withdrew into the etchings on the chair.

"Moses last gift makes him a wizard. Earth, wind, fire and water will respond to his command. He has also been given the same mysterious gift that was given to Allison. Perhaps this mysterious gift is linked to their ability as healers."

Moses moved and Ben took his turn. He felt the cold metal chair against his back. As Ben sat down he thought about the gifts he wanted to receive. He really wanted to be a wizard and control the elements. Strength and speed were his second and third choices. He thought it would be really cool to get all three gifts. Those gifts added to what he already had would make him a real super hero unlike anything the worlds had seen before. No one could stop a strong fast wizard with the ability to transform into a dragon and move great distances just with a thought. Ben held his breath waiting for at least one of the hoped for gifts to manifest itself. He knew that three was the normal number and he already had two gifts, but Allison had just been given two additional gifts even though she already had two, and as he sat on the chair he believed the same thing was about to happen to him.

The light did not respond instantly and when it did come it was understated. Light slowly seeped out of the Celtic knots and flowed in and around Ben before gently withdrawing and disappearing back into the chair. Miss Templeton came and laid her hands on Ben and closed her eyes. "Ben has been given the ability to see in the dark," she finally said after an extended period of silence.

Ben's heart sank. "That's it? Seeing in the dark is the only gift I get?"

"What more do you want?" Miss Templeton asked. "You are already able to transform into a dragon and move yourself and others from one spot to another. Isn't that enough for you? The Guardian seems to think it's enough!"

Ben was stunned into silence by the harsh tone in Miss Templeton's voice. "Yes, it's enough," Ben finally said, trying to hide how disappointed he felt by this one rather insignificant gift. It felt like a big hole had opened in his stomach, akin to hunger.

"The rest of you can go on to the room of portals. I want to have a word with Moses before we join you," Miss Templeton instructed.

Ben, Denzel and Allison were waiting for Miss Templeton when she arrived with Moses. She went to the door directly across from the one they had come through and opened it to reveal a brick wall.

"Denzel, because you are strong and fast, and I don't know what's waiting for you on Farne, I'm going to send you first," Miss Templeton said. "Close your eyes and walk toward the wall. The portal will open and you should fall into a pool of water."

Ben had always hated being in water over his head. The first time he went through a portal he would have died if a mermaid hadn't found him. He wasn't looking forward to falling into the water this time either, but at least he'd learned to swim, and understood its importance. The water had magical properties and insured that nothing harmful went from one world to another.

Ben watched as Denzel took one step and then another towards the wall. He'd never watched someone else go through a portal before. He had always been the one with his eyes closed walking through what appeared to be a solid brick wall. The bricks never disappeared, but Denzel seemed to walk right through them. After a few moments

Allison and Moses walked towards the wall holding hands. Ben couldn't help but wish he was holding Allison's hand. As soon as they disappeared Ben stepped forward. When he got close to the wall he reached out and touched it, thinking the bricks were an illusion, but they were solid. He closed his eyes and stepped toward the portal. He fell through the air, but not into the water he expected. He might have broken an ankle if the Watcher of Farne had not sent a current of air to cushion his fall.

CHAPTER EIGHT

"D" DAY ON ZARGON

Mack sat across the desk from Zoey Zanderson as they waited for Zinc to appear. As was often the case, he was late. Zinc seemed to have a need to make the point that no one could tell him what to do. Mack wondered once again why the Guardian chose Zinc.

How, Mack thought to himself. Is Zinc ever going to be able to work with the others? Out loud, he said, "How are you feeling about going off-world with Zinc? Have you two been getting along any better?"

Anger flashed in the beautiful dragonborn girl's brilliant green eyes. "He's not worthy of being a Chosen."

"Why do you say that?" Mack asked, not letting on that he agreed with Zoey.

"I know his secret."

"What secret is that?" Mack asked.

Zoey looked at Mack in surprise. "Don't you know he was the one who betrayed his father to Zork? King Zane wouldn't be missing or dead if it weren't for his son." Her voice was tense and her nostrils flared as she glared at Mack. When her hands started to shake she clasped them before her.

Mack closed his eyes and was silent for a moment. Not for the first time, he wondered if the Guardian was wise to choose Zoey to go with Zinc to Farne. "The Guardian's ways are higher than our ways," he finally said. "The Guardian chose to give Zinc a second chance and who are we to argue?"

"Zork killed my mother in the mines."

"I'm sorry for your loss, but Zinc was not the one who sent your mother to the mines. He was not there, and even if he had been he could not have stopped your mother from dying."

"How could he betray his own father? It was not just his family he betrayed, but all the dragonborn clans."

"His mother and her family were behind him, pushing him in that direction," Mack said.

"That is no excuse," Zoey gripped the arms of her chair. "He should have his own conscience that he listens to."

"Zinc regrets his actions and feels a deep sense of shame," Mack wasn't completely convinced that the words he spoke were true, but hoped they were.

"I don't like him and he doesn't like me. Perhaps that's why he hasn't shown up today, he's changed his mind about going to Farne with me. I hope so. I'll feel better if I'm going without him."

"He will show up and you need to let go of the anger you feel towards him or it will be hard for the two of you to do what needs to be done."

Before Zoey could respond there was a knock at the door. Mack had been distracted by his conversation with Zoey and didn't know how long Zinc had been standing outside listening. When he came in Zinc glanced at Zoey disdainfully, before pulling the empty chair beside her further away prior to sitting down.

"So you've decided to go to Farne?" Mack asked.

"Of course, who else is going to find my father and restore him to the throne?"

"I am, with or without you, preferably without," Zoey said.

"The two of you are part of a team that has been called together to do the Guardian's work."

"The others don't care about my father as much as I do," Zinc said.

"Is that why you betrayed him to Zork?" The scorn could be clearly heard in Zoey's voice. "Although you didn't get what you wanted. Your mother isn't on the throne and neither are you. Zanderella is and she is proving herself worthy of being a Queen of the Dragonborn."

"My father will take the throne back when I rescue him."

Zoey was going to say something more, but Mack ended the conversation, "King Zane must be found and brought back to Zargon before we can address the question of who will rule. Both of you have been chosen for this task. If one person alone could do it, only one of you would have been chosen. Instead five people and a brownie are going. I repeat, differences need to be laid aside for King Zane to have any chance of returning to Zargon."

Zinc and Zoey both silently stared at Mack.

"Well, what do you say? Will you work with each other and the Chosen from Earth?"

"Yes," Zoey mumbled, while Zinc gave a brief nod.

"Let's find out what gifts the Guardian has for you." Mack stood up and walked to the gold chair covered in Celtic knots that sat in the corner. It matched the one on Earth. Zinc was heading for the chair when Zoey darted ahead of him and sat down. Zinc frowned and looked like he was about to say something, but closed his mouth and backed away instead.

"What," Zoey said, glaring at Zinc. "Did you think you should be first because you're a Prince?"

Shortly after Zoey sat down light streamed from the center of each knot. The light flared three times before disappearing. Mack laid his hands on Zoey's head. "Your gift is healing. It is a gift that has always been within you waiting to be discovered. The Guardian has enhanced your natural abilities and made them stronger. The good news about this gift is that you will not lose it when you come back. We will be glad to have another healer on Zargon. Your second gift is one I don't recognize and since I've been given the memories of past Watchers it means none of the previous Watchers ever encountered it. Perhaps because the Guardian has only enhanced a gift already there, you've been given a third gift. You have the gift of invisibility."

Zoey wore a broad and happy smile that added to her beauty as she got up from the golden chair. Zinc scowled at her as he moved to take his turn.

The light came forth from the chair and flared twice after Zinc sat on it. Mack put his hands on Zinc's head. "Zinc, you have become a dowser."

"What in the world is a dowser?" Zinc asked.

"On Earth it is someone who can find water with a forked stick."

"You're joking. Who needs a gift like that?"

"You will not live long if you can't find water," Mack said. "Neither will those who travel with you. It's an important gift."

"What is my second gift?" Zinc asked impatiently, dismissing the first as being of little consequence.

"It is also a gift related to seeking and finding. You will know when you move in a direction if it takes you closer to your father or further away."

Zinc looked like he was about to complain about this gift too, but then he smiled slightly, closed his eyes, and leaned back against the chair. "I will find my father," he whispered. "I will find him." Then he opened his eyes and turned to Mack. "Will I need a forked stick?"

"No, I don't believe so; however, the memories given to me reveal that this gift has never been given to another Chosen from Zargon. And there is no memory of anyone acting as a dowser on this world, which makes sense as there is water everywhere."

"I'd like to take one with me, just in case. I'll be back in a minute." Zinc walked toward the door.

"I'm sure you don't need…" Zinc slammed the door behind him before Mack could finish his sentence. Mack stared at the door with an annoyed look on his face. "I guess it won't hurt for Zinc to take a stick."

Zinc was back in a short time with a forked branch from a fruit tree growing in the valley below Stonehaven. Mack led him and Zoey to the room of portals where Zinc pushed ahead of Zoey and stepped through the portal first. Zachery cushioned Zinc's fall and then Zoey's with currents of air.

"Welcome to Farne. I'm this world's Watcher. My name is Zachery Zaltzburg." Zachery wore a broad smile and his words were punctuated with joyous laughter. He was literally dancing with excitement.

Zinc raised his eyebrows and his mouth fell open as he watched one of his ancestor's brothers prancing and laughing. He then frowned and looked across to Zoey who was staring at Zachery with narrowed eyes, a grimace on her normally attractive face.

Zachery was what Ben had been in danger of becoming when he had been unable to make the transformation from human to dragon and back again. Zachery appeared human, but was covered in green scales. He was neither fully human nor fully dragon.

"I thought we were supposed to fall into water to protect this world from things we might bring with us from Zargon," Zoey said.

"Finding water in this world is very hard, but don't worry this world is not in danger from anything you might bring with you," Zachery said.

"It's a good thing the Prince was given the gift of being able to find water," Zoey sneered.

Zachery looked at Zoey with a puzzled look on his face, then his face cleared and he giggled. "Please follow me." He leapt into the air, twisted and landed with his back to them. There were gasps of surprise and suppressed chuckles from all six of the Chosen. Coming out of a slit in Zachery's trousers was a stubby tail that hung just above his knees.

CHAPTER NINE

DAY ONE: FARNE

Zachery led them through an ancient town. All around them was rubble from brick buildings that had not endured the passing of time. As they walked, Zachery talked non-stop in a dry raspy voice. When he wasn't talking he was giggling. He would ask a question and then not wait for an answer. "I haven't seen a living soul that talks on this world in all the time I've been here," he said, speaking rapidly. "I've longed for this day more than you can possibly know. My fondest dream was having just one single visitor come through a portal and now I've got six."

"Is there no one on this world to talk to?" Zoey asked.

"There is nothing living that remembers how to talk. Some who can talk should be silent."

"What do you mean by that?" Ben asked.

"You can talk to the demons in Sheol if you like, but they are tricky and can get you into trouble." Zachery giggled.

"You talked to the demons in Sheol? That's not a good idea," Allison said.

Zachery stopped and stared at Allison. "Yes, you're right. It's a good thing you came so I don't have to talk to them again."

"Why would you ever need to talk to them?" Allison's eyes were wide beneath the frown on her forehead.

"You can ask me that question when you've been alone for almost a thousand years."

Zachery led them to a large building made of stone that was the only one still standing. They went up two flights of stairs to a dining hall with several round tables, all but one covered in dust. He grabbed two dust-covered chairs and moved them to the dust free table. Denzel and Ben grabbed more chairs so that there was enough for all of them. Zachery sat on a stool, which allowed his tail to hang over the edge. Ben suppressed a giggle. Zinc and Zoey both laughed out loud. Zachery scowled at them, giggled, and scowled again.

"Did none of the Farnean people survive the war?" Ben asked when they were all seated around the table.

"I don't think so, but if they did, then they are now something other than their Creator intended. If they see you, I have no doubt they will want to take you home for dinner, and not as their guests, if you take my meaning." Zachery laughed so hard he fell to the ground, which made him laugh even harder. He climbed back onto his stool. "I think it's best to stay away from every living creature on this world, even if it looks humanoid. Anything that survived will be very dangerous."

"But you don't know that for sure?" Ben asked.

"Stands to reason," Zachery said. "This is a hard world to survive on."

"I don't understand," Ben said, puzzled. "You are the Watcher of Farne. Why don't you know more about what lives here?"

"Shh. Don't tell," Zachery whispered, looking around. "This Watcher does not have a strong connection to the world he watches. Farne is sick. It is tainted. He sends his mind out across Farne and he cannot stand it. He brings his mind back and puts it safely in a box." After saying this Zachery giggled so hard he almost fell off the stool again.

Ben sat in stunned silence. Zinc laughed out loud. The Chosen all stared at one another and at Zachery with wide eyes.

Great, just what we need, the Watcher of Farne is crazy, thought Ben. "If you have no connection with this world how are you going to help us find the King of Zargon?" he asked out loud.

"Good question," Zachery said. "Are you sure the King came to Farne? I never saw him." This time he spoke without giggling.

"So he didn't come through the portal like we did?" Ben asked puzzled.

"Anyone a Watcher sends through a portal comes here," Zachery said. "At least I think they do. You are the only ones that have ever come."

"King Zane didn't leave through a portal, he left through a gateway. Would it not bring him here?" Allison asked.

"King Zane has a gateway! You must leave immediately and go find it," Zachery jumped off his stool.

"The gateway stayed with the Watcher of Zargon," Ben said, his growing frustration showing in his strained voice.

"Oh too bad," Zachery sat back down on the stool.

"You didn't answer our question. Would a gateway not bring him here?" Zinc asked.

"Gateways are ancient and predate the war on this world. It likely took the King to the previous Watcher's home and school. That area was badly contaminated by the war, which means there is little doubt that the King is dead. You may as well stay here with me."

"My father is still alive," Zinc's voice was loud. "And I'm going to find him and take him home."

"You've survived," Denzel said. "What makes you think the King could not?"

"I'm the Watcher of Farne which means I have special powers. Besides that, I stay here where it is safer than the rest of the world."

"We need to find my grandfather," Ben said. "That's why we've come to Farne."

"It's a good thing we don't need you to find my father," Zinc said disdainfully. "One of the gifts I've been given is the ability to know what direction he's in."

"And have you figured out how to work that gift yet?" Zachery asked, laughing.

Zinc bit his bottom lip and clenched his hands. Worry lines appeared on his forehead.

Allison stared at Zachery. A frown etched on her face. "Don't worry," she said to Zinc. "You've been given a gift, and you'll learn how to use it. The Guardian wouldn't have given it to you otherwise."

"Yes," Zoey whispered. "The Guardian would not have sent us if King Zane was dead or given us gifts if we couldn't learn to use them."

"I think the Guardian sent you to visit me. You are here to keep me from going mad." Zachery giggled. "We can play games and tell each other stories."

"You're already mad if you think we're going to stay here and play games when my father is missing," Zinc said.

Zachery stared at Zinc with a stricken look on his face. "The Watcher doesn't like this one," he whispered to himself, in a voice just loud enough for everyone to hear.

"I'm sorry, sir," Ben said, "but we've been sent to find my grandfather. What we need you to do is teach us about Farne as it exists today. The books in our libraries did not cover anything that happened after the war. The only thing we were told is that you became the Watcher and the world was still recovering from the war."

"Teaching you about Farne will take a very long time. I wouldn't count on setting out to find the King for at least six months." Zachery giggled and grabbed the table to keep from falling off the stool again.

"We leave in the morning," Zinc said.

Ben's head jerked up and his eyes narrowed as he looked at Zinc. "Wait a minute. We haven't talked about when we're leaving yet. I think we need to stay long enough to learn what Zachery can teach us about surviving on this world. We should stay a couple of days, but no more."

"I agree with Ben. We should stay and learn what we can. What do the rest of you think?" Allison asked. Moses nodded in agreement.

"How much can a Watcher who has no connection with his world teach us?" Zinc asked. Zoey nodded her head in agreement.

Ben looked from Zinc to Zoey. It worried him that they were divided by what world they came from. Then he looked at his friend Denzel. Denzel looked away. "Okay, Denzel agrees with Zinc," Ben thought. "Not good."

"Okay," Ben said. "Let's stay tomorrow and at the end of the day evaluate whether to stay longer."

Denzel looked at Ben and smiled.

"I don't think we should stay here for even one day," Zinc said. "Let's take a vote. Who agrees with me?"

Zoey scowled at Zinc as she raised her hand. As soon as she noticed there were no other hands up, she put hers down.

"It appears that we are staying here tomorrow to learn about Farne from Zachery," Ben said.

Zinc said nothing, but smoke issued from his nostrils.

"You need to tell me what your gifts are, perhaps I can give you advice on how to use them in this world," Zachery said. "Ben, tell me, what gift did you receive?"

Ben named the one gift the Guardian had given him before coming through the portal to Farne. "I can see in the dark," he said with little enthusiasm.

Zinc smirked. "Is that it? You can see in the dark. Your gift is even more pathetic than mine."

Ben glared at Zinc. "I can also transform into a dragon and as a human I can move myself and a couple of other people great distances in the blink of an eye."

"The gift of transporting great distances is not a gift you can use here," Zachery said.

"What! Why?" Ben asked.

"You can't use the transportation gift because of the danger of toxic rain. You can't know what the weather is like until you arrive somewhere. If you arrive when the wrong kind of cloud is forming it would strip the flesh right off your bones." Zachery seemed to find that funny and started to giggle and dance. Laughter and dancing did not fit with Zachery's appearance. They were actions better suited to a child, than to an ancient lizard man with a tail. Zinc, Zoey and Denzel giggled out loud.

Zachery immediately stopped dancing. "It's time to eat. I spent a lot of time looking for food when I knew you were coming."

Nothing more was said about the gifts they had each been given.

The meal Zachery worked so hard to prepare was sparse and unpalatable. It consisted of very small portions of a finger-sized rubbery meat and a bland woody vegetable. Zachery gave them a lesson on what was safe to eat as they shared their meal. The list was not very long and included slugs and grasshoppers when one was lucky enough to find them. Zachery assigned sleeping quarters and the Chosen retreated, glad to be away from the non-stop talking of the Watcher of Farne.

CHAPTER TEN

WATCHERS JOURNAL YEAR 937

I'm so happy I can't seem to stop laughing. My guests are certain I am mad and I'm afraid they're right. When they are out of sight I wonder if they exist only in my imagination, but then I tell myself that I wouldn't imagine anyone as annoying as the Prince of Zargon.

Strange things are at work. A brownie has been chosen and given the most highly valued gift, he is a Wizard.

I tried to connect with the Guardian yesterday. It's been a long time and the connection was weak. All I heard was one word: rebirth. I'm not sure what it means, but I like the sound of it.

CHAPTER ELEVEN

THE SALT MINES

Early the next morning, before anyone else was awake, Moses walked through the ruins until he found a quiet spot hidden from sight. He opened the bag that hung under his left arm beneath the vest he wore. Moses pulled out the objects the Guardian had instructed Miss Templeton to give him. There were three objects; two square frames made of iron covered in elaborate Celtic knots and one iron stand also covered in knots. Moses put one of the square frames on the stand and placed it on the ground near the remains of a brick wall where it was unlikely to be seen. Moses stared at the iron square on the floor and thought of the place where he had last seen his parents and sister. He watched in alarm as his hand began to stretch and fade as it was drawn toward the frame. Soon his whole being was drawn toward the iron square, which seemed to get bigger as he moved close. He blinked and when he opened his eyes it was to discover that he was no longer on Farne, but had been transported to the salt mines on Zargon, the last place he'd seen his family. He was in the prison barracks he'd slept in for six months.

This was the place he was running from when he first met Allison. It was a place of suffering and death, from what Moses could tell it still was. It smelled of sweat, urine, vomit, and blood. Moses heard brownies moaning and crying outside the door. He had a sick feeling in the pit of his stomach. This was the place where nightmares came to life. He had watched many of them right outside the barracks.

Moses quietly walked over and peeked through a crack in the door. Outside, two brownies, a male and a female, were staked to the ground. Their hands and feet were tied to posts. Piled around them were the eggs of dinosaurs in the process of hatching.

The dinosaurs would be greedy for their first meal, eager to eat anything that was close at hand. They would strip the flesh off the brownies, one small piece at a time. Moses had seen a brownie killed this way for trying to escape and knew it was a terrible way to die. The brownies were forced to watch with the hope that it would make them too afraid to run away. It worked on most brownies, but Moses has made his escape anyway.

Two of the baby dinosaurs had already hatched and one stood near the pile of eggs looking around for its first meal. It spied the brownies on the ground and made a few hops toward them, then it stopped and looked back at the second dinosaur that had just hatched. The dinosaur decided to feast on one of the dragonborn guards rather than the brownies staked out for their meal. The dinosaur that was the first to hatch decided the second one was getting a better meal and left the brownies to join the attack on the guard. The other two guards watched their friend and laughed at his efforts to turn the persistent dinosaur away from him towards the meal intended for them. He was using the flat side of his sword to push the baby dinosaurs away. They would fall over, shake their heads, and get back on their feet to attack the guard again.

Moses silently left the barracks and made his way to the brownies staked to the ground. He hoped the guards would keep watching their friend and not notice him until it was too late. He squatted and started with the ropes that held the female brownie to the ground. The guards did not notice Moses was there as they laughed at the dinosaurs attacking their friend, but the brownie prisoners silently watched Moses at work. When the female was freed, Moses crawled over to release the male brownie. One of the guards noticed that the brownies slaves were staring intently at the prisoners staked to the ground. He turned, expecting to see more newly hatched dinosaurs, but instead saw the free female and Moses working to free the male.

"Hey, where did you come from?" He took out his sword, but before he reached Moses a third baby dinosaur ran in front of him, jumped up, and pecked him in the groin. The guard bent over in pain and the dinosaur bit his nose. Meanwhile, the other guards were alerted and on their way toward Moses who had just freed the brownie male.

"Join hands and come with me." Moses grabbed hold of the female's hand as he took the metal square he'd brought with him from its bag and held it away from his body. He willed himself to go back through the gateway to Farne as he stared at it. The female brownie, whose hand he was holding, cried out in alarm as Moses and her arm began to stretch toward the frame. Moses held her tight as she struggled to escape being drawn through the gateway.

Moses, two brownies and two baby dinosaurs that had just been in the process of taking their first bite out of the male brownie materialized in front of Zachery, who jumped back in surprise.

"Where did these brownies come from?" Zachery asked in shock.

"I bring them," Moses said. "No choice. If stay, they die."

"Take them back. They're not allowed to be here," Zachery made a shooing motion with his hands.

"Can't take back," Moses said. "Zargon salt mine not good place for brownie."

"They're not a good place for anyone." Zachery danced away from the baby dinosaurs that had decided Zachery would be their first meal. "But someone's got to mine the salt."

"Many die there, my mother, father, maybe sister too. Guards feed dinosaurs with these two."

Zachery stopped dancing and the closest dinosaur caught up and nipped at his leg, making a hole in his pants. He sent the baby dinosaur flying through the air with a swift kick. "Wait. There is a more important question. How did you bring them here?"

"Guardian give Moses gateway."

Zachery stopped dead in his tracks and stared at Moses. "You have a gateway? I can't believe it. I've waited centuries for one and now one has been brought to me."

Zachery held his hand out toward Moses. Instead of placing the gateway in Zachery's hand, Moses took a step backwards as he put the gateway back into his bag, before turning and picking up the one he'd left on Farne. He stood up and turned toward Zachery. "Earth Watcher tell Moses keep safe."

"What better way to keep it safe then to give it to me." Zachery held his hand close to Moses.

"Moses keep safe." Moses backed away from Zachery and turned so that his body was away from him.

A scowl appeared on Zachery's face. When Zachery moved toward him, Moses was afraid that he was going to try to take the gateway by force, but then Zachery stopped, clenched his fists, closed his eyes, and appeared to be thinking about his next step.

When Zachery opened his eyes, he moved toward the unnamed brownies and looked closely at them. The brownies were very thin and showed signs of abuse. They had bruises on their faces, open sores on their hands, and there were places where dried blood coated their fur. Their arms were wrapped around each other and they were weeping.

"They really don't treat brownies very well at salt mines, do they?" Zachery observed.

Moses moved towards the wounded brownies. He laid his hand on the female and closed his eyes so that he could concentrate. He sent his healing power into her to see how extensive the injuries were. When he opened them again, he was surprised that the bruises on her face and the wounds on her hands were gone. His previous experience as a healer had been with the dragonborn and they'd been harder to heal. He didn't know whether it was easier now because this was a brownie or whether it was easier because of the recent gifts he'd received from the Guardian.

"You are a healer," Zachery said in amazement. "You also have the coveted wizard gift. What other gift has the Guardian given to you?"

"I got gift Miss Templeton never see before. Allison got same gift. She also healer," Moses said.

"Amazing! Simply amazing! A brownie cannot only be a Chosen, but they can be given the most extraordinary gifts of all. Not only that, but this one has been given the most precious gift—a gateway that can take me off this cursed world." Zachery began to giggle.

Meanwhile, the second baby dinosaur had moved behind Zachery and was about to take a bite from his tail. Zachery danced away from it giggling. Moses couldn't tell how much of the dance was to avoid the baby dinosaur and how much was excitement over what Moses had just told him. As Zachery danced, Moses laid his hands on the male brownie and healed him.

Finally, Zachery stopped dancing with his face inches away from Moses' own. "You are a brownie and a Chosen and you've been given gateways by the Guardian. Did Miss Templeton say why the gateways were given to you?"

"No," Moses said, a worried look on his face.

"So maybe the Guardian intended you to give the gateways to me?" Zachery words turned into a howl as two baby dinosaurs nipped him. One bit his finger and drew blood.

"No, Guardian give Moses. Miss Temp'ton say I look after. She say I go Zargon and know what do."

"What did you know?" Zachery asked.

"Guardian want me help these brownies," Moses replied.

"So now that you've rescued these brownies, I think you should give the gateways to me. I will look after them for the Guardian."

Zachery held out his hand until one of the dinosaurs jumped up and nipped it.

Moses was silent for a moment. There was a look of concentration on his face. "No, Guardian want Moses keep them. Maybe find sister. Maybe rescue more brownies."

"What will you do with all those brownies you rescue?" Zachery asked as he danced away from the dinosaurs taking him further away from Moses.

Moses stared into space for a moment. "I bring brownies here. They need world. You need brownies."

Zachery stopped moving to stare at Moses and one of the dinosaurs got in too close and nipped his leg through the torn spot in his pants. He howled in pain and then started to giggle. "Imagine that. I could be the Watcher on a world with brownies on it. Yes, I like it. Of course, I'd need to teach them how to talk."

The brownie female spoke for the first time, "No need teach. We talk."

With those words Zachery forgot about the dinosaurs and danced a jig of pure joy. He turned his back on the baby dinosaurs and one of them nipped his tail again. Zachery pointed to Moses' sword and held out his hand. "I've forgotten what dinosaur tastes like. It will be a nice change from slugs and those wretched gourds."

Moses handed Zachery his sword and the Watcher used it to keep the dinosaurs away from his legs and tail. "What are you still doing here," he said to Moses as he danced around in a circle. "Go get more brownies."

"Okay," Moses started to take the gateways back out of his bag.

"Wait till night. Go when brownie in barracks. Safer," the male brownie said and Zachery danced over to him.

"Brownies, on a world of their own need names. Zachery pointed the tip of the sword toward the female brownie. You will be Rose and you will be Thorn." He pointed the sword tip at the male. Then he giggled. "Let's not tell the others about brownies making Farne their home just yet. Let's wait until the Chosen come back from their quest. The Chosen from Zargon may not approve and there's no point in upsetting them before they leave. If they don't come back then we won't need to upset them at all." Zachery laughed as if he had just told a joke. "Besides, the Guardian told you to keep the gateways secret, right?"

"Yes, I keep secret," Moses replied.

"You have two gateways," Zachery said. "Are you sure that one was not meant as a gift for me?"

"One is anchor. One not work alone," Moses said. "When I go back Earth, I give to Miss Temp'ton."

"I think you should leave one with me while you're on Farne. I will keep it safe and if you run into a problem you can't solve on your own, or your lives are in great danger, you can come back here and get my help."

Moses stared silently at the Watcher with a frown on his face.

"You wouldn't want anything to happen to Allie would you? You would feel very badly if she died because you wouldn't give me one of the gateways."

Moses stared at Zachery for a moment. "I leave one here. You promise give back. It belong Miss Temp'ton."

"Okay," Zachery said, without actually making a promise. Zachery held out his hand and Moses laid one of the gateways in it. Zachery bit his lip to keep from giggling.

"Please take the dinosaurs to the kitchen," Zachery said, handing Moses the sword. "I will find a safe place for our guests to stay and come to the kitchen as soon as I can. We will make dinosaur soup."

Zachery took off at a run with Rose and Thorn following behind him. The still-living dinosaurs squawked and took a few running steps after them before turning around and making a run at Moses. They appeared to decide that a brownie standing still was a better menu choice then the rapidly disappearing lizard man. Moses led the dinosaurs to the kitchen. They only got close enough to nip him once.

When they got to the kitchen, Moses maneuvered them inside and closed the door that separated the kitchen from the dining room.

Zachery took Rose and Thorn to a room set apart from the others and promised to bring them food and water. He then went to his office and removed a picture from the wall. To the naked eye the wall seemed without flaw or break, but Zachery waved his hand and a drawer slid out. He took a box out of the drawer and set it on his desk before removing the lid. In the box was a square that looked exactly like the one Moses had just given him. Next to the square was an empty space. He laid the gateway Moses had given him in the box next to its twin. It fit perfectly. He now had two gateways in his possession.

"Finally," Zachery said to himself as he closed the lid. "I no longer need to stay on Farne if I don't want to."

He put the box back in the drawer and waved his hand over the wall. The drawer disappeared and he hung the picture back in place.

It was only after the box was securely hidden away that Zachery allowed himself to giggle.

"The Chosen came to find a Watcher and a Watcher I will be, te do dum dee, te do dum dee." He sang absentmindedly. After singing he sat in his chair and stared into space, scratching his chin with a perplexed look on his face.

"Of course," he finally said. "Of course, I can't be a Watcher, without the Guardian's medallion. Where did I leave that thing?"

Zachery searched through the debris on his desk, but did not find it. He opened each drawer and pulled what was inside out onto the floor. Then a vague memory came back of hanging the Guardian's medallion on a hook underneath the desk. He felt for the hook and found it, but it was empty. He got down on his hands and knees and crawled underneath the desk. He moved aside one item after another until his hand touched a chain. He banged his head on the underside of the desk as he pulled the medallion from where it had lain for several centuries.

He brushed the dust and cobwebs off and hung it around his neck. With the medallion in place he sent his mind out across Farne. What he learned surprised him. "There's more life on this world than I thought," he whispered to himself. "When did that happen?"

CHAPTER TWELVE

THE BREAKFAST OF CHAMPIONS

When he arrived at the kitchen, Zachery wasn't expecting living dinosaurs. Nor was he prepared for the mess they could make. He dealt with them as one must, when dinosaur is a menu item. When breakfast was ready Zachery sent Moses to tell the others to come. Soon they were all seated at the table. Zachery invoked a blessing on the day and on the food. As he did so, he realized that a very long time had passed since he had last blessed his food or the day that was before him.

"Eat." Zachery picked up his spoon and took a taste. "Delicious, if I do say so myself."

"Somehow I doubt that." Zinc took a small bite. A look of pleasure replaced the scowl on his face and he took a larger spoonful.

Soon everyone was enjoying the food.

"This is good. It reminds me of home," Zoey said.

"Yes," Allison agreed. "This reminds me of something we ate on Zargon. What is it?"

"It is a creature rarely found on Farne," Zachery said giggling. Moses giggled with him, which caused Allison to give him a perplexed look.

"Well, tell us the places where it's rarely found so we know where to look." Zinc scraped the last mouthful out of the bottom of his bowl.

"Look where you least expect and who knows what you'll find," Zachery said and started to giggle uncontrollably.

"At least tell us what it looks like, so we'll know one when we see it," Zinc said.

"It has claw tipped feet on the end of thick legs. The arms are short. It has a tail, and a pointy-head with some razor sharp teeth. If you see a full grown one and can't transform into a dragon, run because they are hard to kill, but will have no trouble killing you." Zachery giggled once more.

"Sounds like some of the dinosaurs we have on Zargon." Zoey scraped the bottom of her bowl for the last bite of stew.

Both Zachery and Moses burst out laughing. Allison looked at the brownie in surprise, wondering what had struck Moses as so funny. She'd never heard him laugh out loud before.

After breakfast Zachery excused himself and took some food and water to where he had hidden Rose and Thorn. When he came back the lessons as to what to expect on Farne began.

"You are best to spend the night on solid rock or on concrete if you can find it in good condition. Watch out for cracks. Whatever you do, avoid sleeping directly on the ground. Nasty things hide in the soil that can deliver a painful bite, sometimes lethal. One person should always be on guard when you sleep. You need to not only watch for big things that look dangerous, but for small things that do not."

"What sort of things are we watching for?" Denzel leaned forward, concern written on his face.

"Snakes, scorpions, creepy crawlers, and other things that have no translatable name. The snakes are edible and any white slugs are also edible. White slugs are what we had for supper last night. The best place to look for slugs is in the basement of ruined buildings, but that is also where the dangerous creepy crawlies hang out. When you hunt snakes make sure not to get bitten."

"So they're venomous, but safe to eat?" Allison asked.

Zachery nodded, and was about to go on, but Denzel stopped him. "Do they taste better than the slugs?"

Zachery shook his head, then continued. "Water will be hard to find, mostly you will find it inside some plants or by finding underground streams. You need to be careful with the water that falls from the sky. Some will be good, but most will not. If you see clouds gathering, especially if they have a greenish tint, run. Do not let the water that falls from the sky touch your skin and don't drink it. Also avoid the sun, it will blister your skin and cause you to go blind if you are not dragonborn. It's best to leave the humans behind as they cannot safely travel on Farne, but don't worry, I'll take good care of them, we will play games and tell stories."

"Allison and I will be perfectly safe." Denzel called forth the gift he and Allison had been given. Brownish green scales covered his body, and his eyes changed from round to snake-like with a ridge on his forehead to provide shade for his eyes when out in the sun.

"I see," said Zachery annoyed. "The Guardian thought of everything. You are as safe as anyone traveling on Farne can be, but always remember that Farne is not a safe world, not even for dragonborn. There are many things that can kill you on this world besides the sun and the rain."

"Would we be safer traveling at night and staying underground during the day?" Ben asked.

"Only if you can find an intact building like this one and even then I would not advise it. Dangerous things hide in buildings. I think it best to be awake in the daytime so you can watch for the rain clouds. It rarely rains at night, and when it does the rain is usually safe. Any rain when the sun is at its highest is almost always toxic. One minute there will be no cloud and the next a cloud forms right in front of you and rain falls that can strip the flesh right off you in almost no time.

There is one more thing I need to tell you. I sent my mind out across Farne this morning and made a connection with something vaguely familiar. King Zane may still be alive. I felt his presence near the place where I believe the original school was. You need to travel in the direction of the setting sun for several days to find him, if what I sensed is the King. Did your gift already tell you what direction to go?" Zachery asked, looking at Zinc.

"Of course," Zinc said, looking away uncomfortably. Zachery laughed and Zinc flashed him an angry look.

"What about Farnian portals? Don't you have portals like the other worlds do, linking one place on this world to another?" Ben asked.

"Those portals are not operational," Zachery said. "I'm afraid you must travel by dragon wing." Zachery looked away. He was embarrassed that he did not know where the intraworld portals were.

CHAPTER THIRTEEN

EMANCIPATION

When the sun went down Moses met Zachery in the dining hall. The watcher led him to the room where Rose and Thorn had spent the day. Zachery suggested Rose accompany Moses to the female barracks on Zargon and that Thorn go with him to the male brownie's barracks. Rose and Thorn agreed the brownie slaves would be more likely to trust them rather than a strange brownie who showed up unexpectedly in their midst.

"I wasn't thinking of that, so much, as the fact that you know where there is an open space. I wouldn't want Moses to arrive on top of the stove or in the latrine bucket," Zachery said.

"Moses know male barrack, but not female. Rose choose place." Moses carried a gateway in a bag under his vest so it could be used for the return trip.

When everything was settled, Zachery took the portable gateway Moses gave him out of his pocket. He held it in his hand and directed Rose to look into the gateway and think about a spot in the barracks where she had spent the last two years of her life. Moses took her hand and stood beside her.

It took three trips to move the thirty-five female brownies from Zargon to Farne. When they arrived Zachery gave each of them a name of their own. Moses looked at each one carefully, knowing that his sister could have changed a great deal since the last time he saw her, but she wasn't among them. With a heavy heart he went through the gateway with Thorn and before long the male brownies arrived and were all named.

Once everyone was safely through, Moses visited each brownie. He asked those he thought he recognized from his time at the mine whether they knew what had happened to his sister. Most just shook their head, but one woman said, "Think I know. Sister escape mine. Never found."

Moses closed his eyes and breathed a sigh of relief. He didn't know where his sister was, but at least she wasn't dead.

After he asked his question, he laid his hands on the escaped brownies to see if they needed healing. Almost all were suffering from the effects of malnutrition and abuse. Moses sent his healing power into those with serious injuries. He was especially glad to heal the brownie who thought she remembered his sister.

Zachery followed behind Moses. He laid the Guardian's medallion on each hand to see if there were any Chosen among them. The medallion did not move for any of the brownies they rescued that night. Zachery was disappointed. He was staring down at his medallion with a bleak look on his face when Rose stepped in front of him. "Test me," she said. For the first time that night the medallion opened up and revealed the days, months and years of the calendar. Rose stared at the medallion in amazement.

"Hee, hee, hee… I have my first brownie Chosen!" Zachery spun around and around laughing and dancing. A thought struck him and he stopped turning in circles. "Where is Thorn? I haven't tested him yet either."

Thorn stepped forward and Zachery laid the medallion on his open hand. "I have my second Chosen!" Zachery whooped with joy when the dials began to move.

Rose and Thorn looked at each other, unsure of what it all meant. "Is good to be Chosen?" Thorn asked with a confused look on his face.

"It is very good," Zachery said. "We must have a school. Where will I find teachers?" With that question in mind Zachery spun around and looked at Moses. Moses knew what he was thinking and shook his head no. "I go Earth with Allie."

"We'll see," Zachery said. "For now we'll find a place for these brownies to rest. They must have food, but where to find it."

"I take Rose and Thorn. We bring food from Zargon"

Zachery held out the gateway, Moses and the other two brownies stepped through it. In his mind Moses carried an image of the school for the Chosen. They made two trips and brought back enough food for the next day.

CHAPTER FOURTEEN

WATCHERS JOURNAL YEAR 937

I have my own Chosen. They are only brownies, but still the Guardian has chosen them. I might stay on this world just to see what happens. Besides, I haven't made up my mind what world to go to yet. Are there any worlds where a lizard man can find acceptance and friendship?

CHAPTER FIFTEEN

THE QUEST BEGINS

The six Chosen left by dragon wing the next morning to begin their search for the King. Ben carried Denzel, Zoey carried Allison, and Zinc grumbled as he carried Moses. Allison and Denzel called forth the gift to change their eyes and cover their skin in protective scales. Moses' toes, his hands, and his face were not covered by fur, but his exposed skin did not seem to need protection. Zachery had given him goggles to help protect his eyes from the intense glare of the sun. Moses was delighted with his goggles and made sure that each one of the Chosen knew they were a special gift from the Watcher.

As they flew away from Zachery, they noticed something special about the area where the Watcher lived. It was an island of green in a world that was dry and barren in every direction they looked. The world around the watcher had always been healthier than other places in Farne, but since the arrival of the Chosen new life was springing forth from seeds that had long lain dormant in the soil.

They landed for lunch at the base of a mountain in an area where they'd seen a few scraggly bushes from the sky. Moses and Denzel went to look at the greenish brown plants to determine if they were the ones that grew the gourds Zachery had dried and given them to carry in their backpack.

Ben did not go with them because he was tired. One of the downsides of being forbidden to transform on Earth was that he had not exercised his wings for a long time. He wondered how he could keep flying for the rest of the day let alone for however long it took to find his grandfather. He closed his eyes and laid his head on arms resting on his knees.

Allison sat beside him. "Are you okay?" Ben lifted his head and looked at her. He could hear the concern in her voice, but he couldn't see concern in the lizard eyes that stared at him from her scale-covered face.

When Ben didn't respond Allison rested her hand on his. The place Allison touched tingled and warmth flowed from her hand into the rest of his body. At first, he thought it was just the touch of the girl he adored making him feel better, but then he realized Allison was using her healing power on him.

He snorted and pulled his arm away. He didn't want Allison's pity and he didn't like the fact that the only reason she was touching him was to ensure he could continue to fly. Then he felt like a cad. "Thank you," he mumbled as he got up to go find Moses and Denzel. As he walked away he thought of their last awkward conversation that had ended in a disastrous kiss.

"You're welcome," Allison whispered as she looked wistfully at Ben's retreating back.

Moses, Ben and Denzel returned with some fresh gourds which meant they did not need to eat the dried ones Zachery had placed in their backpacks.

"I think I would rather starve, than eat more of these," Zinc complained.

"That's your choice. I, for one would not be unhappy if you did. It's too bad you're the only one among us with a gift for finding water." Zoey's lip curled and she wrinkled her nose. "It would seem the Guardian has made you indispensable."

"King's son find water now," Moses said.

"I'll find it when I'm good and ready. A brownie isn't going to tell me what to do." Zinc turned his back on Moses.

"Need to find before gone," Moses held up the water gourd he carried over his shoulder and sloshed the water around to show how empty it was. Zachery had given each of them their own water gourd to carry.

Ben shook his own water bottle. "We should all be careful with how much we drink. Zachery said water was hard to find on this world."

"You're right. Who knows whether the Prince will even be able to use the gift he's been given," Zoey sneered.

Zinc gave the dragonborn girl a dirty look as he took out his gourd and drank deeply from it. When he put the lid back on he could tell that his gourd was almost empty and silently cursed himself for letting Zoey goad him into doing something so foolish. Why did he drink so much? What if he couldn't find more water?

The gourds Moses and Denzel harvested were tasteless and woody, but everyone forced them self to eat some. They spit the seeds out and watched them roll down the side of the rocky hill and into the soil below.

Zinc sat by himself and ate very little. He stared out into the distance, in the direction of the setting sun, with a worried look on his face. He then took out the forked stick he carried in his backpack and held it in his hands. He closed his eyes and waited for some indication it would speak to him and tell him where to find either water or his father. He felt nothing, and wished again that he hadn't drunk so much of his water.

When their lunch was finished, the three dragonborn transformed from human back into dragons and their passengers climbed on board. As they left, they failed to notice the seeds already sprouting not far from where Allison sent healing power into Ben. Shoots were pushing their way down into the soil to become roots.

CHAPTER SIXTEEN

ZINC, THE DOWSER

They followed the remains of an ancient road for much of the day. It went through the ruins of one community after another. In mid-afternoon the land below them changed and the road disappeared. The dragonborn and their riders saw no sign that anyone had ever lived in this part of Farne. The crumbling ruins vanished. Nothing grew. Whatever once existed appeared to have melted and run together to create a flat shiny surface. Ben wondered what kind of weapon made the land below them look like glass. Was it akin to an atomic weapon? Could the same thing happen to Earth?

Without talking to one another, the dragons flew faster until the glass ended and the normal dry and barren land, with a few stunted gnarled shrubs and the ruins of towns and villages, re-appeared.

They stopped when the sun was low on the horizon. Each of them went out to take care of personal business with instructions to look for the gourds or anything else on Zachery's list of edible foods. They all came back empty handed. Supper consisted of some of the dry gourds Zachery had packed for them.

"These things are hard enough to eat fresh, let alone dried." Denzel took a drink from his water bottle to wash the distasteful food down. After drinking, he swished the water in his gourd back and forth.

"Zinc, my water is almost gone, you need to put your gift to work and find us some soon."

"Obviously," Zinc said with a hint of annoyance in his voice. He took a small sip from his own water bottle and tried to wash down the dried gourd he was eating. He choked on it and had to take a larger drink.

"It's not food meant for a Prince, is it?" Zoey asked with a smirk.

Zinc stared at the dragonborn girl with a look of distain on his face. He was irritated by the way she spoke to him and hated the mocking tone of her voice when she called him Prince. He watched her take a bite of a dried gourd and chew without drinking any water and realized her gourd must be very empty. His first thought was good. Then he sighed, picked up his pack and walked away.

When the others were out of sight Zinc took out the forked stick he had brought with him. He held it in his hands the way Mack had described, one hand holding each branch of the fork with the single end pointing out and down. He tried to block out every impression coming from the world around him and focus only on the stick in his hands. He waited expectantly, but nothing happened. He could not sense the stick pulling him in any one direction. He closed his eyes and imagined water just below the surface. He waited, hoping for a tug or an impression or anything that would tell him what direction he needed to walk. He moved further away and repeated the same procedure over and over again.

"Maybe there is no water close by," he muttered to himself. Zinc then replaced the image of water with the image of his father. He turned slowly in a circle with his eyes closed and the stick held straight out in front of him. Mack, the Watcher of Zargon had told him he would always know what direction his father was in, but there was no tug on the stick and no impression telling him what direction his father was in. He just hoped they had been going toward him and not further away.

After several attempts he opened his eyes and threw the stick angrily on the ground. He was so frustrated that his eyes were tearing up. He hated to cry and when he did it made him angry. He kicked the ground with his foot, then clenched his hands and started back to where the others were, but then stopped, retraced his steps, picked up the stick and put it in his pack.

"There's no water close enough," he said to the others. "You'll need to be careful not to drink too much until I can find some."

"So you couldn't find water," Zoey croaked. "That's not a surprise. Can you at least tell us if we are still going in the right direction to find the King?"

"Yeah, he's that way," Zinc glared at Zoey, as he waved his arm in the general direction they'd been traveling. Before the others could say anything else, he walked away, rolled out his bedding and laid down with his back to them.

Allison frowned at Zoey and shook her head. "Zoey," she said. "Zinc, is doing his best, just like we all are. You need to cut him some slack."

"What does that mean?" Zoey asked, but started to walk away without waiting for an answer.

"Sniping at one another will not help us find the King." Ben said loudly. "We need to work with everyone whose been chosen even if we don't like them."

CHAPTER SEVENTEEN

TERMITE WORMS

Zoey was on watch when the sun began to lighten the night sky. Zinc was crying out in his sleep and thrashing about in his bedding. At first she assumed he was having a bad dream. When he didn't stop, she walked over for a closer look and caught sight of the crack in the rock and the white worm like creatures that were crawling through it toward Zinc. The front end of the three-inch long worms was the width of a thread, while it got bigger toward the tail end. Zoey gave a cry of alarm that woke everyone up, including Zinc, when she noticed one burrowing its head into Zinc's arm. Zinc cried out and threw off his sleeping bag to discover there were white worms crawling all over him.

"Get them off me!" Zinc screamed as he grabbed one and pulled it away from his body. When he tried to throw it away the worm wrapped itself around his hand. It drove the narrow end of its head into his palm. He grabbed it with his other hand and managed to cast it away, barely missing Zoey. Ben, Denzel and Moses grabbed the worms off of Zinc's body and threw them as far as they could. Zoey and Allison found rocks and brought them down on the worms still crawling toward him.

When there were no more worms visible on Zinc's body, he took off his shirt and pants. Denzel took them and shook them out, which dislodged three more. One of the worms had buried most of its body into his bicep. Moses grabbed that worm and started to pull it out. He ended up holding the tail end in his hand, while the head was buried inside Zinc's arm. What remained of the worm was disappearing. Ben grabbed it before it could disappear, and very gently, but firmly pulled back, taking great care not to break it again. When it was out he threw the partial worm to the ground where Zoey crushed it beneath a rock. Further up Zinc's arm they could see the tail end of another worm. Most of this worm was buried in Zinc's arm. Ben grabbed for it, but the tail slipped out of his hand and more of the worm disappeared.

"Wait," Zoey croaked through dry lips. "If you try and pull that one out, it will break apart and the Prince will have one stuck in his arm until he dies, which won't take long as that thing eats him from the inside out."

"You'd like that wouldn't you?" Zinc said, as he grabbed for the tail himself.

Allison grabbed his hand and stopped him from pulling on the worm. "Zoey's right. If you pull on that one it might break off inside. Ben, could you grab it and keep it from disappearing and I'll see if I can get it out using my power as a healer."

Allison closed her eyes and rested her hand on Zinc. She found not one worm, but two. One was down near his ankle and had disappeared completely. She focused on the one in his arm first. She treated it like the slivers she'd been called to remove at Fairhaven when she was first learning how to be a healer. She pushed backwards on it toward the hole it had made when it entered Zinc's arm. The worm resisted in a way that a sliver never did, but Allison managed to push it most of the way out, until Ben was able to grab it close to the head and pull it the rest of the way out.

"There's a second worm in your leg," Allison said.

Tears of fear, rage and frustration appeared in Zinc's eyes. "Please, get it out now."

Allison tried to push the worm out the way it had come, but it was more firmly entrenched than the first one. It was also larger than the hole it had gone into. Allison didn't want to think about the reasons why it was larger. Zinc was indeed being eaten from the inside out. Meanwhile, the still living worms were on their way to where the Chosen sat intent on finding a host they too could enter. When Allison looked down and saw one near her foot, she shuddered and realized she needed to be somewhere free of these things to concentrate on removing the one in Zinc's leg. "Let's move from here," she said. "Ben and Zoey, can you carry two of us to a safe place where I can try again? I'd prefer that Zinc not transform until we can clear his body of the parasites."

"No problem," Ben said.

"I'll carry Allison and the brownie," Zoey was looking at Zinc with a disgusted look on her face.

"I want to know before we go, who was on watch?" Zinc asked.

Zinc's question was met with silence. Finally, Zoey spoke, "I was."

"I should have known," Zinc glared at Zoey. "You probably laughed when you saw those things crawling all over me."

"N...I...it was dark. I never would," Zoey began. Then she stood up straight. "Those worms must like the taste of traitor." Smoke was issuing from her mouth with each word she spoke.

Fire and smoke issued from Zinc's mouth as he struggled to his feet. For a moment it looked like the two of them were going to do battle, but then Zinc turned away.

They flew to what remained of the foundation of a large building and landed. Zinc sat down on a broken chunk of concrete and put his leg up.

Denzel looked at the large lump just below Zinc's knee and his face went pale. "I'll go and see if I can find any food near here."

"I'll go with you," Ben said.

"I'll go too," Zoey added.

"Zoey, I need you to stay and help heal Zinc," Allison said.

"I don't want her to touch me," Zinc growled.

"You don't have a choice if you want that thing out of your leg," Allison said. "Moses, I also may need your help."

"Moses help Allie," Moses said.

When Ben and Denzel walked away, Zoey started to follow them, but then turned back with a scowl on her face.

Moses stood on one side of Allison, while Zoey stood on the other. Allison put her hands on Zinc and sent her spirit as a healer into his body. What she discovered was disturbing. The termite worm, as she named them, had grown even bigger and moved further up Zinc's leg. Allison shuddered as she thought about what would happen if this worm left Zinc's leg and made its way to the vital organs at the core of his body.

"Does it hurt?" she asked.

"No, I wouldn't know it was there if you hadn't told me."

"It must have the ability to dull pain in its hosts," Allison said. "There will be pain as soon as it is removed from your leg. Moses, I want you to use your gift as a healer to manage the pain."

"Moses do," Moses moved closer to Zinc so he could lay his hands on him.

"Unfortunately, there is only one way to get this thing out. It needs to be cut out." Allison took her knife out of its sheath.

"Are you sure?" Zinc eyes were wide and his face was pale.

Allison nodded, "I'm sure.

"You've done this before?" he asked.

Allison considered lying. Zinc needed to feel confident even if she wasn't. In the end she didn't lie, but she didn't admit to never using a knife on a person before.

"Don't worry, this kind of healing is common on Earth. It happens all the time. Healers are always cutting people open to deal with problems they can't fix from the outside. You are lucky, you have not just one healer, but three. Once we cut you open and the worm is out, we can start healing the wound." Allison handed Moses her knife. "Moses please call forth fire and sterilize this."

Moses took the knife and held it by the handle as he called forth a ball of fire with his other hand. He moved the fire up and down the knife blade and when he was finished Allison took it from him. She motioned for Moses and Zoey to hold Zinc down.

Zoey held Zinc's feet together while Moses sat behind Zinc's head and held his arms. Allison placed the knife against Zinc's skin, over the bump made by the termite worm. Her hands shook and her breath was quick and shallow. She had never cut someone open or even seen it done. On Earth, Fairhaven healers set Earthling Chosen to the hospital where a doctor with more surgical experience could look after a problem like this. The only time they themselves might do surgery was if the person was a Chosen from off world whose physical makeup was different than human.

Allison bowed her head and said a silent prayer. When she opened her eyes, she pressed down on Zinc's leg with the point of the blade. After the blade made a small opening, she ran it under the skin alongside the lump. At first it was hard to see the worm for the blood, but then it moved and its tail popped out of the cut. Allison slipped the knife under Zinc's skin at the top of the wound she'd already made and cut across to make an L shape. The head of the worm was exposed, but it quickly started to burrow deeper into Zinc's leg. Allison grabbed it just above the spot where the body tapers down towards its head and pulled. The worm was out and wrapped around Allison's arm. Its head lashed out and attached itself to her arm and began to burrow. Zoey grabbed the worm, yanked it off Allison and threw it to the ground before stomping on it. Blood spurted out and stained the ground red. Zinc screamed in agony. With the worm out of his leg, he felt the pain. Moses sent his spirit as a healer into Zinc to control the pain.

"Thank you," Zinc murmured.

Allison jumped up and ran a few steps away from Zinc before throwing up what little remained in her stomach. She kept retching even when there was nothing left to throw up. Then she wiped her mouth and turned around to begin the work of healing Zinc's leg.

"Zoey," Allison said. "Please come help me. Put your hand over mine and think about going inside the leg. As a healer there is a part of your spirit that can move outside of yourself and into the body of another person. The Guardian can use your gift to send healing energy into Zinc."

Zoey did as Allison asked and put her hand on hers, so their spirits were linked as Allison sent healing power into Zinc. When they finished there was an indentation the size of a golf ball below the knee. Only this golf ball had a tail. Allison knew without being told why she had been unable to heal Zinc completely. Some of Zinc was inside the worm that lay crushed on the ground. Thinking about it made her feel queasy again. She walked away gagging, but there was nothing left in her stomach to throw up. She picked up her water gourd and used some of her precious water to wash the foul taste out of her mouth. Then she returned to Zinc, opened her medical bag, took out some cloth, and gave it to Zoey, who put Zinc's leg in her lap and very gently wrapped the cloth around it. When Zoey finished, she placed a hand on each side of the bandage and sent healing energy into Zinc's leg.

When Denzel and Ben returned from their search for food, Zinc was sitting up. He was pale and shaking.

"Oh gross," Denzel said, looking down at the smashed worm. "How did something that big get inside the Prince's leg?"

"Grew inside," Moses said.

"We couldn't completely heal his leg because there is flesh missing, but we'll keep working on it," Allison said, still feeling sick to her stomach at the thought of what happened to the missing chunk of Zinc's leg. "By the time we're finished it should be almost as good as new."

"From now on, we sleep closer together to make it easier for the person keeping watch," Ben said. "And I think that Moses and I should always be on watch during the darkest part of the night. Moses can use his wizard fire to make light and I will use the one gift I received for coming to Farne. Seeing in the dark will be a useful gift after all."

Allison smiled. Ben on watch meant she would sleep better. She trusted Ben to do everything he could to keep them all safe. She couldn't think of anyone she trusted more.

"I don't think I'll ever sleep again," Denzel said. "But the good news is that we have food." Denzel held up the fresh gourds he carried in his hand. "And we found water."

"Denzel's the one who found it," Ben said. "He figured that plants can't grow without some water so he started digging in the depression where the plants with the gourds were growing."

"My gift of strength and speed came in handy," Denzel said with pride. "It didn't take me long to make a fairly deep hole in the ground."

"He dug deep and water rose to the surface."

"We'll take your gourds and fill them up before we eat," Denzel said, reaching out his hand. Allison and Moses gave him their gourds.

Zoey picked up Zinc's water gourd from where it lay on the ground and gave it to Ben, along with her own.

"Prince, I gather there was no water where you found the gourds yesterday?" Zoey asked with a shake of her head and a mocking tone in her voice.

Zinc glared at Zoey and mumbled a word that made her eyes flash in anger.

When Denzel and Ben returned they ate and then flew off with Zoey carrying Allison and Moses, and Ben carrying Denzel and Zinc. When Allison looked down she noticed something different about the land surrounding the old foundation. She could have sworn it was greener then when they first arrived.

That day and the following night went without incident. They saw clouds and rain in the distance, but stayed away as Zachery instructed them to do. Allison had Zoey help her every time she sent her healing power into Zinc's leg. By the third day he was recovered; however, he had a scar that would remain for the rest of his life. Denzel used his strength and speed to dig in likely places whenever they stopped, but was not able to find more water.

CHAPTER EIGHTTEEN

WATCHERS JOURNAL Year 937

I don't know how to explain what is happening here. There is new life around the school and it seems to be spreading. There are plants, some I've never seen before, growing everywhere. In a week there will be an abundant crop of gourds, which is good, otherwise my brownies would go to bed hungry. I never thought about how I was going to feed them all when I said they could come. I can't keep sending them through the gateway to raid kitchens on Zargon. Eventually, one of them would be caught and there'd be some difficult questions asked. What questions? Well to start with, "What does the Guardian think of you taking things that don't belong to you?" I would have no answer to that question because I don't know. All I know for sure is that it is wonderful to have plenty of good tasting food reminding me of home. I've also discovered that brownies are surprisingly good company. They like playing games.

CHAPTER NINETEEN

ZINC AND THE FORKED STICK

When they stopped at midday, the companions drank sparingly from their water flasks.

"We'll need water again soon," Ben commented as he shook the contents of his flask back and forth.

"I didn't see any likely places from the air. Not much is growing in this area to suggest there is water," Denzel said. "But I'll look later."

"It's the Prince's job to find us water," Zoey said. "Otherwise he's not much use."

"Zoey," Allison said. "Give Zinc a break. He's not the only one with a gift he hasn't figured out how to use yet."

"Moses has gift needs to learn," Moses said. "Moses learn, so will Prince."

"I have a gift like that too," Zoey admitted.

Zinc briefly smiled at Moses before turning his full attention on Allison with a look of admiration on his face. He never took his eyes off her as he finished what was left of his dried gourd. When he finished eating, he rose to search for water.

"Wait," Ben said. "Where are you going?"

"Where do you think I'm going?" Zinc replied.

"You shouldn't go off on your own," Ben said. "We decided that after our first night here."

"I don't remember deciding anything," Zinc said.

Ben pushed himself up off the ground. "I'll go with you."

"You don't need to. I haven't seen anything out there that is a danger to someone who is dragonborn, so I can take care of myself. If there's any real threat I can't deal with I'll just fly away."

"Only if you see the danger coming and recognize it as a dangerous when you see it," Ben said.

"Yeah, you can't always take care of yourself. You were the one the worms got into," Zoey said.

"I was asleep then. I'm awake now." Smoke rose from Zinc's nostrils.

Allison gave Zoey a dirty look. "Zoey, you'd be the one with the scar on your leg if you'd been closest to where those worms came out of the ground." She then spoke to Zinc. "Ben has a point, Zinc. We should always have someone with us. If anyone of us is lost then it makes it less likely that our quest will succeed. Please let Ben go with you. I'd feel better if you did."

Zinc silently stared at Allison, searching her scale covered human face with its lizard eyes. "I'd do anything for you," he finally said to Allison, before turning to Ben. "You can come with me. Just give me some privacy."

"You've got it," Ben said.

Zinc transformed into a dragon and Ben did the same thing. Ben followed Zinc as he flew a short distance away before landing and turning back into his human self.

"Don't follow me," Zinc said.

"Okay," Ben responded.

Zinc walked past a cactus-like plant into a bit of a valley and took out the forked stick he'd brought with him from Zargon. He held one end in each hand and pointed the tip downward. He closed his eyes and began a desperate search for water. With all his heart Zinc wanted to be the one who would find water this time. It would be far too embarrassing if it were Denzel who found it again. He clenched and unclenched his jaw as he went around in circles with his eyes closed. When there was nothing to indicate there was water, no sensation, no pull on the stick, he opened his eyes to walk a bit further on where he repeated the procedure. He did this several times. With each repeat he became more and more desperate to find water.

He walked past another cactus to try one more time. He was holding the stick in his hands when Ben's voice broke the silence. "What in the world are you doing?"

"Go away. You agreed to give me some privacy," Zinc said, keeping his eyes closed.

"I will, but first of all tell me what you are doing with that stick?" Ben asked.

"You ought to know. You're from earth where people dowse for water," Zinc replied. "No one looks for water on Zargon. It's everywhere."

"So the Guardian of the Six Worlds gave you this stick to use in searching for water?" Ben asked.

"No," Zinc admitted.

"Then Mack gave you the stick?" Ben asked.

"Not exactly," Zinc replied. "Mack told me about how it was done on Earth so I went out and got this stick."

"Throw it away," Ben demanded. "A stick from Zargon will be no use to you on this world."

"What!" Zinc's eyes flew open. "Do you think it has to be a stick from Earth to work?"

"The gift is in you, not in that stick," Ben said. "The stick is a distraction. It's getting in the way. As long as you are trusting in that stick, rather than in yourself and in the gift the Guardian has given you, you will never find water or your father."

"You're sure about that?" Zinc asked.

"I am," Ben replied.

Zinc gently dropped the stick on the ground and slowly turned around in circles. Instead of sensing water, he sensed the stick lying on the ground waiting to be picked up. Zinc made a couple of turns and then stopped to pick up the stick again. Before he could grab it, Ben pounced on it.

"Give that to me!" Zinc said. "I need it!"

"No you don't."

"I can't find water without it."

"Yes, you can."

Zinc reached out his hand and grabbed for the stick, but Ben backed away. Zinc transformed into a dragon and flew at Ben. Ben became a dragon seconds before Zinc charged into him. Ben was thrown backwards by the impact. He quickly got up, turned his back to Zinc, threw the stick into the air, and sent out dragon fire toward it. The stick burned as it fell to the ground and broke apart so it no longer had the two branches that made it work as a dousing stick.

The two dragons tumbled on the ground as they bit and scratched at one another. They landed against one of the prickly cacti. If they'd run into it in their human form the cacti would have left them bleeding from the wounds it inflicted. In their dragon form all they felt was a prick, but it was enough to stop their fight. They moved apart and turned back into their human selves.

The cactus had split apart and a stream of water flowed out of it. Ben ran and got his gourd and held it in the stream. When his gourd was full, he took Zinc's and filled it as well. Then they turned and walked back to camp together in their human forms.

When they returned to the others, Ben spoke first, "Zinc found water."

Zinc gave Ben a look of gratitude. "Give me your gourds," Zinc said. "I'll go fill them up for you."

"Moses help Prince," Moses said. He was on his way to get Allison's gourd, but Zinc stepped in front of him.

"I like to have the pleasure of filling this one myself," he said.

Allison moved closer to Ben. "I appreciate how you do that."

"Do what?" Ben said.

"Give credit to others and build them up. I know, without being told, that Zinc found water because you were with him. You could have taken some of the glory, but you didn't."

"How can you know that?"

"I don't know, I just do. You are a good man, Benjamin Taylor." Allison reached out her hand and gave Ben's arm a slight squeeze before walking away to join Zoey.

Ben had a smile on his face as he watched Allison leave.

That afternoon the clouds Zachery warned them about took shape all around them. One moment there was no cloud in sight and in the next the air in front of them would start to churn and a cloud would form. They spent the afternoon zigzagging to avoid green tinged clouds. As they zigzagged Zinc became aware of something important. He always knew where his father was, no matter what direction they were flying in. Ben was right. The stick was getting in the way. Not that he planned to ever admit that to Ben.

They didn't stop until they came to a place free of clouds. As the sun went down all the clouds, even those they could see in the distance began to disappear. At supper, Zinc took a seat near Ben and said a quiet 'thank you.' It wasn't a word he'd used often in his life. Ben gave a simple nod of his head and briefly smiled at his uncle.

Allison looked over at them and smiled warmly.

CHAPTER TWENTY

WATCHER'S JOURNAL YEAR 937

I decided to send Rose and Thorn through the gateway. One of the brownies that I named Salty talked about the farm he used to live on and the good crops they grew. I sent Salty with Thorn and Rose to bring back some seed. They not only brought seed, but Salty's wife and children and some of those wonderful domesticated birds that lay eggs. I had my first egg in almost a thousand years. It was wonderful. I am going to let some of the eggs hatch into chicks.

When some of the other brownies saw Salty's wife and children, they asked that their own wives and children be allowed to come. I said they had to wait until there was more food. Not only that, but I am wondering about the ethics of stealing property. A few seeds are one thing, and the birds are plentiful and no real loss, but no dragonborn family would willingly part with brownies who have served their family for generations. Unless they have proved to be more trouble then they're worth. Then they're sold to the salt mines. I thought of sending Salty's wife and children back, but when I saw how happy they were to be reunited, I couldn't do it. Tomorrow we will plant the seeds. I will set a brownie to watch for toxic clouds. When they come I will use my power as a Watcher to send the clouds away. Only good rain will fall on my gardens.

CHAPTER TWENTY ONE

TOXIC CLOUDS

It was early morning and the sun had risen when the first rain fell. Zinc was on watch and he failed to notice when a cloud formed right above them. The wind that picked up should have been a clue. And it was, but he was scanning the horizon rather than looking directly above them. The others slept on the remains of a parking lot. Beside them was the ruin of a large building with ground floor walls still standing, but it had not looked safe enough to spend the night in.

The first rain drops to hit exposed skin brought howls of pain. Zinc did not need to wake the others; the rain did that without his help.

"The building," Ben yelled as he grabbed his backpack and bedroll. The others followed his direction and everyone was soon racing for the open door. As they ran, Allison and Denzel called forth their gift of scales to cover their bodies, rightly reasoning the rain would do less damage in their altered form. Moses' fur offered him some protection, but the rain was causing his fur to frizzle and curl in the places where it hit. Ben, Zoey and Zinc transformed into their dragon selves for the few minutes it took to run to the building. They had to become human again before plunging through the open door.

Much of the roof had fallen in. All that remained intact was the entryway that once welcomed people into the building.

"Allison hurt," Moses said and laid his hands on her so he could heal her.

"Zachery wasn't fooling when he said the rain was dangerous," Denzel said, examining the raw angry looking welts on his scale-covered skin. "I can't imagine how much worse it would be in my normal skin."

"He also said these old buildings can hide dangerous creatures," Ben said. "Keep your eyes open."

"I think I've learned enough as a healer to take care of those wounds," Zoey said to Denzel. "Do you mind if I try?"

"Good idea," Allison said, "It will give you some good practice as a healer, but let me heal you first."

After Zoey was healed she laid her hands on Denzel and put into practice the skills Allison was teaching her. Denzel smiled as the pain left his body. "You are beautiful. I love you," Denzel said. "Marry me."

Zoey didn't know how to respond to those words, so she gave Denzel the most radiant smile and punched him gently on the arm.

"You are very beautiful," Denzel said. "If I'm not careful, I really will fall in love with you."

Zoey smiled as she rubbed the place on his arm she had punched.

"It's against the rules for Chosen to get involved with someone not from their own world." Zinc pushed his way between Denzel and Zoey until he stood in front of the dragonborn girl. "Use your healing powers on me," he demanded.

For a brief moment it looked like Zoey was going to refuse, but then she took his hand in hers, closed her eyes and sent her healing power into Zinc.

In the meantime, Allison healed Ben. Once he was healed, Ben walked to the open door and looked outside. He understood why the land was so dry and barren. It was a wonder that anything grew when rain that could turn anything living into a skeleton fell from the sky.

The others came and stood silently beside him to watch it rain through the open door. It was good they moved for most of what remained of the roof collapsed behind them. Ben stumbled out into the rain, which had gotten heavier, screaming as he did so. He fell to his knees on the ground and stopped the scream.

"Ben," Allison howled.

Ben had closed his eyes as he fell into the rain, now he opened them and put his hands out so they formed a cup. When he caught enough water, he drank it and then laughed because of the sheer joy that came with still being alive when he expected to die a gruesome death.

"Oh, Ben," Allison breathed in relief as she stepped into the rain to join him. She put her arm across Ben's shoulders as she fell to the ground beside him. Soon all of the Chosen stood in the rain so that it could wash them clean of several days worth of grime. They stood with their faces raised to the sky and their mouths open. After the rain passed, they ate their breakfast as the sun dried their clothes.

"Do you think that happens all the time?" Zoey asked. "Do you think the rain always starts out as toxic and then becomes fresh?"

"I don't think so," Denzel said. "We've seen clouds start green and stay green. There must be a reason why this one lost its green tint and became normal."

"Do you see what's happening around the building we were in?" Allison asked.

"It's greener. How could that be happening so fast?" Ben asked.

"I noticed the same thing at the place where we healed Zinc, but there was no rain there," Allison said. "As we were leaving it looked greener than when we arrived. I thought it must just be my imagination."

"I've never seen anything like this. You can actually see those plants growing," Zinc said.

"Hey Prince, this is a different world. Perhaps things just work differently here and things grow faster," Zoey said.

"Could this growth be connected to the use of the gift of healing?" Ben asked. "What we're seeing is beyond normal on any world. It seems more like a gift from the Guardian."

"It truly is amazing," Allison said, "but I've never heard of the gift of healing bringing new life to the world around it when used. I think there is more to it than that. In fact, I know it. It is the gift of healing when used by someone with the Guardian's unknown gift. The gift is called..." Allison paused as if listening to a voice that none of the rest could hear. "The gift is called re-genesis. It has never been given before because no world has needed this kind of re-birth before."

"I was given an unknown gift as well," Zoey said. "Or at least I was given a gift the Watcher of Zargon did not recognize. I thought it was just because he was young and a new Watcher, but he claims to have the memories of all previous Watchers. Maybe I was given whatever gift Allison and the brownie have."

"The brownie's name is Moses," Allison said firmly with a frown on her face.

"In our world names are not given to brownies," Zinc said. "We call them the garden brownie or the kitchen brownie or the cleaning brownie. What we call them is more a function of what they do."

"I be Moses, Chosen and named by Guardian. Moses be freedom brownie," Moses said.

"You give a brownie a name and they forget their place," Zoey said.

"Moses is with us on this quest. Like us, he has been selected by the Guardian, and he deserves to have his name used," Allison stared at Zinc with her arms crossed and her lips pressed together.

At first Zinc looked like he was going to argue, but then he smiled at Allison. "Anything for you," he said.

"Oh please, give me a break." Zoey rolled her eyes and made a gagging sound.

As they sat in the sun the wind picked up and clouds formed around them. The ones closest to them were normal, but the ones further away were the toxic green. Rain squalls appeared and disappeared with no predictability.

"This unsettled weather will make our flight more challenging today," Ben said frowning.

At just that moment a cloud formed right where they sat. Without a word five of the six companions stood up and packed their bags, preparing to move quickly. Moses started packing, but then he stopped, stood up and raised his hands toward the cloud. He closed his eyes as he gathered the air around them and sent it as a current toward the cloud to blow it away.

The Chosen from Earth congratulated Moses.

"Well that should make today's flight safer," Ben said.

"Sorry, no think before. Wizard gift mean no dodge clouds," Moses said.

"I don't get it Prince," Zoey said quietly to Zinc. "You're given the gift of finding water. That is a gift that should belong to a brownie slave. And the brownie slave gets the gift that by rights should belong to a Prince. It doesn't seem right to me, and I don't even like you."

Zinc glared at Zoey, but then his eyes softened and he smiled. "For once we agree on something," he said. "A Zargon Prince should not be looking after mundane things, while a brownie slave has the gifts of a wizard."

A brief smile flitted across Zoey face, but then she scowled at Zinc before quickly transforming into a dragon. It was time to begin their day.

CHAPTER TWENTY TWO

AN OCEAN CROSSING

Throughout the morning, the green dragons with their blue tipped wings flew through the sky. All around them clouds formed. Some of the clouds they dodged. Moses used his power to send others away. Still others were turned from toxic to sweet with the gift of re-genesis. Ben was in the lead with Denzel on his back when they encountered a body of water that stretched as far as they could see before them and as far as they could see to the left and right. Ben landed on an old foundation close to shore, one of many lining the banks of the dead ocean. Zoey and Allison landed a moment later.

"This is a major body of water," Ben said.

Zoey landed next to Zinc and stared out across the ocean. "It looks like it goes on forever," she said wearily before turning her head to look at Zinc. "Prince, is this the direction we must go to find the King?"

"Yes," Zinc said, pointing in exactly the direction he knew his father to be; a direction that led straight across the body of water.

"Does anyone know if this could be an ocean?" Zinc asked.

"Didn't you read about Farne in your library?" Denzel climbed off Ben's back so he could stretch his legs.

"Most of the books in our library were burned by Zork when he attacked Stonehaven, otherwise the Prince and I would have read all about it," Zoey said, surprising everyone, including herself, by coming to Zinc's defense.

"What we read in the library on Earth tells us that Farne has two very large bodies of water. This might be one of them," Ben said. "If it is, then it might take us days to get across."

"We can't fly for days without stopping," Zoey exclaimed.

"There may be islands," Ben said doubtfully.

"But what if there are not? If we fall into the water, I doubt any of us will survive," Zoey said. As they looked across the water there were several green clouds forming and disappearing after dumping their payload of toxic rain into the sea below. "I don't think we can do it."

"I agree with Zoey," Denzel said. "This quest has just gone from foolhardy to impossible. I'd like to find the Zargon King, but not at the expense of my life. Perhaps we should turn around and go back."

"Wow, you surprise me, Denzel," Ben said. "You've never given up on anything in all the time I've known you. You are the most foolhardy person I know."

"I've never been faced with the real possibility of death before," Denzel said.

"Except for the time you decided to climb the outside of the castle," Ben replied.

"It didn't seem foolhardy at the time and I still ended up dead." Those from Zargon gave Denzel a puzzled look and he gave a brief account of what happened. "I knew there was something more going on at the school than anyone would tell me. So I put the rock climbing skills they taught me into practice and climbed the outside of our school. I fell and broke my neck. I would be dead if not for the quick thinking of a visiting healer. Dying was no fun. I don't want to do it again so soon. So my vote is to give up this quest and go home if we can't find a way around this ocean. If we try to cross it we will die."

"There's got to be a way across," Zinc said, sounding desperate.

"I agree with Zinc, there's got to be a way," Allison said. "The Guardian sent us here and must know there are seas to cross. I believe we have been given what we need to do so. Perhaps the unknown gift can change the water from toxic to fresh."

"There's too much of it," Ben said, shaking his head.

"We need to try," Allison replied, looking at Moses and Zoey.

"I don't know how," Zoey said. "But I want to try. This quest is too important to give up on."

Zinc looked at Zoey, surprise written clearly on his face.

"Let's try having the three of us stand together and stretch our hands towards the sea while sending healing through our hands," Allison said.

"I try," Moses said. Zoey nodded her agreement.

At first it appeared that they were going to succeed. The water went from being a murky green to clear. The clouds close by lost their greenish tint and rained down pure clean water. However, the effort soon drained them and when they dropped their arms the murky water infiltrated the good clean water they had just created. The clouds above the water that had been touched by their healing power remained free of the green tint, but the sea itself did not.

"I didn't think it would work," Denzel said. "We have no choice but to go back."

Moses dropped his bag on the ground and pulled out the gift the Guardian of the Six Worlds had given him. "We have choice," Moses said. "Guardian gave Moses gateway."

"The Guardian gave you a gateway?" Ben and Zinc said almost in unison, both of them thinking they would have been better choices for such a gift. Ben because he saw himself as the natural leader, having already been on two previous worlds, and Zinc because he was the King's son and as far as he was concerned the right choice for leadership and any special gifts.

"Moses give gateway to Zachery so can go back," Moses said.

"So do I understand this correctly?" Denzel asked. "We can start our flight across the water. If we can't fly all the way then we can use the gateway and it will take us back to the Watcher of Farne. Why don't we just go back there every night and sleep where it is safe, and every day we can just resume our journey from where we left off?"

Moses scratched his arm and looked perplexed for a moment. "Ask Watcher."

"I don't think a brownie is the best person to decide how a gateway should be used," Zinc said, reaching to grab it out of Moses' hand.

"The gateway was given to Moses by the Guardian of the Six Worlds," Allison said. "We can't take it away from him if the Guardian wanted him to be the one to have it."

Zinc pulled back his hand and looked at Allison. If it had been anyone else he would have argued. Ben had stepped forward to grab the gateway if Zinc tried to take it by force, but he now stepped back from a confrontation with Zinc.

"How do you propose we use this gateway?" Ben asked.

"Moses hold gateway. If everyone touch, we all go through," Moses said.

"So if we go through, what happens tomorrow?" Ben asked.

"We go spot where stop and fly from there," Moses said.

"You're sure it will work?" Denzel asked.

"So if we are flying we hold onto the tail of the dragon in front of us and make a tight circle. I fly through the gateway with Denzel, Zoey follows with Allison and Zinc comes last with Moses still holding the gateway. Will that work?" Ben asked.

"Moses says yes," Moses said.

"Wait a minute," Zoey said. "We could fly right into a toxic cloud and have the flesh stripped off of us."

There was silence for a moment and then Allison spoke. "I will go through first and as I do, I will use the gift of re-genesis."

"I don't like it, I don't like it at all," Ben said.

"There is no other option, and I am the logical choice, because the gift of healing and therefore the re-genesis gift in strongest in me," Allison said.

CHAPTER TWENTY THREE

WATCHER'S JOURNAL YEAR 937

I have been in touch with the other Watchers. I have not told them everything, but only that my world is experiencing a re-genesis and can now support life. I asked them to send me breeding stock for animals they think will do well here. The first animals are set to arrive today. I know this contravenes the Guardian's rule that nothing living other than the Chosen go between worlds, but I believe the Guardian approves. I told the others that. They don't know that my link with the Guardian is weak, but they don't seem to doubt I've heard these words straight from the Guardian.

I am trying to restore my link with the Guardian. Every day I go to my office and sit in silence with an openness to hear what the Guardian would say. All I've heard so far is the word re-genesis, which is one reason I feel it is okay to bring in creatures from other worlds. What good is a world that can sustain life, with no life on it?

The brownies are doing well. The sun does not seem to be a problem for them, but I have asked them not to be out in the sun when it is at its strongest. Actually, I think the sun could be less damaging now than it was before.

The brownies keep asking me to bring more of them here. I am still thinking about it. I cannot go through the normal channels, but it feels wrong to keep going through a backdoor. I know without doubt it would lead to the new Watcher on Zargon's death if he agreed to help in sending brownies here. The dragonborn would rise up and put an end to their Watcher and close the portals linking their world to others.

I'm leaning towards using the gateways to bring more Brownies here. They are happy on Farne. They laugh and I laugh. We play games and tell jokes and it's wonderful.

I've decided to name the school for the Chosen on Farne, Firehaven. I forgot what it was called before, but Firehaven seems like a good name after what this world has been through.

CHAPTER TWENTY FOUR

UNWELCOME GUESTS

Zachery stood near a recently planted garden as the sun was going down, waiting for Rose and Thorn to return. When a gateway opened, he was surprised it was the Chosen who came through. Ben crash landed when his legs gave way and fell face first on the ground. Denzel was thrown off his back and hit the ground hard. Zoey landed and sank to her knees to make it easier for Allison to dismount. She knelt as a dragon, but when she stood it was as a human. When Zinc landed, he shook Moses off his back.

Denzel had the wind knocked out of him and lay on his back. "Ben, buddy, you've got to work on your landings," he moaned before rolling over and pushing himself onto his feet.

Allison knelt beside Ben and sent a little of her healing energy into him. Looking at her, Zachery didn't think she had much energy to spare, but she shared what little she had and helped Ben stand.

"What are you doing here?" Zachery asked them, displeased at their sudden appearance.

"I thought you would be happy to see us," Denzel said. "When we came to Farne you wanted us to stay with you and play games."

"Hmmm," Zachery responded unsure of what to say. "Yes, but I've realized you have an important quest. You should be out there looking for the King. You need to leave right now and get on with the rescue."

"The dragons couldn't fly any further," Denzel said.

"Then they should have stopped flying," Zachery responded.

"There was nowhere to land. We were flying over an ocean you didn't tell us about," Zinc said.

"There's an ocean?" Zachery asked, clearly surprised, then he said, "Of course there's an ocean. Doesn't every world have an ocean?" Zachery didn't want the Chosen to know how little he knew about Farne. Watchers were supposed to know about the worlds they lived on. They were supposed to have a connection with their world.

Zachery didn't know what to do with the Chosen. They would expect him to feed them in the dining hall, but if he sent them there they would find the brownies whose turn it was to prepare the evening meal. He was still trying to decide what to do when Ben and Allison came and stood beside the others.

"Wow. You've been busy while we've been gone," Ben said. "This garden wasn't here when we left. How did you do all that work in such a short time and where did you get the seeds?"

"I have been busy," Zachery said and then he laughed hysterically, which effectively put an end to any more questions.

Zoey was unstable on her feet after their long flight. "I'm going over to the dining hall to wait for you," she said, and started to walk away.

"No, you can't go there," Zachery said, thinking of the brownies who were preparing the meal. "I'll find another place for you."

Just then a gateway opened beside Zachery and Rose and Thorn came through with gardening tools in their hands, and sacks of food hung over their shoulders.

Zachery giggled uncontrollably. All of the Chosen but Moses stood in stunned disbelief. The two brownies dropped their tools and ran for a nearby ruin.

"Where did those brownies come from?" Zinc asked.

"From Zargon, of course," Zachery said.

"How did they get here?" Zinc asked.

"Through a gateway, of course," Zachery said. "How else do you think they got here?"

"A gateway like we just used?" Zinc asked.

"That's right," Zachery replied. "I came here through a gateway, but the magic did not work to take me back to Zargon." Zachery wondered if the Guardian had removed that gateway to prevent him from returning to his home world. "I couldn't use the one I had until Moses left me one of his. I've waited for centuries to go back to Zargon, but now I might stay and be the Watcher of Farne."

"I thought you already were this world's Watcher," Zoey said, with a snarky tone in her voice.

"Now I am a Watcher with something to watch." Zachery giggled and clapped his hands.

"So you used the gateway Moses left you to bring these brownies from Zargon?" Zinc asked, his voice expressing a mixture of disbelief and outrage.

"Moses bring brownies," Moses said.

"You had no right to do that," Zinc shouted.

"Why? Guardian name me Moses. Moses job to free slaves," Moses said.

"Where did you get the stupid idea that the name Moses had anything to do with bringing Brownie's to Farne?" Zinc demanded.

"Denzel read book. I name Moses for reason. Moses sets free slaves."

"Denzel should not be putting ideas into the head of a brownie," Zinc said.

Zoey nodded her head in agreement. "These brownies belong to a dragonborn family on Zargon. They need to go back there."

"Rose and Thorn be in salt mine," Moses said.

"Then they should go back to the mines immediately," Zoey said. It was Zinc's turn to nod in agreement.

"Never," Thorn shouted from where he was hidden. "We be dinosaur food. Moses free just in time."

"They be staked to ground, near dinosaur eggs," Moses explained.

"I guess if these two brownies…" Zinc began.

"Name be Thorn and Rose," said Moses.

"I guess," Zinc began again. "The brownies from the mine can stay here since they were about to die anyway."

"Other brownies stay Farne too," Moses said.

"There are more brownies here?" Zinc voice became high and loud. "You can't tell me the miners were going to kill them all."

"Mines not good for brownies," Moses said.

"That doesn't change the fact that the brownies belong to the owners of the mine," Zoey said loudly.

Zachery, meanwhile, had been dancing a jig and giggling. He danced in front of Zinc. "I'm planning to keep all the brownies here and maybe even bring more."

Zinc was stunned into silence and stood staring at Zachery for a minute before speaking slowly and quietly. "I can understand why you would want to bring the brownies from a salt mine here. How they are treated is not right and they die quickly. It is something my father needs to fix when he is back on Zargon as King."

"King had long time to fix. Never did," Moses said.

Zinc ignored Moses and kept speaking. "The fact remains that you have stolen property belonging to the owners of the mine. They need brownies to produce salt for the dragonborn. You can keep these two, but as the Prince of Zargon, I insist that you send the rest back."

Zoey smiled openly at Zinc, she clearly approved of what he was saying.

"All brownies stay Farne. They not happy on Zargon," Moses said and walked away as if the matter was settled.

"Whether brownies are happy or not, doesn't matter," Zoey said. "Their purpose is to serve the dragonborn and no one cares what they want or think."

It was Zinc's turn to look at Zoey with approval written on his face.

"Moses is not a slave. Rose and Thorn are not slaves. No brownie who comes to Farne will be a slave, and they will all have a name of their own." Zachery laughed out loud, delighted by his own words. It was the first time he'd really thought about the position of brownies on his world.

Zinc started to speak, paused, and finally said, "We will discuss this further, but for now we need rest, food and water. We have flown much further than dragonborn should ever fly in one day."

"After supper, which should be waiting for us, I want to speak with Allison, Moses, and Zoey about the unknown gift they've been given," Zachery said. "Something strange has been happening here: A good strange, but still strange. I think they might be part of it." Zachery skipped away from them, laughing as he went.

Ben and Allison walked to the dining hall together. For the first time since coming to Farne they were alone. "I'm sorry about the kiss," he whispered.

"It just caught me by complete surprise," Allison whispered back.

"I really am sorry." Ben blushed and his ears turned red.

"About the kiss or about the surprise?" Allison was also blushing.

"Both."

"I always thought we were good friends."

"We are."

"I hope we'll always be that."

"We will." Ben was looking at his feet and missed the brilliant smile lighting up Allison's face when he said those words. He knew he should be happy that Allison wasn't mad at him and wanted them to be friends, but the truth was he wanted so much more. He would never forget how wonderful it felt to touch Allison's lips with his own. Try as he might, he could not reconcile himself to the idea of Trevor as Allison's boyfriend. However, it was her choice to make and if she thought Trevor would make her happy, he had to let it be. A childhood rhyme he'd learned came unbidden to him: Allison and Trevor sitting in a tree K.I.S.S.I.N.G. Ben wished with all his heart that it was him sitting in the tree with Allison.

CHAPTER TWENTY FIVE

RE-GENESIS

Early the next morning Zachery took the Chosen out to the place where the green of re-genesis ended and the dry barren land with its few hardy shrubs began. They were instructed to use the mysterious gift.

Zachery sent Ben flying to a hill that stood higher than the others with Allison riding on his back. He sent Zinc and Moses off to the west with instructions that they were to land where the green came to an end on the highest hill they could find. He kept Zoey and Denzel with him. When everyone was in place Zachery waved and Allison, Moses and Zoey raised their arms and sent the energy of the unknown third gift out towards a center point between all three of them. In that point where their energies met clouds began to form. It was the largest bank of clouds Zachery had seen in all his time on Farne. The clouds were heavy with rain and had no tint of green. They spread out in every direction and rain fell from the sky, washing the earth clean. The rain soaked into the soil and found seeds that had lain dormant for centuries. Zachery did not avoid the rain, but ran to the place where it was heaviest. He raised his arms heavenward and laughed and danced as the rain washed him clean. Then he began to somersault. He flipped three times and then fell, sat up and put his head back with his mouth open to catch the raindrops.

Meanwhile, Ben brought Allison back by flying straight through the clouds. He offered to take her around, but she insisted that a shower was just what she needed. When they arrived Ben transformed into a human and went to help Zachery up off the ground. The Watcher waved him away and jumped to his feet. Zinc and Moses returned and soon they were all standing in the rain with their mouths open to catch the raindrops as they fell from the sky. Ben felt a strange urge to dance in the rain alongside Zachery. He might have resisted if Allison had not started to spin around and around as she laughed joyously. Ben, Denzel and Moses soon joined her. Zinc and Zoey stood off to the side and watched for a while and then joined in so that all the Chosen and the Watcher were dancing and laughing in the rain.

"Great," Ben thought, "Instead of us helping Zachery become more sane, we are starting to do the same crazy things he does." Ben laughed joyously and did a summersault in the rain even though some part of him felt foolish doing so.

"I know the name of the unknown gift," Zachery shouted to no one in particular. "It is re-genesis. We will have new life on Farne thanks to the gift you brought. Thank you, thank you Guardian for sending these Chosen with the gift of re-genesis. I pledge myself to do my best to protect this world that is being reborn."

Zachery summersaulted and landed on his back on the ground. He howled in pain as he landed on his tail. Ben walked over and offered his hand to help the Watcher up. This time Zachery took it. "We should go back," Ben said. "We need to have breakfast before we leave."

"Leave? You can't leave today," Zachery said. "You need to go east and west and north and south and bring re-genesis to all the lands around here."

Ben shook his head. "No, we need to continue our quest."

"We will likely be back here tonight and in the morning you can send us out again," Allison said.

"No, no, no, this is far more important than a paltry King," Zachery wailed. "A whole world depends on you staying alive and using the gift of re-genesis."

"Today we will continue our quest and then we will return tonight," Ben said forcefully.

"The good news is that Moses and I can use the gift of re-genesis when we are passengers on dragon wing," Allison said. "We can be healing the land as we travel."

Zachery was about to continue the argument. He stood with his mouth open, but then he closed it and gave a brief nod. "Just make sure to stay alive. Don't take any chances. Come back before your energy runs out."

"Can I heal the pain falling on your tail caused?" Allison asked.

"No, it's okay," Zachery began. "No wait. Yes, you can take away the pain." Zachery moved towards Allison. As she reached out her hands he closed his eyes. When she finished he opened them. "The tail doesn't hurt anymore, and I heard clear words from the Guardian. The King needs you to hurry and rescue him." Then he danced a jig as he repeated the same words over and over again. "I heard from the Guardian. Yah, yah, yah."

The Chosen's breakfast was once again prepared and served by brownies.

"I don't understand why we can't use a gateway and go directly to where my father is," Zinc said.

Zachery laughed. "First of all, you don't know where he is. And even if you knew generally where he was, there would be no guarantee that you wouldn't materialize inside a rock. You need to have been in the place where you are going and have a picture in your mind of where you want to arrive."

"What if there's been a wall built since the last time you were there?" Denzel asked.

"Then you could be in trouble," Zachery said.

"Why does it work to come back here when we only have one gateway with us, but we need two to leave?" Zoey asked.

"The gateway will always take you back to the place you started from if its partner is there, but you can never use it to go somewhere else. To travel forward you need two gateways, to return it is okay just to have one," Zachery said. "I should have been able to use the gateway I had to go back to Zargon, but when I tried it wouldn't work."

"So the only reason you are able to bring brownies here is because Moses gave you a gateway," Zinc said.

Zachery nodded and a small giggle escaped before he could stop it.

"Moses not give. Zachery borrow. It go back Miss Temp'ton." Moses looked up and fixed his eyes on the Watcher as he said this.

"Perhaps you should take it back now," Zinc said.

"Watcher keep for now," Moses said. "He use good. Brownies need own world."

One of the few brownie youngsters, a grandson of Salty's, came and stood beside Moses. He silently stared at the brownie Chosen with shining eyes.

"Something you want?" Moses asked.

Salty walked over and laid his hand on his grandson's shoulder. "Grandson not talk, but want you bless."

"What?" Moses asked with surprise.

"You special. He wants you touch," Salty said.

Moses laid his hands on the brownie youngster and sent a tiny bit of his healing power into him. When he finished the boy grinned and spoke his first words, "Tank you."

A handful of other brownies pressed forward so that Moses could bless them with his touch. The eyes of those who had been at the salt mine looked a little less haunted after being touched by Moses.

Soon the six Chosen went back through the gateway to the position they left the night before and resumed flying over the ocean. They flew for much of the day and as they flew Allison and Moses used the gift of re-genesis until they were too tired to continue. When the dragons were exhausted they returned to spend the night at Firehaven.

The next morning Zachery took them out in a new direction and Allison, Moses and Zoey used the gift of re-genesis. They continued this way for the next four days. They flew over the ocean during the day and then returned to Firehaven for the night. Every morning they started the day by bringing life to the blighted land around where Zachery and the brownies lived. The land around Firehaven became greener with every passing day. Like a ripple caused by a stone thrown into a pond, re-genesis spread out from every place Allison, Zoey and Moses went.

There also seemed to be new faces among the brownies every time they returned. And every time they returned there was a line-up of brownies wanting a blessing from Moses. Zinc and Zoey scowled as the brownies received their blessing. At one point they walked out of the dining hall together.

"This should not be happening," Zinc said to Zoey.

"I agree," Zoey said. "I'd like to stop it, but I don't know what to do."

"Short of stealing the gateway, I don't think there is anything we can do."

"Do you think we should try?"

"Rescuing my father is of utmost importance. Zachery is using the gateway to help do that, so we need to let him keep it for now, but if he shows no sign of returning it to Earth's Watcher, then we need to do something. Are you willing to work with me?" Zinc looked into the dragonborn girl's eyes and thought, not for the first time, how beautiful they were.

"Of course," Zoey said. "We can't let this continue. We need to put aside our differences long enough to stop it."

On the fifth day of flying over the ocean they sighted land. A collective cheer rose up from them all. They had not quite reached it when they decided to return to Firehaven for the night.

CHAPTER TWENTY SIX

FARLAND

The land they traveled over the following day was different from what they had flown over on the other side of the ocean. Grass and small bushes grew in scattered clumps along with the cacti and gourd-bearing vines they were familiar with. Lines that appeared to be tracks left by living creatures crisscrossed the land below them. There was no sign civilization existed here before the war. They saw no ruins or ancient roadways.

The sun lost some of its intensity and most of the clouds they saw did not carry toxic rain. Denzel wondered if he even needed to have the scales and protective ridge over his altered eyes, but kept it just in case.

As the day drew to a close they looked for flat rock or concrete to spend the night on, but there was none to be seen. Finally, they had no choice. The dragons could not keep flying so they landed on the top of a rise that would give them a good view of the surrounding area.

"Do you think sleeping on bare soil could count as an emergency?" Zoey asked Denzel who had ridden with her.

The sun was low on the horizon so Denzel dropped the scales and protective ridge over his eyes and smiled at Zoey. "If you say so, I'll agree."

"Not emergency," said Moses, who had overheard their conversation. "Watcher say not return Firehaven when find land. I decide. I say no emergency."

"Yes, but we were told to sleep on rock or concrete and there is none," Zoey said. "I wouldn't want to discover that there are termite worms here."

"Not emergency," Moses said stubbornly.

"Don't worry," Denzel said. "Those worms won't get you while I'm on watch. I'd stay on watch all night if I have to."

Zoey gave Denzel her most brilliant smile. "That's not necessary, but I appreciate the offer."

"Would you like to come with me to gather some gourds?" Denzel asked.

Zoey's eyes went to Zinc, who was listening to the conversation she was having with Denzel. He was staring at her, but there was no warmth in his face. Zoey turned to Denzel and smiled again. "Sure, it would be good to exercise my human legs."

"If all we have to eat are those dried gourds that should qualify as an emergency," Denzel said.

"Agreed," Zoey said laughing.

"Not emergency," Moses said again.

"Fine, we heard you the first time." Zinc ground his teeth.

"Give me your water bottle," Zoey said to Denzel. Then she took both their bottles and pressed them roughly into Zinc's hand. "Hey dowser Prince, fill these up for us while Denzel and I gather some gourds for food."

Zinc scowled at Zoey, but took the water bottles from her hand. He had no trouble finding water now that he was not concentrating on a stick.

Ben gathered up the bottles that belonged to Allison and Moses. "I'll go with you to get water," he said to Zinc.

"What did the books in your library say about the land on this side of the ocean?" Zinc asked Ben as they walked.

"The books said that the north had few people living in it. I assume that we are further north than we were before because the sun is not as strong. There were no cities and no strategic military bases here. It is very possible there were no direct attacks in this area. If life survived anywhere on Farne, this would be the place."

"Was the school for the Chosen on this land mass?" Zinc asked.

"No," Ben said. "If my guess is right, we will fly over another body of water before we get to where the school was."

"The connection to my father is much stronger then when we started. It gets stronger with every day that we fly in this direction." Zinc pointed in the direction they'd been flying.

"You have some very useful gifts," Ben said. "The gift of being able to sense where grandfather is will be very helpful when we get closer and we would all be dead by now if it were not for your gift of being able to find water."

"I wasn't happy when the Watcher first said I'd be able to do that," Zinc said. "I couldn't imagine any use for such a gift. On Zargon water is everywhere. I didn't realize how important it would turn out to be here."

"So how is Mack?" Ben asked.

"Being the Watcher of Zargon is not easy, but I think he'll be okay. I made life hard for him and I'm not the only one." Zinc said. "How well did you know him on Earth?"

"He was my roommate for a couple of months. If you'd told me he was going to be the Watcher on Zargon, I'd have said you were nuts. He lacked confidence and was afraid of everything."

"It would seem that the Guardian has a way of changing people so they can do great things." Zinc stopped walking and pointed off to the left. "There is water in that direction."

They found something they had not seen before on Farne. Water bubbled up through a crack in the hillside. The water flowed down and pooled in a basin at the foot of the hill. All around the pool, a profusion of green plants covered the ground. They climbed the hill and filled the gourds at the spot where the water came out of the rock.

As they were leaving, Zinc grabbed Ben's arm. "Look," he said and pointed at a muddy spot on the ground.

"Is that a footprint?" Ben asked.

"That's what it looks like to me."

"It's a pretty big animal, if it is, but we have seen no sign of anything living."

"We should tell the others," Zinc said. "Maybe they only come out at night."

When Zinc and Ben returned they discovered that Moses and Allison had gathered some dry branches for a fire. Zinc used dragonfire to ignite the branches. When Denzel and Zoey returned they had some of the fresh gourd that had become a mainstay of their diet. They passed the food they'd found around the circle. Denzel and Zoey sat together and engaged in private whispered conversation and laughter. Zinc watched them with a scowl on his face.

After supper they all gathered some dead branches so the fire could be fed during the night. When the sun went down this part of Farne was colder at night then what they were used to. Ben planned to sleep for the first part of the night so he could be on watch when the night was at its darkest. He'd just fallen asleep when the howling began.

CHAPTER TWENTY SEVEN

NIGHTMARES WALK AT NIGHT

Ben looked up at the stars as he sat beside the fire with his arm around Allison. It was a beautiful night and he was helping her find the planet Venus. Allison held his arm and rested her head on his shoulder. Wolves howled in the distance. Denzel sat on the other side of the fire with Zoey, answering the wolves with a howl of his own. There was a nasty smell and Ben thought it must be the fish frying on the fire. Something was wrong with it. It smelled like it had sat in the hot sun for days before being cooked.

"Denzel, you're an idiot," Ben said. "How would you feel if your howling brought real wolves to our camp?"

Allison leaned in closer, gripping his arm with a trembling hand.

"Don't worry. I'll protect you," he murmured with a smile.

"Ben, you've got to wake up," a voice cut into his dream. He opened one eye. It wasn't Allison holding his arm, but Denzel who was using it to shake him awake.

Ben struggled to open both eyes. "Those howls are not just in my dream," he said as he sat up. "Neither is the awful smell of rotting fish. Where is it coming from?"

The world around them had come alive since Ben fell asleep. The howling wasn't the only animal sound, just the closest and the creepiest. A howl behind them caused Ben to jump off the ground and spin around. He thought he saw eyes and called forth his gift of seeing in the dark.

"Yikes," he said. "These things belong in a nightmare."

The only thing the others saw were the eyes until Moses called forth wizard fire to illuminate the surrounding area. At first the wolves ran away, but soon one was cautiously creeping toward them again.

"Very scary," Denzel said. "I think we should get out of here." He grabbed his backpack and stuffed his sleeping bag into it without taking his eyes off the wolves.

The Chosen quickly gathered up their belongings and shifted around so that every rider was near a dragonborn. Denzel stood near Zoey instead of moving closer to Ben. As soon as Zoey transformed, Denzel climbed onto her back.

More wolves stepped into the light cast by the fire. Three times the size of any wolf on earth, large fangs protruded from their mouths. They did not appear to be healthy; their bones stuck out on the thin bodies, open sores covered them and mucus drained from their eyes and noses. The saliva dripping from their jaws showed these creatures planned to make the Chosen their next meal.

The wolves looked to their leader, waiting for the signal to attack. The lead wolf yipped and lunged toward the dragonborn, who took to the air. Ben was not fast enough and a wolf latched onto his right hind leg. He lifted it off the ground with him, but a second wolf leapt up and dug its teeth into his left leg. Ben howled in pain, but kept trying to lift himself off the ground with wolves holding onto his hind legs. Moses called forth his wizard fire and used it to keep the other wolves at bay, but from Ben's back he could not direct the fire at the wolves holding onto his legs.

The wolves on the ground were desperate to get their own teeth into some fresh meat. They did not run very far even when Moses sent fire their way. One wolf darted forward and Moses used his wizard fire to stop it, but while he was busy with that one, another wolf attacked from the other side. One leapt through the air in an attempt to knock Moses off Ben's back. It might have done so, but Zinc blasted it with dragon fire and sent it tumbling through the air. He roared in triumph.

Ben tried to reach the wolves whose teeth were sunk deep in his legs. He was too close to the ground to reach around and under himself to grab them without getting his head too close to the rest of the pack. Zinc and Zoey could not help him without getting too close to the attacking wolves. The weight of two heavy wolves kept Ben from flying higher. Finally, in desperation, he reached down and snapped at the wolf on the right. A third wolf leapt at him and latched onto his nose. He roared in pain and released a huge blast of dragonfire. The wolf on his nose let go and fell to the ground where it lay whimpering.

Zoey sprayed the ground with dragonfire. The mix of dragon and wizard fire drove the wolves back, and Zinc moved closer to Ben. He grabbed one of the wolves by its neck and threw it into the darkness. Before Zinc could grab the second wolf it let go on its own. The wolves howled in frustration as they stared at the dragons soaring above them. They were answered by the howls of many more wolves, coming from all directions.

Blood oozed out of the punctures on Ben's leg and fell to the ground below. The wolves all wanted to be in the spot where it was falling from the sky. They reminded Ben of sharks in a feeding frenzy. They leapt into the air to catch the drops of blood before they hit the ground and it was bad luck for any wolf that had blood land on their fur.

Zinc sent dragonfire into the midst of the milling wolves causing them to scatter, but they were soon drawn back to the scent of blood. He was too far away for dragonfire to be effective, but getting close enough was risky. Zinc started to move toward the wolves, but Zoey flew up beside him. "You've done well, Prince. Your father would be proud, but it's time to leave the battle. You need to stay alive."

Zinc eyes widened and the nostrils on his dragon face flared. He looked around at the wolves running toward him from all directions.

"You're too close to the ground," Zoey yelled from just over his shoulder. Zinc roared as he put all his strength into climbing higher; a wolf's teeth clacked together just below his tail.

When Ben looked around he saw a world alive with creatures. The wolves were neither the most numerous or the largest, but at the moment they were the only ones intent on making a meal of the dragonborn and their riders.

"More wolves are coming. They all want a piece of us," Ben's words trailed off in a moan.

"We need to find a place to stop long enough so Ben can be healed," Allison said.

"Can't Moses do it?" Zinc asked.

"Moses is getting better every day, but dragonborn are hard to heal."

"Moses try," Moses said.

"Good job, Moses," Ben sighed in relief. "Whatever you did took away the pain."

They flew for a few minutes in silence, before Moses spoke. "Moses need Allie help. Leg not heal."

"So we need to land," Allison said.

"Perhaps we don't need to," Zinc said. "If we fly close together and go into a glide, you can touch Ben's wing."

Zinc moved closer to Ben. Allison reached out her hand and touched the tip of Ben's wing, while Moses used his power from where he sat on Ben's back. The world below was silent as the gift of healing was used. When they finished the night erupted with howls, barks, screeches and roars, as if the animals knew that something extraordinary had happened. Unfortunately, it meant the wolves had more strength to follow the Chosen as their health was improved.

The dragonborn flew through the night. The rising sun revealed wolves still following them. When the creatures saw no sign that the dragonborn were about to land they made a mournful howl, which would have broken Allison's heart, if she hadn't spent the night escaping them. As they flew in the early morning light fewer and fewer wolves followed, until there were only two. Finally, as the sun rose higher they disappeared into a hole in the ground. When the wolves disappeared other animals came out to frantically feed before the sun drove them underground too. Zinc swooped down and caught two beasts with long ears for breakfast.

Soon the world below them looked like it had the day before when they first flew in off the ocean; the only sign of life was the trails crisscrossing the ground.

They landed near some large boulders, and Denzel took the first watch while the others slept close together in the shade. As they took turns standing watch, the Chosen saw few rainclouds, and none that were toxic. Nothing else moved as the sun made it ways across the sky.

At sundown the wolves began to howl and by the time they were in flight the night was alive with sound.

"Looks like we'll be travelling at night for a bit," Denzel said.

None of the dragonborn responded, saving their strength for flying.

CHAPTER TWENTY EIGHT

THE GREEN EYED DRAGON

When the sun was risen enough to drive the predators underground, they found a place with shade and landed. The dragonborn flopped on the ground exhausted, while the others prepared the long eared creatures the dragons caught for breakfast. They slept through the hottest part of the day. Before it got dark enough to bring out the wolves, Ben and Allison harvested some of the gourds. For the first time since that fateful kiss, Ben relaxed and enjoyed the return of an easy friendship with Allison.

They ate their meal as the sun went down, and just before night fell the dragonborn transformed from human to dragon. When Allison moved to fly with Zoey, as she'd done every day except for the last one, Denzel cut in front of her and put his hand on the female dragon. "Do you mind?" he said to Allison. Denzel didn't wait for her answer, but stepped forward to climb onto Zoey's back. Zoey chuckled and turned her head towards Denzel. She used her nose to give him a boost, such a strong boost that Denzel ended up hanging by his arms on the other side of her back. Zoey laughed out loud as she brought her nose around and boosted Denzel into place.

"Humph," rumbled Zinc. "Allison, I'd like it, if you would fly with me."

Ben gave himself a mental kick for not speaking up before Zinc did.

"I don't need a boost," Allison said, as she put her foot on Zinc's wing, and grabbed a scale on his back to pull herself up.

"I guess you're with me," Ben said to Moses. He tried to keep the disappointment out of his voice so the brownie would not feel unwanted.

Zinc took the lead. His ability to sense what direction his father was in, kept them flying through the night in the right direction. Rising from the ground was the sound of wild things on the hunt. As they travelled, Allison and Moses sent forth the gift of re-genesis until their energy was depleted.

In the morning the land below them was changed. The grasses and brush had disappeared. The only thing still growing was the cacti and vines that produced the gourds they'd harvest for future meals. They found a place with shade and landed to eat and sleep.

"This ought to constitute an emergency." Zinc sat on the ground beside Allison looking at the gourd Moses had placed in his hand.

"Not emergency," Moses said. "Eat gourd, then fly."

"I saw more toxic rain clouds today then yesterday," Denzel said.

"Me too," Zoey said next to him. "I sent healing power at one close to us to make it pure. Needn't have bothered, it moved away on its own."

"We should change them anyway," Allison said.

"Why bother?" Zoey snorted. "What we can do is a drop in a bucket in such a big world."

"You never know what other forces are at work. What you do might provide the tipping point. And even one cloud changed makes a difference for whatever the rain is going to fall on."

"The cacti and pukey gourds don't seem to mind the toxic rain," Zinc looked disdainfully at the gourd in his hand.

"That's not true," Allison said. "If the rain falls directly on them, the vines shrivel up."

"A cloud formed close-by when I was standing watch," Denzel said. "I woke Moses up so he could blow it away with his wizard's power."

"Next time, wake me up," Zoey said quietly in his ear, but loud enough so everyone could hear.

Zinc grunted and threw what remained of the gourd he was eating away.

Zoey looked at Zinc and smiled. Then she moved closer to Denzel so there was no space between them.

Zinc turned his body away so he couldn't see her. "I wonder why there are more toxic clouds here."

"I suspect we're getting closer to the coast," Ben said. "If I'm right, we have another ocean to cross, but it will not take as long as the last one. If my memory serves me right, there is a narrow passage between this continent and the one we are going to. We may even be able to cross over in one day."

"I would love an excuse to go through the gateway back to Firehaven," Zoey said. "The brownies make a good meal and even if we have to sleep in the dining hall it is safer and more comfortable then here. There are no termite worms or wolves. I still don't understand why we can't go back there every night."

"Maybe Zachery just didn't like you and Zinc giving him a hard time about the brownies," Ben said.

"Do you think those wolves are still tracking us?" Allison asked.

"I doubt it," Ben said. "I'm sure they found easier prey to catch."

"I'm not sure that you're right about that Ben," Denzel said, and as if on cue, a wolf howled nearby.

"They're waking up," Zoey said. "We should go."

Ben was about to ask Allison to fly with him, but she looked at Zinc. "Ready to go?"

Zinc transformed from human to dragon. As Ben watched Allison climb onto Zinc's back, he tried to push down the familiar burning pain in his stomach. He wasn't going to let jealousy ruin his friendship with Allison. Too bad his body wouldn't listen. A whiff of dragon smoke emitted from his nostrils.

"Let's go, Moses," Ben said and transformed into a dragon.

CHAPTER TWENTY NINE

TRIALS AND TRIBULATIONS

They flew steadily onward while the stars made their way across the sky. The sun had not yet risen when they flew into trouble.

"Stop!" Ben yelled. "There's a massive cloud bank right in front of us." The dragons braked hard and spiraled up.

"I wondered what happened to the stars," Zinc said. "Which direction should we go to get around them?"

"I don't see any break in either direction," Ben said.

They landed on the ground in an area that seemed free of animals and the three dragonborn transformed back into their human forms.

"Are the clouds toxic or clear?" Zinc asked, looking at Ben.

"I think they're normal clouds, but my night vision is not good enough to be sure. I think we need to wait until the sun rises to see exactly what we're dealing with.

"Well, we may as well catch up on our sleep then," Zinc said. "Moses, you take the first watch."

"Moses take second watch," Moses said, not willing to let Zinc tell him what to do.

Zinc looked like he was ready to argue with the brownie, but Allison stepped forward, "I'll take the first watch," she said.

"I really should be the one on watch since I'm the only one who can see in the dark," Ben said.

"You've flown far and need rest more than I do. I will take the first watch," Allison insisted.

As the night wore on, the clouds came closer and Allison wished she knew if they were fresh or toxic. In the middle of the night she woke Moses up and asked him to use his wizard gift to blow the clouds away. He did so and took the second watch. Allison slept fitfully and woke as the sun peaked over the horizon. She went and stood beside Moses and watched as the bank of clouds started to expand rapidly in their direction.

In daylight the clouds were clearly tinged with green. Moses called forth his wizard gift and Allison used the re-genesis gift. They pushed them away or transform them, only to have more toxic clouds move in. As she watched the clouds, Allison became aware of a foul smell reminding her of the night they first encountered the wolves. She scanned the area around them, afraid of what she would see. The first time she looked around she saw nothing. When the smell grew stronger she scanned the area again and this time she saw eyes, many pairs of eyes, shining in the morning light, on the opposite side of her sleeping friends.

Allison screamed, "Wolves," and everyone was instantly awake. When she screamed, the wolves leapt toward the Chosen lying on the ground. They would have all died if it hadn't been for Moses and his wizard gift. Moses called forth fire and drove the wolves back long enough for those who'd been sleeping to get out of their sleeping bags and scramble to their feet.

Moses stepped in front of Allison and sent wizard fire out in a semi-circle. The light of the fire illuminated gaunt wolves with rheumy eyes. They danced away when the fire got near them, but as soon as it moved around the circle they came toward them.

The wolves' hunger was stronger than their fear of Moses' wizard fire. One darted in and leapt toward Zoey's throat, while another went for her leg. Denzel jumped into the air and kicked one, sending it tumbling away. Zoey, Zinc and Ben transformed into dragons and stood facing different directions in a circle with Moses. Allison stood in the middle of their circle.

They were using fire to keep the wolves from getting too close. In the light created by dragon and wizard fire, Denzel was fighting a battle of his own. He had gotten around behind the wolves that were trying to get past the fire to attack the Chosen in the circle. As Allison watched he grabbed a wolf by the tail and sent it flying through the air to knock other wolves off their feet. The wolves were big and heavy and strong, but Denzel would have been a match for any three who came at him at one time, but there were many more than that.

One of them jumped on his back and he went down. Others surged forward to share in a feast of human flesh. Denzel would have been their next meal if the dragonborn had not moved closer and blasted the wolves with fire. Denzel ran towards his friends bleeding from several wounds.

"Moses and I will hold them off, while the rest of you get ready to fly," Ben yelled.

The mounting procedure would make dragon and rider vulnerable as the dragon had to get down on its belly so that the rider could mount and the rider had to turn their back to whatever threat was attacking.

"Wait. This be emergency," Moses said, as he brought out the gateway. "Wolves and bad clouds mean we go Firehaven."

Moses held out the gateway in the semi-darkness. The dragons kept the wolves at bay as Allison and Denzel went through the gateway. Zinc and Zoey went next. Ben and Moses followed them through, along with two wolves.

Back at Firehaven, the wolves stood next to Moses, drool hanging from their half open mouths, uncertain of what to do next. When Zinc shot a blast of dragonfire at them, the wolves bolted, but didn't go far. They jumped over a sheep enclosure and each killed one before the dragonborn could chase them away. The wolves carried the dead sheep away with them. Meanwhile, Allison and Zoey healed Denzel's many wounds.

Zachery grumbled when a brownie banged on his door with the news that the Chosen were back and there were two sheep missing from the field. He went to the dining hall where he found the Chosen waiting for him.

"What are you doing here and where are my sheep?"

"It be emergency," Moses said, glaring at Zachery with his arms crossed.

"You always seem to be having emergencies. Maybe this quest is too difficult for you," Zachery said grumpily. "Now someone tell me why I have two missing sheep."

Ben and Zinc both started talking at once.

"One at a time," Zachery said.

They both started speaking at the same time again.

"Okay, we will hear from Ben first because I like him best." Zachery turned his full attention on Ben.

A look of annoyance crossed Zinc's face.

"There was a cloud bank in front of us and wolves all around," Ben said.

"Two wolves came with us through the gateway," Zinc added.

"I guess that explains why two of my sheep are missing," Zachery said.

"I want to know where those sheep came from," Zinc demanded loudly. "There were no sheep here when we arrived. What world did you steal them from?"

"If all Zaltzburg's are as nasty as you, I'm glad to be staying on Farne," Zachery said. "I did not steal those sheep. I told other Watcher's what was happening here and asked them to send me some animals. The sheep were a gift from the Watcher on Earth."

"I recognize the one with the black spot over his tail," Allison said. "It was born at Fairhaven my first year there."

"You are forbidden to bring any more dangerous animals back with you unless they are good to eat." Zachery paused. "Do you think wolf is good to eat?"

"Definitely not," Ben said. "They are skin and bone and look sick."

Zachery looked up at the ceiling as he scratched his head. "Use re-genesis gift on them and then maybe they will be good to eat."

"The wolves are getting better than when we first encountered them thanks to re-genesis, but generally, animals that eat other animals are not good to eat, even if they're completely healthy," Ben said.

"Then you shouldn't have brought them back with you." Zachery wagged his finger at the Chosen. "I forbid you doing that again."

"It's not like we decided to bring them back." Ben's voice was louder than normal and sounded annoyed. "They were trying to make a meal of us as we came though the portal. It's a good thing brownies are fur covered. Otherwise we might have left Moses and the gateway behind. They tried to take a bite out of him and all they got was a mouthful of fur."

"Don't be ridiculous," Zachery said. "The gateway is far too precious to ever leave behind. You can leave the Zaltzburg Prince, but not the brownie."

"Moses more precious than Prince?" Moses asked in surprise.

"You are both of great importance," Allison said.

"What are your plans now?" Zachery asked.

"We need to talk about that." Ben sat down at one of the tables. "Perhaps you can help us come up with a plan over breakfast."

Soon they were settled over a substantial breakfast of eggs, bread, and greens.

"This is good," Ben said. "Do you have enough eggs to boil some so that we can take them with us?"

"We can spare a few," Zachery said, "but only a very few. It's not easy to feed this many brownies."

"You should have thought of that before you took them from where they belong," Zoey said. Zinc smiled at her in approval.

"They are happier here," Zachery said. "You stay away and I will have more food for my brownies."

Zinc appeared to be about to say something more, but changed his mind.

"We would be grateful for any food you can spare," Ben said quickly. "Who knows what we will find to eat if we manage to get over the cloud bank."

"I'm so tired of the puke gourds," Denzel said.

"Puke gourds?" Zachery said puzzled.

"You eat them because you have to eat something, but eating those things makes you want to puke."

Zachery scowled at Denzel. "I've had an almost constant diet of those gourds and little else for close to a thousand years."

"You are a stronger man than me," Denzel said. "I couldn't have endured it."

"It's probably one of the reasons he's half mad," Zinc muttered.

"More than half," Zoey whispered next to Zinc.

Ben gave Zinc and Zoey a dirty look and then turned to speak to Zachery. "So when we left, there was a cloud bank in front of us and wolves behind us. If we use the gateway to go back, we might find ourselves in the middle of a toxic cloud. And if there are no clouds, the wolves might still be waiting for us."

"Why so many clouds?" Moses asked.

"The clouds must be forming over the sea that sits between Farland and Caroway. Caroway was the continent where the school for the Chosen was located before the war wiped everything out," Ben said. "If I am right, Farland is the land mass we have spent the last few days travelling over.

"I'd forgotten that," Zachery said. "But it's coming back to me." He giggled and clapped his hands and then pasted a serious look on his face. "If you go back I can guarantee there will still be clouds over that sea. Most of it is shallow and the hot sun causes many clouds to form. There is no time of day when it would be safe to travel over that sea. It looks like your quest is over. There is no way to get to the other side and find the King."

"Wait," Allison said. "There's got to be a way to continue, otherwise the Guardian would not have sent us."

"No, no, no. It's time for the Chosen to give up. You've tried, but there's no way it can be done. You can stay here with me and be teachers and healers at Firehaven, except for you and you," Zachery pointed at Zinc and Zoey. "You will need to find another place on Farne to live."

"What! Ben exclaimed.

"Why are you so ready to get rid of us? What are you up too now?" Zinc asked. "And why wouldn't you just send us back to Zargon, if you don't want us here?"

Zachery began to giggle. Finally, he answered Zinc's question with a question. "What makes you think Zachery is up to something? Maybe he's just tired of troublesome dragonborn."

"None of us are ready to give up," Ben said. "That's my grandfather and Zinc's father we're looking for. We have come too far and gone through too much to walk away from this quest if there is anything more we can do."

"Think, was there anything that would help us continue on?" Zinc asked. Then he answered his own question. "I thought I saw a mountain. It was in the middle of the bank of clouds. The top of the mountain stood up above the clouds. Did anyone else see it?"

"I didn't," Zoey said.

"You need a location to use the gateway to go somewhere, right?" Zinc asked Moses.

"Yes," Moses said. "If I no see, might not arrive on mountain, but in water."

"What if you gave the gateway to me?" Zinc asked. "I could use it, because I have seen the mountain."

"Guardian give gateway to Moses. No one use but Moses."

Zinc frowned and bit his lip, as he struggled to contain his irritation with Moses, then he put his hand out toward the brownie. "Be reasonable and give me the gateway. Zachery uses it, why can't I."

"That be different. He be Watcher," Moses said, but he looked at Zachery and wondered if he would be able to get the gateway he'd given to the Watcher back when it was time to leave.

"Wait a minute. I saw that mountain. I can use my gift to take us there," Ben said.

"What gift is that?" Zoey asked.

"The gift of being able to transport myself and others from one place to another," Ben said.

"It is too far for your gift," Zachery said. "You need to be able to see the spot where you wish to go. Besides, your gift will not protect you from the rain between here and there. You still travel through time and space, even if you do it very fast. You would arrive as skeletons. But don't worry I have an idea. I'll look into Zinc's mind and then I can put the image into Moses mind."

After breakfast, Moses was on his way to the mountain whose image Zachery had formed in his mind. Moses insisted that he go alone to make sure it could be safely done. He also wanted to know that there was a way forward from that mountain. There was no point getting everyone there, only to find there was nowhere else they could go.

While they waited for Moses, Zoey walked over to stand beside Zinc. "Don't worry Prince," she said quietly. "I'm sure there is a way for us to continue. We've come so very far. It can't end without finding your father."

Zinc smiled at Zoey. For the first time he didn't mind her calling him Prince, he did not hear any mockery in her voice. Zoey's presence helped curb some of the anxiety he felt as he waited for Moses.

"Cloud surround island, but mountaintop above," Moses said. "There be other mountains. Ben use gift. We go next island."

"Well then," Zachery said. "It's time to be on your way."

"What? You don't want us to stay and play games with you?" Zinc asked mockingly.

"What kind of son are you?" Zachery asked. "You'd think about staying here to play games with me when your father is out there somewhere?" Zinc couldn't tell if the Watcher was serious or mocking him.

"Nooo," Zinc said emphatically. "I don't want to play games with you. I will never want to play games with you, but you were always trying to get us to do that when we first arrived, and now you can't wait to get rid of us."

"I have brownies and I like them better than you. They play games, they work hard, and they cook good food. They make me laugh and some of them are even Chosen of the Guardian." Zachery liked what he was saying and clapped his hands and laughed.

Zinc scowled. "You must be mistaken. The Guardian of the Six Worlds would never choose brownies to be Chosen."

"Guardian chose Moses." Moses held out the gateway he'd just used. "Give Moses gateway, wizard gift, and gift that heals Farne."

"You're different. You went into the place between time and space and are no longer just a brownie," Zinc said.

"I be brownie. I be Chosen," Moses said stubbornly.

Zachery stopped clapping and stepped closer to Zinc, so they stood face to face. "The brownies are discovering who they really are, and I have no doubt the Guardian has a special plan for them."

Zinc stepped away from the Watcher. "The Guardian's plan is for them to serve the dragonborn. So it has always been and so it always will be."

Zachery burst out laughing. "I am the only dragonborn on this world and I say they will be a free people. What they do for me, they do out of gratitude, not because they are forced."

"You are not dragonborn. You're a lizard man with a tail." Zoey laughed harshly and Zinc joined her.

Zachery swished his stubby tail back and forth with a scowl on his face. "Not nice of you to say so."

"Okay," Denzel broke in. "Are we going to stand here and talk all day? Or are we going to go save the King of Zargon?"

"Yes, it is time to be on our way," Ben said.

"I hope there are no more emergencies," Zachery grumbled. "I am tired of having dragonborn visitors. They never treated me well on Zargon and they don't treat me well even here on Farne where I am the Watcher." Zachery's last words were spoken forcefully as if to remind the Chosen from Zargon that they should show him some respect.

Moses used the gateway to move the Chosen to the island mountaintop. After that Ben used his gift to move them from one mountainous island to another. Below each mountain they landed on, green tinged clouds swirled over a dead sea. Every time they landed on the top of a mountain, Allison, Moses and Zoey sent forth the gift of re-genesis. The last mountain they landed on was not an island, but part of Caroway. There were no green tinged clouds below this mountain.

"We have been going in the wrong direction to find my father," Zinc said. "If Ben is going to keep using his gift to move us we need to go in that direction." The direction Zinc pointed in led away from the mountain range.

"I can't keep doing this. It uses too much energy," Ben said. "We need to go back to flying."

Allison and Moses laid their hands on Ben so he would be ready to fly when the others were. After a short rest Zinc took the lead and they flew off in search of King Zane. Below them stretched an arid land devoid of any sign of life, plant or animal. There were not even the cacti much of their water had come from, or the vines that grew the gourds they had eaten far too much of.

CHAPTER THIRTY

WATCHER'S JOURNAL YEAR 937

I have asked the Chosen not to return to Firehaven unless it is an emergency. Who knew that a Zaltzburg could be so annoying? He gave me no peace over my decision to bring brownies to Farne. I have found two more Chosen among the newcomers and can only assume that the Guardian intends the brownies to be part of Farne's regenesis. The more I think about it, the more convinced I become that the Guardian does not approve of slavery. My only concern is how the dragonborn will respond when they learn these brownies have disappeared because of their link with other worlds.

CHAPTER THIRTY ONE

CATCHING FISH

They flew for three days and saw no signs of life. There were no clouds in the sky, toxic or otherwise. There were no new dangers to face until the third day when their water gourds were empty and no food remained. They stopped in the shade of a sand hill to rest because the dragonborn were finding it increasingly difficult to keep flying without food and water. When they were out of the sun, Allison and Denzel dropped the scales and eye protection the Watcher had given them since keeping it required energy they did not want to spend. Zinc noticed that Zoey's lips were dry and cracked. His felt the same way.

"Okay Prince, it's time for you to put your gift as a dowser to work and find us some water," Zoey croaked.

"Don't you think I've been trying," Zinc croaked back. His mouth and tongue were so dry it was hard to form words. "There is no water to find in this land."

"What direction do we need to go to find the nearest water?" Ben asked.

"I don't know. All I know for sure is that my father is in that direction." Zinc pointed in the direction they had been flying. All they saw in the direction Zinc pointed was more dry and barren land devoid of life.

"For now, you need to stop thinking about grandfather and focus on water," Ben rasped. "We won't do the King any good if we die out here in this desert."

"Ben's right," Zoey said. "We need to find water to keep going. If we don't find it soon, I think we need to declare it an emergency and go back to Zachery."

"If we go back again, I'm afraid he will send you and I back to Zargon," Zinc said. "He was close to doing so the last time we were there."

"Actually, I'm not so sure about that," Zoey said. "He talked about us living somewhere else on Farne, but he didn't say a word about sending us back."

"Listen Zinc," Denzel croaked, "We really need you to find water."

"Easy to say, hard to do," Zinc said. "All I can think of is my father, and how what I did caused him to be marooned on this world." For the first time in his life Zinc admitted making a mistake to others.

"We need water or we give up the quest. Simple as that. Close your eyes and imagine what you would do right now if you had lots of water. Imagine yourself drinking water, dancing in the rain, swimming, then turn in a circle until you get a sense of what direction we need to go in to find the water you are imagining."

Zinc closed his eyes and turned in a slow circle. At first all he felt was a tug in the direction his father was in. But he pushed thoughts of his father out of his mind and thought about water instead. Cool, refreshing water that would satisfy his thirst. He soon sensed that water could be found in any direction they went in, but discovered a source that was closer than the rest. He stopped turning in circles and pointed his finger. When he opened his eyes, he was pointing southwest, toward a mountain standing by itself in the barren desert.

"That will take us further away from my father," he croaked.

"We have no choice for now," Ben said.

"Ben's right," Allison croaked. "It is time to stop talking and fly."

Zinc nodded his head and transformed back into a dragon. Allison walked over to Zinc. A wisp of smoke came from Ben as Allison climbed onto Zinc's back, but he closed his eyes and sighed as he crouched down to make it easier for Moses to climb onto his back.

The mountain was further away than it looked and they flew for the better part of an afternoon before reaching it. A few scattered clouds started to appear. The land below them changed from flat and barren to rolling hills with a few scattered shrubs. The sun was setting when Zinc led the others into a valley where a river once ran. He flew the length of the valley to a place where an ancient waterway had worn its way deep into the hillside. The river valley became so narrow that they could no longer fly on dragon wing. The dragons landed and transformed into their human form. An ancient waterfall had formed a pool at the base of the small mountain. The pool was bone dry and no water flowed from the ledge above.

Zinc led the way into the semi-darkness of a cave behind the dry waterfall. It felt cool after a day spent in the scorching heat of Farne's sun. Allison and Denzel gratefully let go of the energy sapping transformation protecting their skin and eyes as they walked into the cool dark of the cave. At the back of the larger cave there were two openings.

"Which one should we take?" Ben asked.

Zinc closed his eyes. "They both lead to water, but there is a stronger pull from this tunnel." Zinc pointed to the tunnel on the right.

"Wait! It is going to be pitch black in there and only Ben will be able to see," Denzel said. "I found a piece of rope at Zachery's place and put it in my bag. I think we should make six knots and each hold one."

"That's a good idea," more than one voice said and Denzel proceeded to make knots in the rope.

Soon they were on their way into the tunnel with Ben leading the way and Zinc directly behind him. Before too long they heard the sound of dripping water. The moisture in the air brought some comfort to their cracked lips and parched throats. Ben stopped walking when a drop of water hit his nose. He waited for the searing pain that would signal toxicity, but the water just felt cool and refreshing. He stepped forward as he looked up to see where the water was coming from. He took a second step and screamed as he fell through the air. The others felt a sudden tug on the rope they were holding and were pulled forward until they successfully put the brakes on.

"What's happening?" more than one voice asked. Zinc was in front of the others and he called forth dragonfire to illuminate the tunnel.

"Don't let go of the rope. Ben has fallen through a hole in the ground," Zinc said.

Ben's voice came up from the ground below their feet. "You need to pull me up. I'm holding onto the rope at the top of a huge cavern. The ground is a long way down and there are stalagmites below me. It'd be hard to survive a fall."

The five companions started to pull Ben up out of the hole. The tunnel was no longer illuminated and they didn't see that a sharp edge on the rock was severing the rope. All of a sudden the weight on the rope vanished, causing those holding it to fall backwards with cries of alarm.

"Ben!" Allison screamed and the sound of her voice reverberated in the tunnel. Rocks fell behind them. Allison started to weep. "Oh, Ben, Ben, Ben."

Zinc crawled on his hands and knees toward the hole. Sharp rocks dug into the flesh on his knees. He stopped crawling when he put his hand down and found nothing but empty space. "Are you okay, Ben?" he yelled through the opening.

"Yes," Ben said. "The fall is survivable if you can transform into a dragon and see where to land, but the really good news is that there is a pool of fresh water down here."

"How do you know it's fresh?" Zinc asked.

"I landed in it," Ben replied.

"I'm coming down," Zoey pushed past Allison.

"Better not," Ben said. "They are some stalagmites growing from the cave floor. Unless you can see in the dark it would be hard to land safely."

"But I smell the water," Zoey wailed. She dropped her voice when rocks fell behind them.

"It would be wonderful to have enough water to wash with," Allison said, brushing the tears from her eyes.

"Ben, could you fly up under the hole and give each of us a ride down?" Denzel asked.

"Yes," Ben said.

"I'll go first to make sure it's safe," Denzel said.

Zinc called forth a tiny flame of dragonfire to illuminate the dark as Ben flew up and got into place. Starting with Denzel each of the companions crawled to the hole and sat on the ledge with their legs hanging down. When they felt Ben move into position, they dropped themselves onto his back. Zinc was the last one to ride down. When everyone was on the floor of the cave Ben transformed back into his human form. As soon as he did so, Allison came and hugged him. "I am so glad you weren't hurt. I wouldn't want to lose you."

Ben was stunned, unsure of what to say. "I'm glad you care," he finally said and put his arms around Allison and hugged her back. Far too soon Allison pushed herself out of the circle of his arms.

"There is a basin of water higher than the rest," Ben said. "We'll use that to drink from. Moses can make some light for you to see by, while I look around." Ben turned Moses so that he was facing away from the others. "It's safe to use wizard fire here. The cavern is big enough not to be damaged by your fire and the others are behind you."

Moses called forth his wizard fire so they could see where the water was. They stood near the shore of a large underground lake. In the dark, they couldn't see the other side. Scattered on the floor of the cave were stalagmites and hanging from the ceiling there were stalactites.

Ben led the way to a small pool near the edge of the cavern. Water flowed down the side of the cavern into the pool. A small stream of water trickled down from the pool into the lake. Ben drank his fill of water and then left the others and explored the cave. He ended up standing near the lake. He found something leaning against a rock that puzzled him. When he looked closer he discovered that it was a stick with a sharp pointed stone lashed to it. He wondered where the primitive spear had come from and who had last used it. He had no way of knowing how old it was, but he doubted it would have survived from the time before the war in such good shape.

Ben took off his shoes, rolled up his pant legs and waded into the water. He carefully put one foot in front of the other to make sure he didn't step on something sharp that would injure him. The pool got progressively deeper the further he went from shore. He took one step too many and the water was making his pant legs wet when he felt the first nibble on his toe. He looked around and discovered dark shapes lurking underneath the water. He cried out and tried to scramble backward. He wished he'd brought the spear with him. He quickly returned to shore and picked it up and went back into the water. The dark shapes moved toward him. He plunged the spear downward toward one of them. The weight of the wiggling fish almost caused him to fall into the water. The splashing caused by Ben's struggle attracted even more and dark shapes swam toward him from every direction. It also attracted his travelling companions who walked toward the lake to see what was going on. He pitched the fish high up on the ground and sent the spear downward again. A second fish joined the first and soon there were three fish on the ground behind him.

It was at that moment Ben realized he was in trouble. His eagerness to spear fish had caused him to step into deeper water. He struggled to stand as fish bumped against him. They were doing their best to make his toes their next meal. More than one nipped him and broke the skin. Ben howled in pain.

"What's going on?" Zinc yelled.

"Ben, are you okay?" Allison called.

There was blood in the water and the fish were going into a feeding frenzy. They fought each other to get close enough to take a bite out of Ben's toes. It would only be a matter of time before they knocked him over. Ben had visions of fish feeding on his ears and nose. He drove the spear downward again. This time he did not throw the fish on shore, but threw it in the water about three feet in front of him. The water roiled as the other fish attacked the wounded one. The movement and smell of blood attracted even more fish and Ben was no better off than he was before. He fell backward toward the shore. Denzel and Zinc ran into the water still wearing their shoes, they grabbed Ben's arms and dragged him to shore. A couple of fish came out with them, because they had attached themselves to a pant leg. One of them escaped back into the lake, but Denzel grabbed the other one and threw it away from the water.

"Are those fish?" Allison asked.

"Don't they look like fish to you?" Zoey said. "They do to me, although, I've never seen any with eyes that big."

"I wish I could have grabbed the second one before it got back into the water," Zinc said. "We'd have eaten well tonight."

"Not to worry, I've got three good sized ones on shore already," Ben said. "And with the one Denzel caught we have more fish then we need."

"It looks like you need some healing again," Allison came next to Ben, touched him and sent her healing power to his bleeding toes.

"I'm so glad you're here." Ben smiled at Allison. When she finished healing his toes, he hugged her.

Ben stood and walked over to where he'd thrown the fish. He took out his knife and quickly filleted the first one. He held it out in two pieces and Zinc and Zoey grabbed them out of his hands. Ben gave them a dirty look, which they missed in the semi-darkness of the cave.

He quickly filleted the second fish and placed one half in Allison's hand and the other half in Denzel's.

Allison laid hers out on a flat rock. "Moses, do you mind cooking it with wizard fire," she asked.

Moses cooked her fish and then Denzel asked him to do the same with his. Ben filleted the third fish. He gave half to Moses and kept half for himself. Moses and Ben ate their fish raw.

"I guess, I won't be going for a swim in the lake," Denzel said.

Ben looked down at his toes. "I wouldn't recommend it, but there is a small pool near the cavern wall that doesn't appear to be connected to the lake. I'll check it out and see if it's a safe place. If it is, we can bathe there."

"I claim first dibs for Zoey and me," Allison said.

"Come with me then," Ben said.

Ben and Moses walked with Allison and Zoey over to the small pool. There was no sign of fish in it. Ben walked back to join the others while Moses stayed nearby with his back toward Allison and Zoey. He created a flame in his hand and held it up so the girls could see as they took their bath.

"I have never felt so grimy," Allison said.

"I know what you mean," Zoey said.

"You and Zinc seem to be getting along better," Allison said.

"Yes, I guess we are," Zoey leaned back so that only her face was out of the water. "He's not as bad as I thought he was. Or maybe he was and being on this quest has changed him."

"Maybe both. I do think he's changing in some good ways," Allison said.

"He needed to, if he wants to be King of the Dragonborn some day," Zoey said. "He seems to really like you, but you know it's against the rules for Chosen to have romantic relationships with people from other worlds."

"Yes, of course, I know that," Allison said. "But don't worry, it's not me he's interested in."

Zoey sat up and stared at Allison. "Well, it's certainly not me. He hates me."

"Don't be so sure of that. I see him watching you when he thinks you're not looking."

"Really?"

"I wouldn't have said it if it wasn't true."

The girls finished their bath in silence as they were both lost in their own thoughts. They changed into the clean clothes they carried in their backpacks and walked down to the lake so they could wash the clothes they'd been wearing. They let the boys know they were finished on their way.

During Ben's rescue he'd left the spear in the lake. The stone tip was resting on the bottom, but the shaft floated on the surface. Ben walked into the water just far enough to get it.

"Why are you going back into the lake?" Denzel asked.

"I'm getting the spear," Ben said.

Dark shadows darted out of the deep water toward him. Ben grabbed the spear and turned and ran. Once on shore, he picked up the heads and internal organs of the filleted fish and threw them into the water. The water came alive with fish all trying to feed. Ben took the spear in his hand and quickly had three more fish on shore.

"Where did you find the spear?" Zinc asked.

"Leaning against that rock," Ben replied.

"You know what this means, don't you?" Zinc asked.

Ben stared at Zinc for a moment. "Yes, I think so. There has been someone down here using this spear and I don't think it was a thousand years ago."

"Should we take it with us?" Zinc asked.

"I don't think so. Whoever made it might depend on it being here to find fish to feed their family."

CHAPTER THIRTY TWO

HELLO TINY

They filled their water gourds before they left the cavern. Ben flew up to the hole in the ceiling with Denzel on his back. Denzel reached up and grabbed hold of the ledge and easily pulled himself up so he was in the tunnel they had left earlier.

"I sure enjoy the gift of strength," he said as he hung from one hand. "Too bad I have to give it back."

"I'll bring up the others," Ben said. "And you can put your gift of strength to work helping them."

"I'll be ready," Denzel said.

When Ben flew the other Chosen up to the hole in the ceiling, Denzel effortlessly reached down and pulled them from Ben's back to stand in the tunnel behind him. The only real challenge came when it was Ben's turn. He could not get through the hole as a dragon. He had to transform and Denzel had to grab him after he was no longer a dragon and before he fell to the ground as a human. The first attempt failed. Ben fell toward the ground but transformed as soon as he knew Denzel had failed to catch him.

The flight back to where they'd changed direction went faster than the trip to the cave. They flew in the morning and evening, while taking turns sleeping in the hottest part of the day and the darkest part of the night. They started to see a few scattered clumps of hardy grasses that grew in the sea of sand and rock. They saw the remains of highways and the scatted ruins of small towns and farms.

As they flew Allison and Moses sent their healing energy out across the land as they had done every day since discovering they had the gift of re-genesis. Allison believed their power was not only healing the earth, but the creatures living upon it.

Allison woke from sleep when Denzel, whose turn it was to watch, called her name. She opened her eyes and gasped in shock. Sitting on the ground in front of her face was a little creature with no tail that reminded Allison of a mouse. When she sat up the creature scrambled backward, but soon came back and sat on its haunches staring at her. Allison tentatively put out her hand and the creature crawled into her palm. She lifted it and gently stroked the fur on its back. It almost seemed to be purring as she rubbed her thumb against its little head. Others came out from behind rocks and out of holes in the ground and sat and stared at Allison and Moses. Moses wanted nothing to do with the creatures and shooed them away, and soon all of them were gathered around Allison.

Zinc woke up and threw a rock at the nearest creature. In the blink of an eye every mouse had disappeared.

"Why did you do that?" Allison asked. "They were harmless."

"How do you know?" Zinc asked. "Just because something looks harmless, doesn't mean it is. I learned that the hard way."

"Zinc's right," Ben said. Allison stared at Ben in surprise. It was the first time she remembered Ben agreeing with Zinc about anything.

"I just know," Allison said. "There is no doubt in my mind."

"No one can, just know, except a Watcher," Zinc picked up a rock and threw it at some of the mouse like creatures that had reappeared and were getting too close to him. "Are you a future Watcher?"

"No…I don't think so, but I do just know some things, and this is one of those things," Allison looked away from the others and bit her bottom lip. It would be good to know why she just knew some things.

"If Allison says she knows these little guys are harmless, then they are," Ben said.

Allison turned and smiled at Ben in gratitude.

Allison was flying with Zinc, as his passenger, as she had for most of the past week, when she felt something move over her shoulder and down her arm. One of the creatures had crawled into her backpack and was traveling with her.

The mouse squeaked and ran down her leg to the tip of her shoe. It went over her toe and disappeared from sight.

"No!" Allison shouted, afraid her little friend had fallen to its death.

"Are you okay?" Zinc called back to Allison.

Allison saw tiny feet appear as the mouse came back up her foot and ran up her leg. "Yes, everything is fine," she said to Zinc.

Allison picked up the tiny creature and held it in her hands. "Hello Tiny," she whispered. "I'm sorry you got separated from your family, but I promise to look after you." She stroked its back with the tip of her finger and it rubbed its head on her thumb.

CHAPTER THIRTY THREE

SO WHERE IS THE KING?

They flew for two days and saw very few clouds, either toxic or normal. They were at the end of the second day when they came upon the ruins of a small city built at the base of a mountain.

Zinc had become more hopeful as the pull of his father's presence became stronger with every passing day. Below, Zinc spotted the first intact building since leaving the school. Zinc wondered what the building had been when the city was filled with people. After they flew past it, he realized his father was no longer in front of them. He led the others down to the ground where he transformed from dragon to human.

"What's the matter, Prince," Zoey asked. "Are you tired?"

"No more tired than you are," Zinc said. He waited until Ben landed and transformed into a human before sharing his information. "My father is no longer ahead of us. I think he must be somewhere in the ruins of this city, but let me check." Zinc closed his eyes and turned around in circles. He made one rotation and then another just to be sure. When he opened his eyes he was facing the direction they had just come from. "He's back there somewhere."

"Then we need to go back," Ben said.

"Before we do, could we find water and fill up our gourds again?" Allison asked. "Mine is just about empty."

"If my father is here, then there must be water somewhere in the city," Zinc said. "If we go back we will find both."

"Are you sure he's here?" Denzel asked. Everyone turned and stared at Denzel. He caught the disapproving look in their eyes. "What?" He said. "You think Zinc is incapable of making a mistake?"

No one answered him.

Zoey took Zinc's arm. "Come on Prince. Show us where to find your father."

Zinc thought about how his father would feel when he saw his son leading a rescue party. He imagined the pride gleaming in his father's eyes and the words his father was sure to speak. "Well done, my son. I'm proud of you."

Zinc transformed and flew over the city until he came to a place where he realized his father was no longer ahead of him, but was once again behind them. He turned around and went back. Several times he led the others back and forth in the sky above the city. Finally he landed and transformed back into a human. He closed his eyes and turned in circles, felt the pull and started to walk in the direction where he felt the presence of his father. He walked too far and realized what he took to be the pull of his father's presence was now behind him somewhere, so he stopped and turned around. He walked in circles and finally came to a stop.

"All this time I thought I was feeling my father, I wasn't. If I was, he'd be right here, but he's not." Zinc wiped away tears of anger and disappointment. "I've led you all on a wild goose chase." Zinc fell to the ground, bowed his head and wept out loud. "I can't believe it. I was so sure I was feeling my father's presence. What a fool I've been to believe the Guardian would give me a gift and let me be the one to find my father. I should have known the Guardian would never let a traitor be a true Chosen."

The others stared at Zinc in shock, unsure of what to say or do. They were seeing Zinc at his truest; his disappointment in himself and his sense of unworthiness, all the things he took great pains to hide from others. Up to now they had experienced him as proud and arrogant. Finally Zoey stepped forward and laid her hand on his shoulder. "I'd like to know what the Guardian is playing at," she said. "Does the Guardian want to lose the dragonborn Chosen? None of us will offer ourselves to do the Guardian's work if this is how a Prince of our people is treated."

"Guardian not play games," Moses said indignantly.

"You're the biggest joke of all," Zoey said. "I should have known there was no truth in a quest when a brownie was chosen to be part of it."

"No, Zoey," Zinc said. "The brownie was chosen. I'm the one who shouldn't be here. I'm the one who betrayed my father. How could I believe forgiveness was so easy?"

"The Guardian's ways are not our ways. We hold grudges, but the Guardian does not," Allison said. "The Guardian has forgiven you, and you need to forgive yourself. The Guardian sees that you have great potential, which is why you were selected as a Chosen. Your gift is genuine, which means your father is here somewhere. I just know it. There is no doubt in my mind at all."

"Does it really look like King Zane is here?" Zoey asked, perplexed.

"Allison's right," Ben said. "Grandfather is here. You believe he should be right where we stand. Maybe he is, but if he is, then he is underground which explains why he is still alive on a world where the sun and rain are so dangerous."

Zinc looked up at Ben with a face full of pain and grief. Then the light of hope shone from his eyes and his face transformed. "Of course, that makes sense. He is here. I wasn't mistaken." Zinc felt a great weight lift from his shoulders. If he'd been standing instead of kneeling he might have danced with joy or he might have knelt and given thanks to the Guardian for the first time in his life. As it was he spoke his first prayer, "Thank you, Guardian. Thank you."

"Arise, Chosen of the Guardian and take your place with the heroes of Earth, Zargon and Farne who have been sent to rescue the King of Zargon," Allison intoned the words in a voice that was not quite her own. Allison's eyes were wide with surprise.

"Where did that come from?" Zoey said laughing.

"I don't know," Allison said. "But I do know the words were not my own. I am convinced these words just came through me from the Guardian. So Zinc, if I am right and I think I am, you can trust that you belong with us and the gifts you've been given are true because the Guardian says so."

"It will be interesting to hear what Miss Templeton has to say about how you have unexplainable knowledge and speak words not fully your own when we get back to Earth," Ben said.

"Who from Farne?" Moses asked.

"I don't know for sure, but I think it must be you," Allison said.

Moses turned away from Allison with a troubled look on his face. "Moses doesn't want to be from Farne. Moses want be from Earth."

"We don't always get what we want," Zoey said.

"Yeh, like right now I would like something else to eat besides puke gourds," Denzel said.

"Before we eat, maybe we should spend some time looking for entryways to take us underground. There must be something. After all grandfather is down there somewhere." Ben was walking away even before he finished speaking.

They searched for an entrance, but did not find one before it started to get dark. Zinc sensed there was water below their feet, but was unwilling to let either Moses or Denzel disturb the ground without knowing where his father was.

"It's time for us to go look for water before it gets dark," Allison said.

Zinc hesitated. He didn't want to give up looking.

"We can continue the search tomorrow," Allison insisted.

Finally, Zinc took to the air. Riding with him was Moses. Ben carried Denzel and Zoey carried Allison. Zinc led them to a hill beside a dry lakebed. They landed in the middle of the lake and Moses used his gift as a wizard to bring water to the surface.

"I think this would be a good place to spend the night," Denzel said and laid out his backpack near the small pool of water that had accumulated in the center of the lake.

Before they went to sleep Allison, Moses and Zoey sent out their re-genesis gift as they did almost every night. The little mouse came out from Allison's backpack and ran to the tip of her finger. Its nose twitched as it sniffed the air, and it put out its paw to touch the tip of Allison's finger. A light began to illuminate the little mouse. Even after Allison stopped sending forth the gift of re-genesis, the mouse shone.

"What's that doing here?" Zoey asked.

"It crawled into my backpack. Isn't it cute?" Allison held out her hand to show Zoey the mouse.

"I think it's creepy," Zoey said.

The mouse disappeared under Allison's shirt to sit on her shoulder out of sight.

"I think you should get rid of it," Zoey said. "It might carry disease. I'll kill it for you if you like."

"Absolutely not!" Allison said. "Tiny stays with me."

"So you've even given it a name. Make sure it doesn't crawl over me when I'm sleeping. I can guarantee it will be a fried mouse if it does that."

Zoey turned away from Allison and laid out her sleeping bag. Zinc laid his sleeping bag down beside Zoey.

Soon they were all asleep, except for Moses, who took the first watch.

In the middle of the night they had to move. Water kept coming from underground and filling the bottom of the lake.

The next day, when the sun rose, some of the water was taken into the air and formed clouds. Miles away fresh clean rain fell from the sky, bringing with it the special gift of re-genesis. The world of Farne was being transformed.

CHAPTER THIRTY FOUR

SIGNS OF LIFE

The Chosen spent the next two days searching. They found many holes in the ruins that led into basements and underground passageways, but every one of them came to a dead end before they'd gone very far.

The group shared their discouragement as the sun set.

"We will need to leave the city and look for food soon," Denzel said.

"There's not much growing here to eat." Ben picked up a rock and threw it at a vine that had no gourds growing on it.

"We can't leave," Zinc protested. "My father is here somewhere."

"Re-genesis is working, but it will be several days before something eatable starts to grow on the new plants," Allison said. "There's no way we can hold out until then."

"I think we can spare one more day to look for the King," Zoey said. "Then, I agree. We will have no choice but to go look for food somewhere else." Zinc gave Zoey a brief apologetic smile.

"Too bad Tiny isn't bigger. He be food," Moses said. Allison looked at Moses in stunned disbelief.

"Has anyone seen Tiny?" Allison asked, suddenly worried.

"He go down hole," Moses said.

"Where?" Allison asked.

Moses led Allison over to the place where he had last seen the tailless mouse. He showed her the mouse-sized opening in the dirt. Allison was staring at the hole when Tiny came running out of it. The little mouse's cheeks were puffed out and looked funny.

"Tiny must have found a beetle or a worm for his dinner." Allison held out her hand and the mouse ran onto it.

"Maybe not safe," Moses said as he reached to take the mouse from Allison before it dropped a worm into her hand.

The mouse backed away from Moses and began to screech at him. When he screeched food fell out of his cheeks. Beans lay in the palm of Allison's hand. One fell off and rolled across the ground where Ben picked it up.

"Where did you get these?" Allison asked. The mouse was quickly filling his cheeks back up again. Allison picked up the last bean before Tiny could stuff it back into his mouth.

"Look what Tiny found." Allison held the bean out toward the others.

"What is it?" Zinc asked.

"Some kind of bean," Allison said.

"The question is not what they are," Ben said, looking at the one he'd picked up. "But where did it come from?"

"There must be food stored underground." Denzel scratched the dirt with the heel of his shoe.

"It's been stored so well that it looks like a fresh bean," Allison said.

Ben popped the bean he had picked up into his mouth after rubbing it on his none-too-clean shirt. A look of amazement appeared on his face. "It is not preserved at all. It is fresh and delicious."

The companions looked to where Tiny sat eating the last bean he'd brought out of the hole.

"We need to find out where the food came from," Denzel said. "Show us where the mouse was."

Allison and Moses led the rest of them to the small hole Tiny had come out of. When they got there, Tiny ran down Allison's leg and disappeared into it. Denzel used his gift of strength to enlarge the opening. The others moved rocks, dirt and chunks of concrete to the side as Denzel worked to make a tunnel that was large enough for humans to go through. Sometimes it would take three or four of them to move a particularly large piece of concrete or rock Denzel had pushed behind him. Eventually they realized there were steps made of concrete leading downward under their feet.

Denzel stopped digging when he hit a concrete wall. The sun was dropping below the horizon, and the moon was rising. The others were too exhausted to continue moving the debris away from where Denzel dug it out.

"I'll try to break through this wall," Denzel said.

"It's getting dark. Why don't you leave it for tonight," Ben argued. "Then you can try to breakthrough if we don't find a door nearby."

"Yes, we'll decide in the morning when we're not so tired," Allison wiped her face with her sleeve and followed Ben up the stairs.

CHAPTER THIRTY FIVE

A MOUSE LEADS THE WAY

Allison woke to whiskers tickling her nose. The sun was rising, but the world was still in shadows. Tiny sat on the ground in front of her face. He was holding something larger than he was in his front paws.

Allison sat up and put out her hand and Tiny laid his gift on her palm. Then he broke off a piece of the yellowish green leaf, held it in his front paws and nibbled on it. Allison tore a piece off the other side and put it in her mouth. It tasted good and she really wished there was more. She looked around for the person who should be on watch and saw no one. Then Zinc emerged from the path they had made down the stairs carrying dirt in a rusty hunk of metal he had found.

"What are you doing?" Allison asked.

"Finding my father," Zinc said. "What does it look like I'm doing?"

"You're supposed to be on watch," Allison said.

"I couldn't just stand there and watch people sleep when we're so close to finding my dad," Zinc said.

"It turned out okay this time," Allison said. "But as you know only too well, there are dangers in this world that we need to watch for."

Zinc said nothing. He simply dropped his load of dirt and turned around for more. He was sweating and dirty and looked tired. Allison picked up Tiny and followed Zinc down the stairs.

"There should be a door through that wall at the bottom of these steps. They've got to lead somewhere," Zinc pointed to the small portion of a cement wall they had exposed the night before.

"Do you see any holes that Tiny could get through?" Allison asked.

"No, I haven't." Zinc dug into the dirt.

Allison picked Tiny off her shoulder and put him on the ground. The small mouse disappeared behind a rock that Zinc had dislodged. Zinc moved the rock away and the mouse began to dig at the dirt that had fallen from above. Soon he revealed a small mouse-sized tunnel and disappeared into it.

"That is the direction we need to go," Allison said, as she handed Zinc half of the green leaf remaining in her hand.

"What's this?" Zinc asked.

"I'm not sure, but it's good to eat and I think it came from underground," Allison said.

"How can it grow underground? Don't things need sunlight to grow?" Zinc popped the leaf into his mouth.

"I don't know, but it is certainly not like anything we have seen growing on this world."

A second later Denzel and Ben appeared. "Did I hear the word food?" Denzel asked.

"Yes, Tiny brought something else up from underground," Allison said. "I'm sorry there is none left. Zinc and I ate it."

"The mouse may come back with more," Zinc said. "He disappeared through that hole."

"Let's see if we can make it bigger." Denzel moved in front of them and used his superior strength to dig through the dirt. The rest of them carried the dirt up the stairs and out of the way. The concrete wall he was digging beside disappeared. They had found the door they were looking for. Denzel enlarged the hole and stepped through it into a concrete tunnel.

"Get the others," Denzel said. "Let's find out where the food is coming from."

Ben went back and helped Zoey and Moses pack. He picked up Allison and Denzel's backpacks to give to his friends. "We may as well take these with us," he said. "You never know where we'll end up staying tonight."

Zoey had Zinc's backpack. She handed it to him with a slight smile. "May this be the day we find your father, my Prince." Her words caused a smile to appear on Zinc's sweat streaked dirt covered face.

They stepped through the opening Denzel made and Moses used his wizard gift to illuminate the darkness. There was a collective gasp and an instinctive reaching for weapons. Denzel moved with lightning speed and jumped in front of the others ready to defend them. The light Moses created revealed a large, dangerous-looking cat-like creature that appeared ready to pounce. It took a moment for them to realize it was just a painting on the wall. As they walked the light illuminated one painting after another. Many of them had words written across them.

"Just like on earth," Denzel said. "Everywhere you look, there are billboards and ads wanting to sell you something. They promise that you will be beautiful and happy if you buy their product, but they can't really package the things a person truly needs to be happy; like good friends by your side and food in your backpack when you are rescuing a King. We have friends at our side, now all we need is the food."

"The people of this world had a cat-like appearance," Allison said, stopping before a picture of a family on a poster advertising a holiday destination. The members of the family had narrow faces with pointed ears further up the sides of their heads then human ears were.

"How is it that I can read those words?" Zoey asked.

"A gift always given when Chosen go to another world is the gift of being able to understand the languages of that world," Allison said.

"We were told we would understand the language of any people we met; I just didn't realize it would extend to written language as well," Zoey said.

"Look at this." Denzel pointed at the wall. "It's a recruitment poster for the military." The man in the picture was pointing his gun at a couple of men with a particularly nasty look on snarling faces. If you looked past the snarl, the only difference between the men in the picture was the man holding the gun had small perky ears and eyes slanted upwards, while the prisoner's eyes were round and their larger ears folded over to hang down the side of their heads. "If it isn't the color of our skin, it is the shape of our ears that divide us. I wish people could get along and treat others who are different from them with respect."

"Me too," Ben said. "Which way should we go?"

"We should follow the mouse," Zinc said. "He knows where to find food." Zinc pointed to the tiny mouse footprints that had disturbed a century's worth of dust.

Allison moved closer to Denzel. "Can I ask you some personal questions?"

Denzel slowed his pace so they could speak in private.

"Did your family experience a lot of prejudice because of the color of your skin?" Allison asked.

"I'd say so," Denzel said. "My cousins experienced the worst of it. Two of them were on their way home from football practice when some guys jumped them. 'Let's put these niggers in the hospital,' they said. The guys who beat them played my cousins team the week before and lost. They were from important white families and the judge didn't want to ruin their lives by convicting them of a crime, but if my cousins had done the same thing they would have spent a lifetime in prison. James was a good high school football player, and a good student, but he never walked again.

Fairhaven is the first place I've ever been where character matters more than the color of your skin. I never want to leave."

"Most of us leave when we graduate and only come back when we've been chosen to go off-world," Allison said.

"Except for teachers," Denzel said.

"You want to teach at Fairhaven?" Allison asked.

"I've never thought of it before, but that is exactly what I want to do," Denzel said. "I'm going to put my mind to becoming the best student they've seen for a very long time so they'll seriously consider me when I apply."

"That's a tall order. They're some good students at our school."

"I don't have to be the very best, just the best who wants to stay on as a teacher."

"Still a tall order."

"I think I can do it. I hope Miss Templeton won't hold the bone-headed things I've done against me."

"Like?" Allison asked, as she picked up the pace because the light Moses was creating with wizard fire was too far in front of them.

"Breaking into the forbidden section of the library, climbing the outside of the castle so I could look in a window and find out what's going on in a secret meeting, and not so long ago I talked Ben into taking me for a dragon ride when Miss Templeton had forbidden it, just to name a few. We didn't get away with the dragon ride, Miss Templeton caught us."

"You're going to need to be a model student from now on."

"I just need to stop doing and saying the first thing that comes into my mind."

"I'm not so sure that you should be hiding from the world at Fairhaven."

Denzel didn't respond. He just looked at Allison with a questioning look on his face. A look she couldn't see because it was too dark.

"Maybe the Guardian would like you to take on a more challenging job with your life on Earth. Maybe the Guardian would like you to go back to the place where your cousins were attacked and model what it means to live with respect for everyone, regardless of color."

"Easy to say, hard to do," Denzel said. "Besides I don't think some of those people will ever change."

"You're probably right, but someone's got to be a light in the darkness," Allison said. "And I can't think of anyone better suited than you at your best."

"I'll consider it. Now, what's going on with you and Trevor? That guy's a jerk. He's one of the few people at Fairhaven who treats me like I'm beneath him. Ben is so much better than that. Why are you interested in Trevor and not Ben?"

"Trevor treats almost everyone that way, which is one reason I'm not interested in him in spite of the fact that Crystal thinks I'm crazy not to be. At this point in my life, I don't really want a serious boyfriend, because who knows where the future will take me. I could never be serious about Trevor, but Ben-who knows?"

The two of them walked side by side in silence, both lost in their own thoughts. Allison found herself thinking about that disastrous kiss in the library. She suspected it was the first time Ben kissed a girl and a part of her was happy he had chosen her for his first kiss.

They followed the small mouse footprints through the tunnel until a metal grate barred their way. The mouse's footprints continued on the other side of the grate, which was cemented into the concrete wall. Denzel and Allison caught up to the rest at the gate.

"Do you think you can remove this?" Ben asked Denzel.

"Of course," Denzel said as he grabbed the bars and pulled them toward himself. They didn't budge. He changed his tactic. Instead of trying to pull the whole grate out, he pulled individual bars sideways. He started on the outside and worked to the center. When he was finished there was a hole large enough for them to slip through. He stepped aside and gestured for Ben to go first, as he was the one who could see in the dark. Denzel followed him through.

When everyone had come through Moses stepped in front of them and called forth his wizard fire so they could see. He led them to the end of the tunnel and into another one that ran perpendicular to the first. When they got to the end of that tunnel, Moses extinguished his wizard fire because a faint light shone in the large tunnel they were now in.

CHAPTER THIRTY SIX

CAPTURED

They walked along a passageway that appeared to be an underground subway system much like Denzel knew from living in New York City. Instead of tracks on the ground below their feet, there was a single track above their head. The tunnel was wide and high enough for the dragonborn to transform into dragons, but in most places it was not wide and high enough to unfurl their wings and fly.

Ahead of them the track was broken and the ruins of a cable car lay in their pathway. They climbed onto the car and crawled over it. The light was stronger on the other side. The tunnel widened and there was a platform with skylights high above that let the sun shine in. Tiny sat on top of the platform eating a bean. Denzel arrived first and he stood looking at the platform in amazement. "You guys have got to see this," he said. "There is food! Lovely food! It looks like a garden."

Denzel pulled the Chosen up onto the chest-high platform. Each one of them walked a short distance away and fell to his or her knees to pick and eat the food that was growing there. Plants grew in boxes all over the platform. The only place they didn't grow was on the paths laid out between the rows of boxes.

"Maybe we shouldn't eat too much," Ben said, as he stuffed his mouth full of a tasty yellowish green leaf. "We don't know who planted this garden and how they will feel about us eating their food."

"You're right," Denzel said, as he reached for more of the beans.

"We should eat as much as we want, because we may need all the strength we can get to find my father," Zinc said as he picked a round yellow fruit.

"Good point, Zinc," Denzel said.

They ate in silence, glad for the change of diet from the gourds that had been their staple since coming to Farne. Denzel started thinking of the time he got caught raiding a garden.

"When I was a kid we visited my grandmother," Denzel said. "Her neighbor had a garden in the backyard. It was wonderful to eat carrots straight from the ground, but what wasn't wonderful was how mad the neighbor got when she discovered us. My mother grounded me for a month when she found out."

Thinking of being grounded made him wonder about those who planted the garden they were in. Denzel pulled his hand back from a bean he was about to pick and reluctantly stood up. "I think we should be on our way," he said.

Everyone but Denzel picked some more of their favorite food, and put it in their backpacks before agreeing that it was time to go.

"Which way to the Zargon King?" Denzel asked Zinc.

Zinc pointed in the direction they'd been walking.

At first the tunnel in front of them was dark, but as they walked a pinprick of light appeared and grew stronger as they walked toward it. They soon came to another platform that was also covered with plants. They passed more than two dozen platforms where gardens had been planted.

They'd walked for two or three hours before taking a break. They climbed onto a platform and harvested some of what was growing there to eat. They were sitting together eating in silence when they first heard something moving through the tunnel toward them. Denzel jumped off the platform and helped the others down. He stared into the tunnel wishing he had Ben's ability to see in the dark.

"There are people coming," Ben said.

"What can you see?" Denzel asked, feeling a little anxious about meeting the people who may have planted the gardens they'd been raiding.

"There are two rows of four. They look something like the people in the posters. The ones with the perky ears," Ben said. "Behind them is something I can't see. There are several links of chain attached to the cable on the ceiling. I hope they're friendly, because I think they've seen us. There are people coming out from behind the ones in front with what could be weapons."

"I have a bad feeling about this," Allison said just before three Farnians walked out of the tunnel and into the light.

"They're raising their weapons! Run!" Ben yelled.

They turned to run, but it was too late. Several blasts of blue light knocked them to the ground.

CHAPTER THIRTY SEVEN

COLLARED

Zoey had a bad feeling even before the cat people stepped out of the darkness. As they raised their weapons, she remembered her other gift was invisibility. She turned on the gift and threw herself sideways just before the leading cat people sent out blasts of blue light. She hit the ground and rolled so that she was against the wall. She turned and watched as the others fell to the ground. She pressed her body against the wall and watched as the cat people put collars on the others. One of the guards stumbled over her feet without knowing what it was he tripped on. He turned and looked straight at Zoey without seeing her. Zoey made herself as small as possible and stared at the guard who was looking directly at her. When the guard moved away Zoey stood and slid along the wall to a spot farther away.

Prisoners who wore metal collars were attached to chains hanging from the rail on the ceiling that had once been used by cable cars. These prisoners were ordered to climb up on the platform and harvest vegetables. She recognized King Zane right away even though he looked far different than when she'd last seen him. He was thin, with dark bags under his eyes, and one of his front teeth had been knocked out.

King Zane was staring at Zinc and only tore his eyes away from his son when one of the guards ordered him to get busy. The King began gathering vegetables. Zoey climbed up on the platform and knelt beside him so she could whisper in his ear. "The Guardian sent the six of us to rescue you."

"I'm glad to see you or more accurately not to see you, but hear you," the King whispered back. "Is that really my son and grandson down there?"

"Yes, Zinc and Ben are both here."

"Zinc has been chosen by the Guardian then?" King Zane closed his eyes and smiled. "It is worth it all to live to see this day, as long as he survives."

Zoey put her invisible hand on the King's arm, "Zinc has done very well. You have reason to be proud of him."

"Tell me-," the King started, but whatever else he wanted to say was cut off.

"What is going on, Prisoner 92? Are you talking to yourself? You know you are forbidden to speak." One of the guards walked over to where Zane and Zoey squatted at the end of the row.

King Zane didn't look up. He quickly picked ripe beans and put them in his bag. The guard held out his weapon and sent a mini blast of blue light toward the King's back.

Zoey scrambled backwards. "No, don't," Zoey gasped as the blue light hit Zane. The King bit his lip to keep from crying out in pain, but as soon as he heard Zoey's start to speak he howled as loud as he could to cover the sound of her voice.

The guard had a puzzled look on his face. "Who said that?" He looked directly to where Zoey was sitting and took a step in her direction. Zoey moved away as quickly and quietly as she could, but in her haste she did not see the prisoner who had recently arrived at the end of the row next to King Zane. She knocked the floppy-eared cat man over. He and Zoey both scrambled quickly to their feet. The cat man stood with his head bent as a mini-blast of blue light hit him in the chest. He gasped, but did not cry out. The guard blasted him again and when he did not cry out sent a third blast of light into his body. The floppy-eared cat man fell to the ground without uttering a sound.

King Zane crawled over to the cat man. "Sim, my friend," he whispered. "Why do you insist on provoking that guard? You know he likes to make you howl. He targets you because the other daga look up to you."

Zoey reached out and touched the king and sent some of her power as a healer into his body. Then she surprised herself, and lightly touched the cat-man and sent some healing power into him.

"What just happened?" Sim whispered.

"I don't know, but we'd better get back to work," King Zane whispered back.

Zoey considered transforming into a dragon and attacking the guard. As a dragon she could withstand a lot more of their blue light than she could as a human being. However, if more than one of those weapons were pointed at her she knew it was possible to end up as a dead dragon.

Her mother's words came back to Zoey. Always pick your battles. She knew her mother would tell her this was not the right time and place and she would do more for the King and Prince by staying alive to fight another day.

Zoey backed quietly away and climbed off the platform. She went over to where Zinc lay on the ground. She sat beside him and put her finger on his wrist to make sure he was alive.

"Zoey, what's going on?" Zinc mumbled.

"Prisoner 93 will not speak," a voice shouted. A guard walked over and pointed his weapon at Zinc, but was distracted when King Zane coughed loudly. The guard turned and pointed his weapon at Zane. While the guard was distracted Zoey sent some of her power as a healer into Zinc. As she did so, she whispered in his ear, "Be quiet."

"Leave it," one of the senior guards said. "We don't want to damage them. It will take longer to harvest our crops if too many are out of commission." Zoey watched as the senior guard walked over to Moses and kicked the brownie. "What do you think this is?"

"I've never seen anything like it before," the first guard said. "But I think it could be dangerous. Just before the stun gun hit it, I'm sure I saw it make a ball of fire and hold it in its hands."

"Then tie its hands together and throw it on the wagon," the guard in charge said. "Just to be safe put a muzzle on it as well."

CHAPTER THIRTY EIGHT

FAMILY REUNION

Zinc woke up to discover he was lying on the ground. He was sure Zoey was beside him, but when he opened his eyes she wasn't there. He rolled over to discover Denzel's face inches from his own. He pushed Denzel away and that was when he noticed the collar and the chains. He brought his hands up to his own neck and discovered he too was wearing a collar. He ran his hands around it looking for an opening. He found the clasp and pulled as hard as he could, but the collar did not open.

Zinc sat up and looked around. Ben, Denzel, and Allison lay on the ground around him. He looked around for Zoey, but did not see her. He noticed the prisoners up on the platform tending the garden. The Farnean guards all had small perky ears, while the ears of all the prisoners except for one were the bent over floppy kind.

Zinc got to his feet and stared at the prisoner who was different from all the others. He was shorter and looked human. He was picking beans and putting them in a sack. Zinc wondered whether the man knew his father just before the man raised his head and looked directly at him. At first Zinc thought, "It can't be." The man before him had hardly any flesh on his bones. He looked frail and a lot older than a few short months before. The only thing that was the same, were his eyes.

"Father," Zinc called out, just moments before being hit between the shoulder blades by something that brightened the air around him with a blue light.

"Zinc," his father cried out in a ragged voice. Zinc lay on the ground and watched through teary eyes as a blue light knocked his father backwards. Indescribable pain caused his arms to spasm. His eyes watered and he panted for air. It hurt to know his father was going through the same thing and it was all his fault. He wondered how many times his father had been shot by the cat-people's weapons and how he had managed to endure the pain.

"Slaves do not speak," a voice above him commanded.

Zinc climbed to his feet and tried to call forth dragonfire to give the guard a taste of his own medicine. The fire rose, but he couldn't push it past the collar; it stopped at his neck causing a new kind of excruciating pain. A tiny flame was all he managed before the pain caused him to crumple and fall to the ground.

"What was that?" one of the guards yelled.

"What was what?" the senior guard yelled back.

"I thought I saw fire and smoke coming from this one before he fell." The guard pointed at Zinc.

"There's nothing there now," the senior guard replied. "It must be your imagination."

Zinc and his father's screams of agony woke the others who were in the process of discovering their own collars and the chains that held them to the rail above their heads.

"What's going on here?" Denzel asked loudly. A guard directed a current of blue light at his body. "Stop!" Denzel yelled and a second current joined the first one. He fell to the ground, his body arching, and his arms and legs each dancing to a different tune.

"Slaves do not speak," a guard said.

Zinc was trying to stand. His arms and legs refused to cooperate, but desperation to see what happened to his father drove him to keep trying. He finally stood only to see his father lying on the ground. He started to call out, but an unseen hand covered his mouth and his eyes went wide.

"Be quiet," Zoey's voice whispered urgently. "I'll go see how your father is and let you know."

"Zoey, you're free," Zinc whispered. "Do what you can to help us, but don't get caught. I'm so glad you were given the gift of invisibility."

A guard blew a whistle. The prisoners jumped down from the platform by reaching their hands over their heads, grabbing the cable attached to their collars, and swinging down to the ground below. A couple of them stayed behind and dragged the King to the edge, where other prisoners carried Zinc's father over to what remained of a trolley car hanging from the same mono-rail the prisoners' chains were attached to. Much of the shell of the car was gone, what remained was the floor and supporting metal beams. They laid Zane next to Moses. On either side of them were piles of vegetables.

"Get up," a guard ordered the five chosen. Ben helped Denzel stand and took one of his arms to support him. Allison helped Zinc. An invisible Zoey took Zinc's other arm. "Your father is still alive," she whispered to him.

The cat people turned and walked in the direction the six chosen had just come from. Those with weapons made it clear the prisoners were to follow. Some of the cat prisoners pulled on ropes attached to the cable car so that it moved along behind them. They walked until they came to the next platform where vegetables were growing. By the third stop, all the chosen, but Moses, were required to climb up on the platform and join in harvesting whatever fruit and vegetables were ripe.

When they got to the last platform they were soon finished for there was little left the Chosen hadn't eaten when they stopped at it earlier in the day.

When the prisoners finished their harvesting early and the sacks were mostly empty the guards responded in disbelief. One of them climbed up to take a look. When he saw there was nothing left he shook his head at the guards below.

"Slaves do not eat without permission," a guard yelled, pointing his weapon at Allison.

"We didn't know," Ben said as he stepped in front of her.

"Slaves do not speak," the guard said and sent a blast of blue light. It was a short blast and didn't knock Ben off his feet, but it did leave him hunched over and gasping in pain. The guards motioned for the prisoners to get down from the platform. Ben's friends helped him stand and Denzel and Allison each took an arm to support him.

The guards ordered them to turn around and walk back toward their place of capture. The Chosen had already made this journey twice and after a short time it became a struggle to keep walking, but they kept going for they knew if they stumbled and fell, they would be dragged by the collars they wore. They put one weary foot in front of the other.

CHAPTER THIRTY NINE

SLAVES

Everyone but Moses was led into an area which smelled so bad it made their eyes water. They stood outside a large cage with a heavy metal gate. Each prisoner stopped outside the gate while a guard unhooked the chain that connected the overhead rail to the collar they wore. It was a relief to have the weight of the chain taken away, but Ben wished they would take the collar off as well.

As King Zane's would be rescuers went through the gate they were each given a battered metal bowl with a handle on one side. Once they were all in the cage a large barrel was rolled in. The other prisoners retrieved their own bowls and scooped up the soup made from the peelings of vegetables and other items of unknown origin. The soup looked and smelled unappetizing. A second barrel, this time filled with water was brought in before the heavy gate was rolled across the doorway and locked. The only light came from the other side of the gate and from a large hole in the ceiling that opened to the outside world. The sun was low on the horizon and there was no light coming directly into the cage.

King Zane retrieved his own bowl and scooped up some of soup. "It's not what we're used to, but eat it anyway," he whispered to his son. "Keep yourself strong for when we get a chance to escape."

Ben took some soup and sat on the ground beside his grandfather. Zinc sat on the other side of King Zane. Ben took a sip of the soup and discovered it was cold and tasted as bad as it smelled. The other Chosen sat down with them and Ben introduced his grandfather to Denzel, who was the only member of the captured rescue party the King didn't already know. Allison took a sip of her soup and immediately spit it back into the bowl.

"You must eat," King Zane said.

"I can't, I just can't," Allison replied.

"You must eat so when the time is right you are strong enough to rescue me," King Zane whispered.

"Rescue, there is no rescue," one of the droopy-eared cat people sitting nearby said.

"Rescue is almost guaranteed now that my son and grandson have arrived with their friends," King Zane whispered back. "Sim, my friend, it is even possible we can take you with us."

"Take me too," several voices whispered at once.

"Slaves do not talk," boomed a voice from outside the gate.

Ben caught Denzel's eye and nodded at the gate that barred the entrance they'd come through. "Do you think you could manage it?"

"I'm not sure. The bars are really thick. I think our best hope lies in getting these collars off so we can leave by the hole up in the roof," Denzel whispered back.

Ben looked up at the hole. It would be impossible for a dragon with its wings extended to get through. In fact, it would be very difficult to fly up to it in dragon form. Moses could call up air and lift them to it, but who knew where Moses was. Ben hoped that wherever he was, he was still alive and well.

"Does anyone know how to get these collars off?" Ben asked in a loud whisper.

"They only come off the day you die," a woman said. "Happen soon enough, too much work, not enough food. The chaka will need to capture more daga soon." The woman pointed to hooks on the wall outside the locked door where unused collars hung.

"Too much work, not enough food," several voices whispered in agreement.

"Daga? Chaka?" Ben asked.

"We are the daga. The others are the chaka," the woman said.

When Ben looked at the daga sitting on the floor with him, he could see that many of them were little more than walking skeletons, whose bones could be counted through the soft fine hair covering their bodies. It was a wonder some of them were able to do the work they did each day.

"Tomorrow," King Zane said. "They will probably leave you behind to find out who you are and where you came from. If they don't like the answers they will torture you. The chaka have ingenious ways to torture. Don't tell them you came from another world; they will never believe it. Tell them you came looking for me, which is the truth. Tell them there are many people where you are from and that it is far from here, but you're not exactly sure where. I finally told them I was looking for a new home a few hundred of us could move to as we were outgrowing the caves we lived in. When I told them that, the torture stopped, but not before I lost this tooth." King Zane pointed to the spot in his mouth where a tooth was missing. "They're not going to look for a community that large, or brave the sun and rain for as long as it would take to find it."

After everyone had eaten their soup, they used the bowls to get water from the other barrel. A thick layer of oil lay on the surface of the water. The Chosen still had water in their gourds so they were spared the need to drink from the barrel, but if they didn't get out of the cage soon they would have no choice. Whispered conversations died out as the prisoners lay on the ground and went to sleep.

The next morning a thin porridge was served without the benefit of milk, salt or sugar. Such a diet could not sustain a dragonborn for very long, not even in their human form. Ben's grandfather was near the end of his ability to endure.

After breakfast King Zane and the other prisoners were taken out and reattached to the cables hanging from the rail. As the King predicted, the Chosen were left behind where they waited anxiously for what would come next. The guards eventually came and took them away one by one. Soon it was Ben's turn.

"Who are you and where do you come from," a perky-eared cat person asked.

"My name is Ben and I live in a community several days from here," Ben told them the story they had agreed to the night before.

"Our records do not tell us of a people who look like you," the interrogator said. "What is your history?"

"There are stories, but I don't know if any of them are true," Ben said. "One story says our ancestors traveled through space to escape a doomed planet. The spaceship was disabled and they couldn't reach their destination so they ended up here. Another story says our ancestors were chosen to come through a portal from another world to offer assistance to this one, but they came too late and got trapped here. Another story…"

"Enough stories," the interrogator thundered. "I want to know about the one covered in fur. What is it and where does it come from?"

Ben didn't know what to say. They hadn't come up with a story the night before to cover Moses's presence with them. He was afraid that if he answered the question in a different way than the others did, they might all end up being tortured.

"I really don't know for sure, but Moses has been on this world as long as I have."

"We found no weapons on you other than knives and swords, but a guard reported the creature with fur had a ball of fire in his hands. How did he do that?"

Ben could tell from the sound of his voice that the interrogator was skeptical about the ball of fire. "I'm sorry, but I can't help you with that. I didn't see it myself." And in truth, Ben had not seen Moses make a ball of fire.

"Why did it come with you?"

"Moses was chosen to come."

"Why?" The interrogator slapped a heavy rope imbedded with metal on the table in front of Ben.

Ben's eyes got wide and he shrunk back. "I don't know?" he said, his voice shaking.

"Are there many of these creatures in your community?"

"No. He's the only one?"

"Is it intelligent?"

"Somewhat?"

"Does it understand what we say?"

"Maybe."

The guard scowled and hit the table again.

"He understands some of what you say," Ben corrected.

"How about the old one? He is the same type of creature as you. Do you know him?"

"Zane is my grandfather," Ben said. Telling the interrogator what they had agreed to the night before. They had agreed to stay with the truth as much as they could, but avoid telling the chaka anything they might not already know.

The chaka interrogator kept coming back to the same questions over and over again, trying to catch Ben in a lie. He was particularly interested in Moses and the location of the community he claimed to be from.

Ben was exhausted when they returned him to the cage, but he had avoided any serious injury. His knees buckled and he sank onto the moldy straw. Allison rushed over to share some healing energy with him, but he grabbed her hand.

"Save your strength, I'm okay." Ben didn't let go of Allison's hand. They sat together and found comfort in each other's company.

CHAPTER FOURTY

ZOEY

Zoey followed them until they got to the platform where the others had been taken captive. She fell to the ground to rest for just a moment, but was soon fast asleep. When she woke up she had no way of knowing how much time had passed. She assumed she'd slept for some time as it was dark and it wasn't when she'd closed her eyes. She called forth dragonfire and discovered she'd become visible after falling asleep. *I must make sure to hide before I sleep again.* She climbed onto the platform and moved behind the gardens to a spot where she would not be easily seen and closed her eyes to wait for daylight. She was soon fast asleep.

The sun was shining through the skylight when she woke up for the second time. She went to the spigot she'd seen the guards use to get water, drank, and filled up her gourd. Her stomach growled so she looked for any vegetables that had been left behind. She found more than enough to eat.

When she was ready to go, Zoey moved to the entrance of the tunnel and leaned against the wall. She would never admit it, but she hated walking through the dark tunnels even when she was with the others. The thought of walking through them on her own without knowing where she was and where she was going terrified her. She knew it was crazy to feel that way. After all, she was dragonborn. As long as there weren't too many of the cat people, she could transform and blast them with dragonfire. She wouldn't hesitate now that she knew the pointy-eared cat people would capture her and turn her into a slave if they could. Once the collar was on she suspected it prevented the metamorphosis needed to send forth dragonfire. She had seen the pain on Zinc's face when he tried and failed.

She wished she could transform into a dragon, she would not be as frightened then, but the tunnels were too narrow for a dragon in flight. She could walk through them as a dragon, but it would be so much harder than walking as a human. It would take more energy and she might need all her energy once she discovered where they had taken the others. She thought about just staying where she was and waiting for the others to come back this way, but then she realized there was no guarantee they would. These gardens had been harvested, but presumably there were other gardens. They may not return to these for several days.

So Zoey stayed in her human form and gathered her courage about her as she prepared to walk alone into the dark tunnel.

I can always change into a dragon if there is any real danger, she thought. Holding the image of herself transformed gave Zoey the courage she needed to take her first tentative steps. Then another thought crossed her mind, one she had never had before. Perhaps she wasn't alone. Perhaps the Guardian was with her as an unseen friend and companion even in this dark place.

"I have no choice. I must walk through these tunnels if I want to find the others. Guardian, please help me. Give me courage," she whispered.

As she took her second step into the darkness she found herself thinking about Zinc and wondering where he had spent the night. She also wondered if the others would look for her if they managed to escape or would they just get away from here as quickly as they could. Thinking it was possible to be left behind when the others escaped was very frightening. She could think of nothing worse than being stranded on this world without the other Chosen. She needed to find the others no matter what happened afterward. It would be better to be a slave with them, than to be alone on this world.

As Zoey walked, she passed many platforms where crops were in various stages of development. She saw no other living thing. She did hear things moving and people shouting, but they were faint echoes, coming from far away; she couldn't tell what direction.

Tired of walking, Zoey decided to stop at the next platform, when she became aware that something was moving in the tunnel directly ahead of her. She shrank against the tunnel wall. She couldn't see what was coming and didn't know if whatever it was could see her. She contemplated transforming into a dragon, but decided that it might be a secret better kept until there was absolute need. As she slid along the wall she felt a break in it and assumed she had arrived at a connecting tunnel. Zoey stepped into the opening. An involuntary scream left her lips as the ground vanished below her and she fell through the air.

CHAPTER FOURTY ONE

A VERY BAD DAY

The next morning the chaka told Zinc and Denzel to stay in the cage while Ben, Allison, King Zane, and the daga were chained up.

King Zane fought against the chain holding him to the overhead rail when he realized his son was to be left behind. "Remember Zinc, you are only human," he called out. "Nothing more."

Light from one of the guard's weapons slammed into King Zane's body. Ben knew it was too much for someone who had worked hard and eaten very little and been weakened by the previous day's attacks. All the color drained from King Zane's face and he convulsed, fell, and lay still on the ground.

Ben dropped on his knees beside his grandfather. A chaka grabbed the chain attached to Ben's collar and yanked him backward, then pointed his weapon at him. The guard was about to fire when the officer in charge grabbed his arm. "The old one will not work today. We don't need to damage the young one too."

"There are not many more days of work left in this one," said another as he poked Ben's grandfather in the side with his foot.

"Throw him back in the cage," the officer commanded. "We will see if he is fit to work tomorrow. If not, his collar will come off."

As the guards forced the prisoners to move away from the cage, Ben turned and looked behind him where his grandfather, his uncle, and his best friend remained locked up. He worried about what would happen to them.

The daga his grandfather named Sim was behind him, "Don't worry," Sim whispered. "Your grandfather is stronger than he looks and the chaka will not hurt your friends too badly. They have too great a need for slaves to work in their gardens."

They spent the day walking from one garden to another. The only break came around noon when they were given some water and the chance to use a washroom. They were getting ready to leave the last garden when Tiny came out of the tunnel and ran up Allison's leg to sit on her shoulder.

The arrival of the small mouse-like creature did not go unnoticed. One of the daga standing nearby snatched Tiny off Allison's shoulder and stuffed the mouse in his mouth. That might have been the end of Tiny, but for a chaka who blasted the daga with its weapon, while yelling, "No unauthorized eating." The daga spat the mouse out and no less than three chaka leapt forward to snatch it out of the air. One of the chaka was about to eat Tiny, until the mouse bit his finger. Free, Tiny jumped off his hand, landed on the ground, and ran toward Allison looking for protection.

"No Tiny, run, run away," Allison's scream ended in a howl as a blast of light hit her in the back. The tiny mouse stood still for just a second and then it turned and ran toward the tunnel as fast as it could go. Blasts of light hit the ground around it. One blast hit so close the little mouse tumbled head over heels. The chaka, whose blast had caught the mouse shouted in triumph. Allison cried out in horror and Ben was sure Allison's little friend was dead. Three chaka rushed towards it, elbowing one another to be the one to get there first. The little mouse slipped through their hands and disappeared into the tunnel.

Ben put his arm around Allison's waist and stood beside her while she rested her head on his shoulder and cried. A guard grabbed the chain attached to Ben's collar and yanked him backward which caused Allison to fall.

Ben had never hated anyone as much as he hated the chaka at that moment. He wanted nothing more than to call forth dragonfire, but knew the collar prevented him from transforming. His grandfather had warned him not to let the chaka know he could transform into a dragon until he found a way to get the collar off. His neck would increase in size, but the collar would not. As it was, dragon smoke drifted out of his mouth and nose because of the fire deep within. He was thankful the dim light made it hard to see. The smoke went unnoticed, although a chaka nearby looked his way as he sniffed the air.

When the workday was over, they walked back toward the cage with Ben supporting Allison on one side, while Sim supported her on the other. Ben didn't think he had ever felt hungrier than he did at that moment. They had been fed nothing all day. The cart was loaded with produce from the gardens and he had to fight his natural inclination to reach out and take something to eat. When he started to put a bean pod in his mouth earlier in the day, Sim had grabbed his arm and stopped him. Now, Ben was not only hungry, but also thirsty. They'd been given water a couple of times during the day from a battered tin cup all the slaves took turns drinking from. He wished they'd stop and give them more water. He wanted to ask for it, but prisoners were not allowed to talk unless the chaka wanted to know something.

Images of the food he wanted to eat came to Ben's mind. They bore no resemblance to the gruel they'd eaten the night before. Dragonborn needed more food than ordinary humans. His friends had always marveled at how much food he could pack away. If he continued to work as hard as he worked today with little food, it wouldn't take long before he was a walking skeleton just like his grandfather and the daga. Ben knew that to leave the daga behind was to condemn them to death and decided he didn't want to leave without freeing them, if it was possible. He had no idea how they could all escape, but knew they had to do it soon.

"Guardian, please help us," he whispered.

Ben worried about his grandfather all day; also about Denzel and Zinc. Sim had said the chaka wouldn't hurt them very much. What did that mean? Would Zinc be able to control his dragonfire if the chaka tried to get information from him through torture? As they drew close to their destination, Ben was both grateful the workday was over and fearful of what he would find when they returned.

CHAPTER FORTY TWO

SAMSON

Zoey felt Zinc stroking her face and heard him calling her sweetheart, as her head rested in his lap. She was trying to decide whether to kiss Zinc or slap his hand away. She loved him. No, she hated him. Which was it? She knew she should hate him because he betrayed his own father and collaborated with the person who caused her mother's death. She did hate him, and one little kiss would confirm it.

"Zinc," she whispered in that moment between waking and sleeping. She reached out her hand and grabbed the front of his shirt to pull him close just as she was opening her eyes. Then she screamed, rolled away, scrambled to her feet, and promptly fell down on her knees. She was too dizzy to stand. So instead of running, which is what she wanted to do, she scrambled as far as the wall behind her would allow her to get.

A small fire burned off to the side, making it possible to see. Her head had not been resting on a lap, but on a bundle of rags. She put her hand on her forehead and discovered it was sticky and painful to the touch. She pulled her hand away and looked at it. There was a sticky green substance on it matching what was in the open jar the creature before her held in his hand.

"Don't be afraid, I'm making you better. This," the man held up the jar, "takes away pain and helps to heal wounds."

Zoey had vague memories of falling through the air. She had landed on her feet and then stumbled forwards and struck her head. What happened after was a mystery.

"Who are you?" she asked, looking at the cat man in the dim light provided by a vent to the outside world in the ceiling high above them. His face was covered in soft fur, turning gray around his nose and mouth. The tips of his floppy ears were also gray. There was no fur on the huge scar that ran from his forehead across his nose to his chin on the other side. The tip of his smashed nose was missing. The scar pulled his mouth sideways in an unnatural angle.

"The more important question is who are you? I've never seen anything that looks like you before."

"I've certainly never seen anything that looks like you before either," Zoey said.

The cat man touched his scarred face, "Hopefully, you never see anyone who looks like me again."

"I will answer your question if you'll answer mine," Zoey said. "Who are you?"

"I'm Samson"

"I'm Zoey."

"Where are you from?"

"I'm not from around here. How about you?"

"I'm not from here either. Are you a friend of the chaka's?" Samson asked.

"I don't know what chaka are," Zoey responded.

"They look like me, but they have pointy ears and no big scar." The cat man pointed to the long scar marring his face.

"No, the chaka are not my friends. They have my king and his son in chains."

"They have my son and daughter in chains too. They thought I was too old to work for them, so they struck me down and left me for dead." Samson touched the scar on his cheek again. "I was not ready to die then, but now I am ready to die if I must to rescue my children."

"Don't talk that way," Zoey said. "You're not going to die."

"I likely will. It is impossible to rescue daga from the chaka, but I must try and therefore I will likely die."

"You are not going to die because I'm going to help you rescue them." A look of sheer determination shone from Zoey's eyes.

"What can a girl and an old daga do?" Samson asked.

"If you don't think you can do anything why are you here?"

"I cannot live without my children. Better to die here and then they will know I loved them enough to try to free them. That is my fate, but you must leave and get far away from this place."

"No, I'm here to rescue my king and his son." Zoey pushed herself off the ground and stood. This time she did not fall.

"If you stay, the chaka will put one of their collars around your neck," Samson pointed at Zoey's neck.

"I won't let them do that."

"How will you stop them? You are just a girl."

"That's what you think," and in a blink of an eye Zoey became a dragon. To make an even more powerful impression Zoey breathed out flame. The space where she had transformed was too small for a dragon, but Zoey managed to get herself turned around so she could see the man's face. Only he wasn't there. He had disappeared.

"Don't be afraid," Zoey said as she returned to her human form. "Please come out, I won't hurt you."

"You don't like the taste of daga?"

"I don't know what daga taste like."

"I will come out if you promise not to eat me."

"I wouldn't consider it."

Samson came out from behind a wall. "I've changed my mind. You can help me rescue my children. And while we're at it, we'll rescue your king and his son too."

"There were others who came with me to rescue the king, so we need to rescue them too."

"We'll rescue all the hairless ones and all the daga we can without getting caught."

"Shall we go?" Zoey bent to pick up her bag and ended up falling forwards and landing on the ground. She was still dizzy from hitting her head.

"I think we need to rest for a while first," Samson said as he sank to the ground.

CHAPTER FOURTY THREE

A VERY HORRIBLE DAY

When Ben and Allison returned to the cage, it was to discover that Ben's grandfather was the only one there. He lay on a pile of moldy straw, his face pale and haggard, his eyes closed. Ben was afraid his grandfather was not breathing as he fell on his knees beside him. Allison was on her knees by the door, exhausted from a workday with little food.

Ben's grandfather's eyes flickered open, "Zenjamin, you're back," he said, using the name Ben had been given at birth on Zargon. "Is Zinc with you?"

Ben shook his head. His grandfather sighed and closed his eyes again. Ben glared at the guards outside the cage. It was the chaka's fault his grandfather was in such bad shape. He felt dragonfire rise from his depths, but doubled over in pain when it hit the collar and couldn't go any further. Smoke came from his nostrils, and tears flowed from his eyes as he forced the dragonfire down.

Sim stared at Ben with a perplexed look on his face, then he shook his head and turned his attention to Zane. "This is bad. Zane needs to be ready for work tomorrow."

"What happens if he's not?" Ben asked.

"They will take his collar off," Sim replied.

"And that's a bad thing?" Ben asked.

"They only take off the collar when you're dead," Sim said.

"But he's not going to die." Ben picked up his grandfather's cold hand in both of his and knew that his grandfather was lucky to have survived the day.

"If he's not able to work, he will die. Maybe not tomorrow, but perhaps the day after that."

"Are you telling me the chaka will kill him?"

Sim gave a brief nod and looked away.

Ben was glad Allison was here, although he worried about her using energy to heal when she was so exhausted. However, if his grandfather was going to survive, he needed a healer's touch and Allison was the only healer in the cage.

Without saying a word, Allison moved closer to King Zane and took his hand in her own. When she did, she could feel his life ebbing away. When she probed his body with her mind she could find nothing specifically wrong. His body had simply grown frail with the poor food and hard work. When the chaka used their weapon on him earlier in the day they had pushed him over the edge. It would take a fair amount of her energy to bring him back from the brink of death, but Allison was determined to heal the king. As she did so, she could feel what little energy she had left draining away. When she finished the King's eyes were open and he was pushing himself up, but no matter how much she fought to stay awake her eyes were closing.

During the night, Ben woke Allison up and helped her eat the food he'd saved for her. He didn't tell Allison she was not only eating her own food, but the best parts of what had been in his bowl.

CHAPTER FOURTY FOUR

TINY RETURNS

Zoey and Samson were eating breakfast when a tiny mouse ran up Zoey's leg and onto her shoulder.

"Tiny," she exclaimed. "Where did you come from?"

Samson reached out and snatched the mouse from her shoulder. "Shall we share," he said, with a hungry look in his eyes.

"You can't eat this mouse. It is a special friend to the Earthling girl who travels with us."

"She'll never know unless you tell her," Samson said.

Zoey reached out and took the mouse from Samson hands. "This mouse might be able help us find your children, because it will want to return to Allison."

Tiny chattered at Zoey before running down her arm and eating the last bit of food she held in her hand.

"Tiny, do you know where Allison is?"

The mouse chattered again and ran to the other side of her shoulder, the one closest to the ladder leading up to the level where the tunnels were. It jumped from her shoulder to the ladder.

"Well," Samson said. "I doubt the mouse knows what you're talking about, but we may as well follow it, if it goes in the right direction. With any luck, we can eat it later. Are you ready to go?"

Samson climbed the ladder first, and Zoey followed.

"What is in that direction?" Zoey asked, pointing in the direction she had seen Samson coming from the day before.

"The tunnel ends not far from here with an exit to the outside world," Samson said.

"So they must be back in the direction I came from." Zoey said. "I must have missed a turn off in the dark."

Zoey and Samson were midway between two platforms when the little mouse appeared in the dim light in front of them and stood chattering. Then it turned and ran off. Zoey called forth a little dragonfire so that she could see where the mouse had gone. It chattered at her and ran around in circles. As she walked towards the mouse there was a noise behind her. She turned to watch Samson fall to the ground when he was hit by a blast of light. Zoey turned on her invisibility and moved closer to the tunnel wall.

"It's only a daga. Not another hairless one," a voice said.

"But I'm sure I saw a hairless one."

"You must be mistaken. All we have here is a daga, but it has no collar on," another voice said.

"Maybe it's a would-be rescuer. Put handcuffs on it until we can get a collar on."

Zoey watched, unsure of what to do. She considered sending a blast of dragonfire their way, but she couldn't attack the chaka without hurting Samson. Besides, if they didn't know she was there, she could follow them and learn where they kept the others.

The Chaka guards waited for Samson to come to, so that he could walk rather than be carried, and Zoey waited with them. One of the guards got impatient and kicked Samson hard with his foot. Samson groaned, but did not wake up.

"It's old and not very healthy looking; maybe we should just kill it now."

"I don't think Sergeant Tonkle would approve. He will want to know where the daga came from and what it's doing here."

"Yeh, you're right." The guard poked Samson with his foot again.

"Leave me alone and let me sleep," Samson mumbled.

"The time for sleep is over. Get on your feet." The same guard who had been poking Samson kicked him hard. Samson howled and his eyes snapped open.

"Get up," the guard growled and pulled back his foot to kick again. Samson tried to get up, but fell over instead. After he tried and failed a second time, the guards each grabbed an arm and stood him on his feet. They held his arms and supported him as they walked through the tunnel.

Zoey dropped her invisibility when they turned their backs to her. She did not want to use up her strength. She kept to the side of the wall and far enough back that she doubted they would see her if they happened to turn around. The little mouse rode on her shoulder. She couldn't always see Samson and the guards, but she could hear their feet crunching on the gravel as they walked ahead of her. At some point, she realized she could no longer hear the sound of their feet walking through the tunnel. The little mouse started running back and forth across her shoulders, before running down her leg and back the way they had just come. Zoey turned around and followed it. She couldn't see where it went, but she could hear it chattering. When she caught up to the mouse it was standing in front of an opening on the other side of the tunnel wall from the one she walked beside. They had walked past the opening in the dark.

"You think they went in that direction?" Zoey asked the little mouse as it ran up her body to sit on her shoulder again. "I guess you do."

Zoey had not walked far when there was the dimmest of lights shinning in the distance. She walked toward it, putting one careful foot in front to the other.

When she reached the light, she discovered it was not just another platform along the way, but a place where several intersecting tunnels connected. A sign on the wall said Milton Station. An open cable car like the one she had seen vegetables put onto stood empty in front of her. When she stepped out from behind the cable car she saw a guard, who also saw her. The guard put a whistle to his mouth. A high-pitched sound pierced the air. As the guard ran towards Zoey, he drew his weapon and fired a beam of light. She quickly stepped sideways and turned her invisibility on, but the beam of light grazed her arm. For a brief moment, she was visible as the pain overwhelmed her. She fought to overcome it, and dropped to the ground as the guard leveled his gun at her again. The blast missed her by a fraction of an inch as she rolled away, once more invisible. Zoey rolled until she was under the cable car. The little mouse had fallen off her shoulder. It chattered and ran towards a tunnel opening. The guard shot a beam of light at the mouse, but it dodged the light and disappeared into the tunnel.

Zoey lay on the ground and watched the guard, too stunned to know what to do.

Meanwhile, guards were streaming in from three of the tunnels leading in and out of the station. An invisible Zoey stood up beside the cable car and put her hand on it to support herself, which was a mistake. The cable car shifted with a screech of metal and the guards all started toward her. She moved unsteadily toward the tunnel she saw Tiny go through, dodging the guards who were moving toward the cable car. It was a wise decision because the guard who had first seen her blasted the area surrounding it. He sent a stream of light from one side to the other, above the cable car and below it. If she had still been standing beside it, she would have suffered a full hit, and become visible when she fell to the ground unconscious. She would have ended up wearing a collar like the others.

"What's going on?" the lone female asked. "Why are you discharging your weapon?"

"I saw one of the strangers," the guard who had seen Zoey said.

"Nothing is there now."

The guard who had seen Zoey opened his mouth and closed it again as he looked around. "It's not here now, but it was just a moment ago."

"Where did it go then?"

"I don't know?"

"You didn't see the direction it went?"

"No."

"Is it possible that it was one of the strangers they brought in yesterday?"

"I don't know. They all look the same to me."

"Was it male or female?"

"Female, I think, but I didn't get a really good look at it before it disappeared."

"Sergeant Tonkle," a guard said, addressing the lone female. "They captured an uncollared daga today; maybe one of the hairless ones was with it."

"Perhaps," Sergeant Tonkle said. "Joss, go and see if any of the new slaves have escaped. Make sure the hairless female is still there. I'll go and alert the commander and organize a search. Dorne and Anjo go stand in front of the tunnels to the subway system so we can be sure it doesn't escape."

Joss turned and headed towards the tunnel the little mouse had disappeared into. An invisible Zoey quickly and quietly followed him. Joss led her right to the cage where the slaves were kept. When she arrived, Allison slept near the wall, while Ben and Denzel sat on the ground with King Zane and the daga. As she stood looking into the cage more guards arrived dragging Zinc between them. She didn't know it, but it was his second day of being interrogated and he looked terrible.

Blood ran down Zinc's chin from a cut lip and his face was battered and bruised. Zoey was outraged. How dare they treat the Prince of Zargon this way? She had to fight the urge to become a dragon and release the flame building in her gut. More than anything, she wanted to attack those who held Zinc by the arms, but knew doing so might get her locked up with the others.

"I have been sent to make sure the female hairless one is here," Joss said.

"She is in the cage with the others," one of the guards holding Zinc said. "Where else would she be?"

"Are you sure? A female hairless one was seen in the Station."

"Look for yourself."

Joss went over to the cage and looked in it. When he saw Allison laying on the ground, he turned and walked away to report his findings.

One of the guards accompanying Zinc opened the cage door and a second one pushed him forward. He fell on the ground and lie there unmoving.

Zoey followed Zinc into the cage and dropped to the ground beside him. She wondered if it was a mistake to enter the cage when the gate banged shut behind her.

"Zoey," Zinc whispered, as her invisible hand gently touched the side of his face. Zoey wondered how he knew she was the one touching him.

"Yes, my Prince, I'm here," she whispered and a slight smile appeared on Zinc's battered face.

Zoey placed a hand on each side of Zinc's head and tried to send as much healing power as she could. It was hard to both stay invisible and use her power as a healer. When the guards walked away, Zoey became visible so that she could more effectively heal Zinc. Before she was completely satisfied Zinc sat up and threw his arms around her. They sat on the ground with their arms around each other for a few minutes.

"I'll be okay, but you need to get out of here just as soon as you have helped my father and Allison."

Voices outside the cage reminded them of the guards who might look in and see an extra hairless female. "You need to become invisible," Zinc said. "We can't afford to have you get caught. You are our only hope of escape."

"What can I do?" Zoey said a little too loudly. One of the guards stepped close to the outside of the cage and peered through the bars with a perplexed look on his face, but by that time Zoey was invisible again.

"The next time they open the cell door, you need to leave and see if you can find the tool they use to put these collars on. We need them taken off to be able to transform and fight the chaka. We can't call up dragonfire with them on."

Ben had moved closer as they talked. "You also need to find Moses and free him," Ben whispered.

"Who cares about a brownie?" Zoey responded.

"I do," Zinc said quietly, surprising not just Zoey, but himself. "I don't know why, but I believe he's important for the success of our mission. He's been sent with us for a reason. His coming might be just for this time we find ourselves in. And besides, he is the only one who has been given wizarding gifts. Those are powerful gifts to have on our side when we go to battle. Not only that, but with any luck he has the portal. My father has told me he won't leave without freeing the daga. The portal Moses has is our best chance of doing that. We need to get ourselves and them as far away as we can, as fast as we can, and using a portal is the only way to do that. The Guardian will help us, all we need to do is work together."

The others stared at Zinc in shock. Ben reached out and briefly laid his hand on Zinc's shoulder and gently squeezed it.

CHAPTER FORTY FIVE

JEON

Moses was not far away. His hands and legs were bound and he lay on the cold stone floor more miserable than he had ever been in his life. Even the salt mines hadn't been this bad. The pain of lying in one position, with his hands tied behind his back was excruciating. He was muzzled and desperate for a drink of water when a visitor came to see him.

"Sh! Don't make a sound." A chaka touched his shoulder. "I'm not supposed to be here. If you promise not to hurt me, I'll take that muzzle off and give you something to drink." There was a moment of silence. "Do you understand me?"

Moses nodded his head, eying the cup the chaka held in his hands.

"Do you promise not to hurt me?"

Moses nodded his head again. The chaka helped him sit up, removed the muzzle, and held the cup to his lips. Moses drank all the water in the cup, except for the small amount that dribbled onto the floor. When they heard footsteps coming, the chaka slipped the muzzle back over Moses' head and scurried for the door, closing it just before a chaka guard appeared.

"What are you doing here, Jeon?" the guard asked.

"I heard there was a prisoner different from all the others and wanted to see him for myself."

"He is different. The commander hasn't decided yet whether to put him in the stew pot or send him out to work with the others. He wants to figure out what it is before he makes a decision."

"If he leaves him in that cage much longer without water the decision will be made for him." The young chaka realized he was holding the cup in his hands and quickly put it behind his back, but it was too late, the guard had seen it.

"I hope you weren't planning to find a way to get in there and give that thing some water."

"No, I've learned my lesson."

"As you've been told before, we can't let sympathy for our prisoners get in the way of doing what we need to for our own people. If we didn't have them under our control, it would be us in a cage instead. We would be the ones working as slaves instead of the daga."

"But I've heard the daga are peace loving and believe in freedom for all."

"Stop being a fool. You can't believe everything you hear. If we weren't stronger than they are, it would be us working as their slaves."

"I've heard they have a rule they follow; do to others what you want them to do to you."

"Perhaps that is one reason they are the slaves instead of us. They are weak and we are strong."

"But I've heard daga and chaka are really one people. That there is no real difference between us except for the shape of our ears."

"I'm going to pretend I didn't hear that. Say those words again when the wrong person is around and you will wear a metal collar and die as a slave. Or if you are really unlucky, they will expel you and send you out into the sun to die."

Jeon nodded his head. "Yes," he said. "You are right. My words are foolish ones to speak out loud."

Neither of the chaka standing in front of the cage knew their conversation was overheard by a girl who'd followed the older guard through the tunnels. Zoey had seen something the older chaka had missed. She saw a drop of water on the cement beside Moses' head and knew Jeon had been inside the cage. When the two chaka walked away, an invisible Zoey tried the door and discovered it was locked. She quickly turned and followed the two chaka down the tunnel. When they went separate directions, she followed Jeon. He had a key, and a heart that had not yet been hardened.

CHAPTER FORTY SIX

THE INVISIBLE HERO

Jeon went to the dining hall and sat beside his grandmother rather than the chaka closer to his own age.

"How's my favorite grandson?" Jachoo asked.

"Gamma, I'm your only grandson."

"Which is exactly why you're my favorite."

"Gamma, I told somebody today."

Jeon's grandmother looked at him sharply and worry lines crept across her forehead. "What did you tell?" she asked.

"That there was no real difference between daga and chaka."

The old woman grabbed Jeon's hand and held it. Her nails dug into his palm. "Did you tell them how you knew?"

"I didn't tell them about you being a midwife and how you were supposed to take any chaka babies born with floppy ears out to die under the sun, but instead took them close to a daga community and left them in the shade for the daga to find. No one but me knows that you saved the lives of daga babies who were born here to chaka parents."

"There weren't very many of them over the years, but every few years a baby with wrongly shaped ears would be born. I should have never told you about them. I should have gone to my grave with that secret. I would have if your sister hadn't been one of those babies. I wanted you to know what happened to her, but telling has put you at risk. We could both be expelled if the commander learns what I have told you. You need to keep it secret."

"Some things were never meant to be kept secret, Gamma, but don't worry I won't say anything more until your time on Farne is over."

"Please be careful even if I am no longer in the world. If you tell, you might join me on the other side before it is your time."

Jeon nodded his head. There was a particularly appetizing bun on a plate in the middle of the table. He reached out his hand to grab it, but before he could, the bun literally disappeared. One moment it was there, the next it was gone. He stared at the spot in shock. He was so focused he didn't hear his grandmother wish him a good day. He was staring at the plate when grain, wrapped in a piece of lettuce, disappeared. Not long afterward some carrots blinked out of existence. He closed his eyes and tried to block out the sound of people eating and talking at other tables. There it was. Across from him and off to the right he could hear what sounded like someone chewing on a carrot. He slid to the right and kicked both his legs out in front of him.

"Ouch," a voice said and a half-eaten carrot fell to the table.

"I don't believe it!" Jeon said. "Who's there?" People turned and stared for he had spoken a little too loudly.

His words were met with silence.

"I know you're there," Jeon whispered. "Speak to me."

No one spoke from across the table, but someone slapped the side of his head. "Stop talking to yourself, Jeon. Get these plates cleared off and go to the kitchen and see what they need you to do today."

"Right," Jeon said to his uncle, who was dressed as a guard. When his uncle was gone, Jeon looked across the table and whispered. "Don't go away. I want to talk to you."

Jeon went from table to table and scraped the leftover food from the plates into a barrel that he rolled along on a wheeled platform. Everything half eaten went into the barrel to be fed to the daga, but there was never enough food left over. Jeon personally always took more than he could eat so there would be more leftovers for the barrel. His grandmother did the same. If Jeon wasn't assigned to clean up after a meal, they took a bite out of everything on the table near them to try to make sure there was more food for the daga. Occasionally, when no one was looking he put some of the untouched food that was supposed to go back to the kitchen to be served to the chaka at a later meal into the barrel.

After he was finished cleaning the plates he went into the kitchen. His job was to clean out the sinks and the waste receptacles and collect anything edible and put it into the barrel with the leftover food. Food that was spoiled, the tops of carrots, vegetable peels and anything that was burned or had turned out badly was considered food fit for the daga. Any water that had been used for cooking was also put in the barrel. Jeon wished he could avoid putting the food waste into the barrel as there was often dirt and mold and sometimes worse in it. However, he had his orders and without the eatable scraps of rejected and spoiled food there would be even less food for the daga to eat. Every time he took the barrel of food to the slave cage he wondered if one of the two younger girls could be his sister.

After cleaning off the tables Jeon left the barrel beside the kitchen door and went back to the table where he had been sitting. "Are you still there?" he asked.

"Yes," a voice whispered back. Jeon was so surprised he stumbled backward. He hadn't really expected someone to answer.

"Follow me," he said and walked away.

When they got to a quiet place where they wouldn't be overheard, he asked the same question he'd asked earlier: "Who are you? What are you?"

In answer to his question, Zoey materialized. Jeon stepped back as she began to take shape and then stepped closer again when she was fully visible.

"You're one of the hairless slaves."

"I'm not a slave," Zoey said indignantly.

"Are all hairless ones able to do that? Can they all appear and disappear at will."

"No."

"How can you?"

"It is a gift from the Guardian of the Six Worlds."

Jeon's eyes went wide and he took a step backward. "We have myths about such a being, but no one among my people believes in them anymore. Well, except for my grandmother. She still believes."

"The Guardian is more than a myth and has sent me and the others to rescue the King of Zargon."

"Zargon! That's one of the mythical Six Worlds in the stories my Gamma used to tell me."

"The worlds are more than myths. I'm from Zargon."

"Seriously?" Jeon fell silent as he sought to digest this information, which seemed impossible to believe. And yet here was this girl doing unbelievable things. If the Guardian was real and had sent her, then it changed everything in his life.

"And the Watchers? Are the Watchers real too?" Jeon's voice was getting louder and higher as he spoke.

"Yes."

"Does Farne have a Watcher?"

"Yes," Zoey said, a little hesitantly as images of Zachery giggling and falling to the ground came to mind.

"How come we don't know about her then? Or is it a him?"

"He lives a long way from here."

"If we left today, how long would it take to get there?"

"With or without my friends?"

"Without. Just you and me."

"Weeks, if we arrived at all, this world is very dangerous, but I'm not leaving without the others and they won't leave without the King of Zargon, who won't leave unless we take the daga with us."

"I'm guessing the King of Zargon is the hairless one who has been here for several months."

"Yes, he's the one we were sent to rescue."

Jeon stepped back until he stood against the tunnel wall and then slid down until he was sitting on the ground. He sat in silence while he thought about everything he had heard. Helping this girl felt like a betrayal of his people, and yet not helping her didn't feel right either. He had this sense that if he walked away, it would be walking away from doing what was right and true. He felt like walking away would mean the dark side won once again.

"I wish I could help you," he said. "I really do."

Zoey silently stared at him.

"I would be afraid of what would happen to my grandmother if I helped you," Jeon said.

Zoey continued to stare at Jeon without saying a word. "My grandmother would want to see the daga freed, but not if it means putting my life in danger. She wouldn't be so worried about herself, but about me. She would worry about the danger helping would put me in, but she would also worry about the damage to my soul if I didn't help when I had the chance. So she actually might want to help and be disappointed in me if I don't help you because I am afraid of what will happen to her. And yet I know she would want me to stay alive."

Jeon fell silent as he thought about disappointing his grandmother and living a life of regret where he would think of the day when he could have stood against the evil at work in his world and chose not to. What would his grandmother tell him to do if she was here? It wasn't as clear as he first thought. She would not only worry about his physical wellbeing, but also about the health of his mind and spirit. If what his grandmother said was true then not to help was to fight against the way life was meant to be, the way this entity named the Guardian wanted it to be. He knew he wanted to stand on the same side as the Guardian, if this being matched what his grandmother had told him. Could he really say no to helping in what was a clear battle between good and evil?

"This Guardian," he finally said, "stands on the side of justice and peace for all people. Right? I've been told that the Guardian has no favorites, but cares for all, both chaka and daga."

"I believe that to be true," Zoey replied.

"So the Guardian is concerned about what is best for the chaka as well as what is best for the daga."

"Yes, I think so."

"What do you need from me?" Jeon asked.

"First of all, I need your help to free Moses."

"Moses?"

"The short one covered in hair. And I need to know how to get the collars off my friends."

Jeon groaned. Releasing the small one named Moses wouldn't be that hard. The cuffs he wore opened with a simple key that hung in the main guardroom. Every pair of cuffs opened with the same key and there were several copies. He could easily steal one, just as he had stolen the key that opened the door to the cells. But taking the collars off would be much more difficult. "The captain of the guard has the device that unlocks the collars," Jeon said. "Unless a new daga is captured or one dies we have no hope of getting our hands on the key."

"When do they put the collars on a newly captured daga?"

"Depends."

"The daga I was with was captured earlier. He was chained up where the others are kept, but when I left he didn't have a collar on yet."

"It might not be too late. The captain of the guard was at supper when I left and I heard him say that he had a meeting with the Elders right afterward. It is almost time for me to feed the daga. With any luck your friend will not have a collar on yet and we'll be there when the captain arrives to put it on."

Jeon did not know where the decision to help would take him, but he was glad to have made it. It felt like the right one. The one his grandmother would be proud of, if she knew. He just hoped this mysterious Guardian really was the same one his grandmother told him about.

CHAPTER FOURTY SEVEN

SAMSON ESCAPES

Jeon showed Zoey the tunnel that would lead back to the cages holding the daga and other slaves. They separated, and an invisible Zoey ran toward the cage while Jeon went to pick up the large barrel containing the scraps from the table and the waste from the kitchen.

"Where did you disappear too?" the chief cook asked. "I was about to send someone else with the slop for the daga. It smells particularly delicious tonight. The daga will love it." The chaka cook spit in the barrel and then laughed harshly. Jeon was sickened by the action and wanted to tell the cook he was a sorry excuse for a chaka, but he bit his lip and kept silent.

Jeon pushed the barrel out of the kitchen and down the hallway toward the slave's cages. On the way past the guardroom he stopped in. "Is my uncle working tonight?" he asked. "I have a question for him."

"Not tonight. You should know that better than I do. What makes you think I am your uncle's keeper?" The guard glanced up at Jeon and then went back to the game he was playing. Jeon quietly took one of the keys for the handcuffs off the hook and left.

 The smell from the bucket made him want to throw up. He guessed this might be a day when most of the food returned to the kitchen uneaten even through it meant the daga would have nothing to eat. They had learned the hard way that sometimes the food was so rotten it was dangerous to eat. He didn't understand why the chaka leaders would allow the daga to be fed food that made them sick. Sick slaves were not very productive and needed to be replaced sooner.

He hated the job of taking the food to the daga and returning the barrels to the kitchen empty, but he knew that if someone else was doing it, the daga would have even less to eat. He hated it even more when the daga judged the food unsafe and looked at him as if it was his fault they wouldn't be able to eat that night. On those nights, he made sure to dump the barrel before returning it. He did that to ensure the food was not served to the daga again the next morning.

Jeon moved through the tunnels faster than normal and slop sloshed around and spilled over the sides of the barrel. He would need to clean it up later or he'd be in trouble. He was moving so fast he was afraid of tipping the entire barrel over before he got to the slave pens, which wouldn't be a bad thing. It would keep the less discerning from eating something that was almost certainly going to make them sick.

Zoey meanwhile, had arrived at the cage in time to hear the captain of the guard speaking to Samson. "Fool, there is no rescue for the daga. All it means is that you will wear a collar and join your children as a slave."

Zoey saw two younger daga, a male and a female, pressed up against the bars and concluded these must be the children Samson came to rescue. They stood in silence, but tears were streaming down their faces as they watched their father get fitted for a slave collar.

The captain of the guard had a chain around his neck. On the end of the chain was a short metal rod with a cylinder on the end that was flat on one side. He pulled the chain over his head and nodded for one of the guards to bring Samson forward so he could put a collar around his neck. The captain was about to touch the flattened end to the collar when an invisible Zoey charged into him. The rod was knocked out of his hand and went sliding across the floor. One of the guards scrambled after it, but Zoey was faster. Just as the guard reached out his hand to pick it up, it vanished.

The chaka guards shouted in surprise and rage. They stood looking at the captain, waiting for orders, unsure of what to do.

"Kill this daga and block the entrance to the tunnel," The captain yelled. "You," he said to Jeon, "Take the food back to the kitchen. Nothing is going into that cage until we find the…"

Samson broke free and ran towards the tunnel entrance with his elbow bent in a strange angle. Only Jeon knew that Zoey was dragging him away. One of the guards leveled a weapon at Samson and fired it. The blast was a fraction off and missed. Two other guards started toward the exit to block it as the first one leveled his weapon again and was about to pull the trigger.

Jeon made a split-second decision. He pretended to slip and knocked the barrel over. Gruesome slop spilled in every direction. A groan rose from the cage as the prisoners saw their only chance for a meal disappear. The slop splashed up the leg of the guard holding the weapon. He jerked his hand sideways and instead of hitting Samson, he hit one of the guards rushing to block the entrance. The blast of light knocked the guard off his feet and he lay on the ground unmoving. The second guard tripped over him and fell. They both ended up soaked in the vile smelling slop that now covered the floor.

Samson was surprisingly agile for an old daga. He leapt over the guards on the ground and disappeared around the corner and out of sight. Jeon assumed an invisible Zoey had escaped with him and wondered when he would see her again. Then the captain of the guard spoke and his gut clenched in fear. He might never get the chance to see anyone again.

"Get a shovel and mop so this fool can clean up the spill, then lock him up. If I have my way, we will be sending this sorry excuse for a chaka away when the sun is at its highest."

CHAPTER FORTY EIGHT

THE KEY

Zoey had not followed Samson out. Instead she had slipped around the guards and was standing outside the cage in the place where the metal bars met the rock wall on the left side.

"No one is to open this cage until we know where the key is," the captain of the guard said. "Search for the escaped daga and bring him to me as soon as you find him. I don't know how he could have taken the key, but it's gone, and he must know something about it. He will beg to tell us everything he knows by the time I'm finished with him."

The captain of the guard noticed some slop splashed up on his legs and stuff he couldn't identify hung on his pants. He stomped his feet to clean it off, but instead of dislodging the sticky mess more simply splashed up and stuck to his pant leg.

"Jeon, you are going to wish you'd never been born," he growled before storming away.

When the captain of the guard left, he took all but two guards with him. One of the two went to find a shovel and a broom, which left only one. The one left behind was turned away from the cage looking out the tunnel entrance waiting for his companion to return.

Zoey didn't think there would ever be a better time to get the key to the Chosen. With her body between the guards and the cage, she put her hand through the bar and put the key quietly on the ground.

When she let go of it, it became visible. The only problem is no one was looking at it. She picked it up and gently tapped it on the ground then let go of it again. This time Zinc slowly crawled over to where the key had materialized. He picked it up and put it over his neck and under his shirt.

"You there," a guard yelled. "What are you doing?"

"Me?" Zinc asked.

"Yes, you."

"I'm hungry and want some of that food over there, but I can't reach it. Would you mind pushing it over this way?" Zinc pointed to a semi rotten pile of vegetable peels on the ground.

The guard walked over and kicked the rotten vegetables into Zinc's face, then he took out his weapon and set it on its mildest stun setting, designed to deliver a painful blast without knocking the victim out. "Move away from the bars," he demanded.

Zinc scuttled backwards and before the guard could blast him pushed his way through the daga so he was at the back of the cage. His father was sitting nearby with his back to the wall. Zinc crouched down beside him and took out the key. He held it up to the collar encircling his father's neck, but nothing happened. Zinc looked at the key and discovered there was a button that needed to be pressed. He slid the key over the spot where the sections of collar joined and pushed the button. This time the collar separated with a snap.

"Leave it on for now," Zinc instructed his father quietly, "until we have used the key on everyone."

Zinc unlocked Ben's collar next. He wanted to be sure the dragonborn were free to transform, as they were most able to fight their captors. Then he gave the key to Ben so he could use it on Zinc's own collar. Next he opened Denzel and Allison's collars. By then the daga all wanted to be next.

"Me next, please, please," they murmured.

"What's going on in there," one of the guards outside yelled. By then the second one had returned. The daga quieted immediately, but they were still eager to get their collars off. They were elbowing one another to be the next one in line.

"Do the daga seem to be behaving strangely?" one guard asked the other.

"Everything they do is strange," was the reply.

"Maybe you should go let the captain know something's up."

"If there's nothing, he'll explode and we might be given extra duty. I'm sure it's nothing. They're probably just upset that they won't get to eat tonight."

Jeon moved between the guards and the cage and started swinging the mop back and forth sending soggy rotten vegetable peels flying through the air, all the while singing a song about how great the chaka were. The guards moved further away from the cage to avoid getting splattered and watched as Jeon danced with the mop.

"This one will be no loss to the gene pool," laughed one of the guards, the strange behavior of the daga forgotten for the moment as they watched Jeon.

Sim took to organizing the daga. He chose who would go next, and sent those whose collars were unlocked to stand between them and the bars with their collars still in place so the guards would not see that Zinc had the key and was freeing daga.

"Are you sure this is a good idea?" one of the daga who'd worn a collar for a long time asked. "We will just make the chaka mad."

"Do you want to die as a slave?" Sim asked. "Or die fighting for freedom."

"Daga are not fighters, we are peacemakers."

"The time for peacemaking has passed," Sim said. "There is a time for everything under the sun. There is a time for peace, and a time to fight against those who destroy the peace of others. There is little hope of escape, but I am prepared to fight against the evil that keeps daga in chains."

"Don't be so sure you won't escape," Ben said. "We have what we need to do so."

Ben walked over to the cage. "Are you going to bring us some food?" he asked the guards. "If so can I request that you bring us some brownies?" Ben raised his voice as he spoke the last line. He looked out of the cage, hoping that if Zoey was still there she heard him and understood what she needed to do.

"Slaves aren't allowed to talk," said one of the guards and sent a blast from his weapon in Ben's direction. Most of the blast hit the metal bar and was deflected away, but Ben still winced in pain.

"There is no slave food left to feed you, and whatever brownies are I wouldn't expect any, ever."

Ben walked back to where the others were. "We will wait a few hours, until most of the chaka are asleep before making our next move," he said.

Jeon finished cleaning up the slop. One of the guards left to escort him to a prison cell.

CHAPTER FOURTY NINE

JACHOO

After Ben requested that the guards bring him brownies, Zoey left to do what she could to rescue Moses. It was getting increasingly hard to keep using the gift of invisibility, but she knew she would have real problems if the chaka caught her walking through the tunnels. One of the problems with staying invisible was that Samson would not be able to see her if she passed by where he was hidden. It would be a shame to leave the old daga behind if he was still alive, but Zinc had convinced her it was important to rescue Moses for their mission to have any chance of succeeding. Rescuing Moses was her priority even if it meant she couldn't help Samson.

Zoey walked in the direction she believed the prison cells were, but soon found she was turned around and lost. She came across a landmark she recognized. Jeon had pointed out the rooms where his grandmother lived and Zoey decided to risk asking the old chaka female for help. She went up to the door and knocked on it. After she knocked she second-guessed herself. Was this really the right place?

Much to Zoey's relief Jeon's grandmother opened the door. The old chaka looked outside and saw no one.

"Jeon is that you? You are a little too old to play tricks on your gamma. Jeon?" When no one answered she started to close the door, but Zoey gently, but firmly, pushed through the opening until she was inside.

Jeon's grandmother stepped outside her rooms to see if there was a reason why her door wouldn't close, seeing nothing she stepped back inside and slammed the door. Zoey could see how worried the old chaka was. When Jeon's grandmother reached out to make sure the door was firmly closed her hands shook. There were worry lines across her forehead as she crossed her arms across her thin chest. Jeon's grandmother opened her mouth to scream when Zoey slowly allowed herself to materialize.

"Please don't scream. Jeon is in trouble and needs your help." Zoey stepped back towards the door as she said these words, prepared to flee if the old chaka let out a scream that would bring her neighbors running.

The elderly chaka strangled her scream before it was fully formed. "Jeon! Why does my grandson need help?"

"He knocked over the barrel containing the daga food, just after the key for the collars disappeared. His actions helped an old daga escape before the guards could collar him."

"I see, and the guards think he might be involved."

"He was and they have taken him to a prison cell."

"What have I done," Jeon's grandmother wailed. "He will die because of me."

"That's not true," Zoey said. "I'm planning to rescue him, but I don't know how to find the cells."

"I appreciate your desire to help my grandson, but I can't see how you can possibly do anything to free him.

"There is more to me, than what you see, I have abilities beyond what is normal. I can transform my shape and in that other shape I can breathe fire, much better than I can in my human form." With those words Zoey breathed some dragon fire and scorched the wall.

Jachoo stumbled backwards and would have fallen, if Zoey hadn't quickly turned off her dragonfire and caught the old chaka by her shoulders.

Jachoo stared at the wall for a moment and then turned to stare at Zoey. She seemed unsure as to whether she should scream for help or thank Zoey for catching her. Her breath was coming out in ragged gulps.

"We will go find my grandson," she finally said when she was able to speak. "We will go there even through it will likely end up with me in prison and you in the slave pen.

CHAPTER FIFTY

THE RESCUE

The guard took Jeon and handed him over to the guards who were looking after the prison cells. They took Jeon and put him in a cell next to Moses, but they did not search him, which was a mistake. In his pocket Jeon had the key that would open every prison door except for the one the daga were in, as well as the key for the handcuffs Moses wore.

The guards were used to chaka prisoners staying where they were and doing what they were told. The penalty was expulsion from the community, which was assumed to be a death sentence. So prisoners tended to stay in a cell even if the door was left open. However, the guards locked Jeon's door since he was known to not always behave in the expected way. Jeon had about fifteen minutes to get out of his cell, free Moses, and decide what to do next before the guards returned to check on the prisoners.

He should have had lots of time, but it was hard to open the prison door from the inside. He had to put his hand through the cage and turn his wrist in such a way that he could get the key in the lock, all without seeing where the key hole was. He dropped the key once, and had a hard time getting it back into the cage so he could pick it up again. But finally the door clicked open, and Jeon let himself into the cell where Moses lay. "Hello Moses," he said. "I'm back."

Moses's eyes opened wide.

"You're probably wondering how I know your name. Zoey told me and sent me to rescue you."

Moses's eyes closed and a single tear formed and slid down his cheek.

Jeon took the muzzle off and unlocked the handcuff that bound his hands behind his back. Next he worked on the rope that bound his feet together. The knot was hard to undo. It took longer than expected and by the time he was finished the guards were returning.

Jeon pulled Moses off the ground and put him on his feet. When he let go Moses fell back down.

"Of course, your feet have lost any feeling after being tied together for so long," Jeon whispered to Moses.

Moses tried to speak, but all he managed was a croak. Jeon helped Moses stand and then hoisted him onto his back. As he stumbled out the prison door, he could hear the guard's footsteps as they walked toward the prison cells. Jeon carried Moses as fast as he could into the dark tunnel in the opposite direction.

The guards shouted behind them when they discovered the empty cells. Jeon tried to pick up his pace, but stumbled and fell, hitting the ground hard.

"Did you hear that?" One of the guards asked the other one. Then he yelled. "Jeon, you're making a mistake. Come back here and bring the hairy prisoner with you."

Jeon bit his lip to stop from groaning.

"I think I see something," the other guard said. "Jeon, is that you?"

Jeon scrambled to his feet as quickly and quietly as he could and tried to hoist Moses onto his back again. It was much harder this time to find the strength he needed. Finally, he lifted Moses off the ground and onto his back, and took a few steps forward before he stumbled and fell again. He was on the ground considering the option of running and leaving Moses behind when a hand grabbed his arm and lifted him up. He swung around ready to attack, but his fist stopped a few inches away from a face he could barely see in the near dark. It was Samson, the daga he had helped to escape when he spilled the barrel of slop. Samson picked up Moses and hoisted the brownie onto his back and they ran down the tunnel away from the guards.

"I was right, there is someone down there," a guard said behind them. "You go back and tell the others the prisoners have escaped. I will probably have them back in the cage before you get back. There was a collapse in that tunnel and they will be trapped at the end of it."

Jeon missed the place he was running to, but only realized the mistake when the tunnel ended in a pile of rubble. He reached out and touched Samson and pointed in the direction they had just come. Samson shook his head no. The sound of the chaka guard running toward them echoed down the tunnel. Jeon nodded his head and grabbed Samson's arm and pulled him back toward the prison cells. The guard was close when Jeon found what he was looking for - a hole at the bottom of the wall. Jeon got down on his hands and knees and motioned for Samson to follow him. He crawled through the hole, then turned around and pulled Moses through. It was a tight squeeze, but Samson managed to follow Jeon and crawl through. They sat and tried to breathe quietly as they heard the guard go by. They waited without speaking until the guard reached the end of the tunnel, turned around, and passed them a second time on his way back to the prison cells.

They were in a utility corridor that held a large rusty water line. There were several holes in the line and water was leaking out and flowing away. Broken cables and power lines hung from the ceiling. A rusty ladder on the wall led to a hole in the roof. Once there had been a hatch covering, but now it was open to the outside world.

"Water," Moses croaked and crawled over to one of the leaks in the water line. He put his mouth over the leak and sucked in some of the water.

"Is this the main water source for the chaka?" Samson asked.

"Yes," Jeon said.

"They will not have water long without a new line." Samson ran his hand along the water line, causing rust to flake off it.

"Everything is rusting and wearing out and we do not have the resources, equipment, and knowhow to fix it. Many things that were part of life when my grandmother was young, no longer work. Grandmother has tried to warn our leaders that life as we know it is coming to an end, but they ignore her and think life will go on as it always has. As long as they have weapons that work they think everything will be fine, but the good news is fewer of those things are still operational. They will truly think the world is ending when the last weapon is gone."

Jeon frowned as he looked at the rusty water lines. It was much worse than he remembered from the last time he had crawled through the hole in the wall.

"Problems ignored can't be fixed and don't go away," Samson said. "Will the others know about the hole in the wall?"

Jeon's face had a worried look on it as he shook his head. "I don't think so. As a child, I used to spend a lot of time on my own exploring. I doubt anyone else knows this entry exists, but they may find it when they start trying to figure out how we got out of the tunnel. We need to be gone from here as soon as we can."

When Moses finished drinking, Jeon gave him some food from his pocket.

"The sun is almost gone," Samson said. "I saw an opening over the prison where the slaves are kept. If we can climb the ladder and find it, I would like to look down and see my children."

"I know where it is," Jeon said. "And that is as good a next step as any. We can go now if Moses is recovered enough to climb the ladder."

Moses struggled to his feet and walked back and forth, stopping every once in a while to shake his legs. In a few minutes he walked to the ladder and started to climb.

CHAPTER FIFTY ONE

PRISON BREAK

An invisible Zoey had her arms around Jachoo's waist as they walked down the tunnel toward the prison cells. When they got to the cells they discovered that Jeon and Moses were missing. Footsteps advanced toward them from the dark corridor on the other side of the cells.

"Jeon, is that you?" Jachoo called out.

"You," a guard said, as he materialized from the dark. "What are you doing here?"

"I'm looking for my grandson. Someone said Jeon was here in your prison."

The guard walked up to Jachoo and Zoey moved behind the elderly chaka as she didn't want to risk being touched by him.

"Jeon has escaped," the guards said.

"But why was he in prison?" Jachoo asked.

"You need to ask the captain that question. I just do what I'm told. Do you have any idea where he would go?"

"No," Jachoo replied.

"Well, if you see him, you let the guard know right away. He's in big trouble and the best thing you can do to help your grandson is turn him in."

"Of course," Jachoo said. She never looked at the guards as she spoke. Instead she looked into the cell where a rope lay on the ground. She turned and walked away with Zoey at her side.

"What do we do now?" Jachoo whispered.

"I need your help to find the cells where my friends are," Zoey replied. "Show me the tunnel leading there and then you go home."

"I'm not convinced home is where I want to be. Perhaps the time has come for me to have the courage to live my convictions. I want to join my grandson in setting the daga and your friends free."

"I don't think there's anything you can do other than show me where to go."

"Who knows what I can do? I want to stay with you in case there is something."

Jachoo and Zoey walked through the tunnels, which were growing dark as the sun went down. The few remaining lights that depended on solar powered batteries flickered to life. Like everything in the underground tunnels they were an innovation from a previous age. Once the last one wore out the chaka would have no light once the sun went down.

"My one concern with helping is what it will mean for my chaka family and friends," Jachoo said. "Life will change for us all and they will have no opportunity to choose which way it changes. I just hope we can all survive the change and in the end it brings a better life for everyone; both daga and chaka."

"I understand your concern. My world will be changed in a similar way if all the brownies decide they are better off on Farne. The brownies are like your daga. They work for the dragonborn and receive no pay, but until lately I always thought they were happy doing so and never questioned that it was their natural place in my world."

"So, they are slaves?"

"I've never thought of them that way. I've always thought of them as working pets."

"I don't understand the word pet."

"Something you keep in your home, you feed it and play with it, but it has no freedom to come and go as it pleases. In the case of the brownies, they are expected to work and if they don't work well they are punished."

"So they are slaves?"

"I guess so, but I always thought it was their choice as well as ours. Brownies who live with dragonborn have a longer life than those who live in the wild. I truly believed they were glad to work for us, even though I knew there were dragonborn who did not treat their brownies as well as my family does."

"It sounds like it is time for change on both our worlds, because it is not right to build a society on an injustice done to those who are weaker than you are."

"I guess," Zoey said, troubled.

Jachoo placed her hand on Zoey's arm and squeezed it. "We need to be quiet now," she whispered. "Just around the corner are the daga prisoners and at least two guards."

"Why are you here?" a guard asked when they arrived.

"I'm looking for my grandson. He should have finished feeding the slaves by now. He was supposed to come see me right afterward, but he never showed up."

"He's not…" the guard began, but his voice trailed off as Moses drifted down and hung in the air between the opening in the roof and the slaves below him. Moses had called forth his wizarding gift to create an air current that was holding him up. He hung in the air and created two balls of electric energy. He flung the balls at the guards and knocked them off their feet.

Zoey turned off her invisibility. "This is Jeon's grandmother," she said to Moses.

"Gramma, don't worry, I'm up here," Jeon's voice called down from the opening in the ceiling.

Moses landed on the cage floor and brought out the portal. "Allie, go first, show how," he said.

Allison pulled off the collar from around her neck and took the hand of one of daga females before stepping toward the portal. As the slaves watched the portal enlarged and Allison and the daga female disappeared. There were several cries of surprise and alarm.

Zoey meanwhile was going through the pockets of the unconscious guards. She was looking for the key so they could get into the cage and leave with the others. However, the key was nowhere to be found. As she stood over one of the fallen guards another one came around the corner. The guard saw what was happening and turned and fled while blowing a whistle to raise the alarm.

Denzel went to the cage door and grabbed hold of the frame. His muscles knotted and he used his super strength to try to pull the door open, but the door did not budge. He ran to where the cage wall met concrete and pushed on the metal frame. The concrete was old, and already cracking in places. As Denzel pushed, the bars began to separate from the wall.

Meanwhile more guards were arriving. Zoey transformed into a dragon just a second before she was hit by a blast of energy. It would have knocked her out in her human form, but it had little effect on her as a dragon. She called forth dragonfire and blasted the closest guards. Those standing near the front howled in pain and fell backwards into their companion's arms. The guards moved behind the wall, dragging their companions with them, and reset their weapons from stun to kill. One of them jumped out and sent a blast toward the dragon standing in front of them. Zoey sent out a blast of dragonfire at the same time. Both Zoey and the chaka guard howled in pain.

Zinc moved over to the wall where Denzel was pushing on the metal frame. He joined his strength with Denzel's, and when the crack was wide enough, he pushed his way through. The chaka guards were taking turns coming out from behind the wall. They were mostly targeting Zoey who was standing in front of Jachoo to protect that old chaka from the blasts, but occasionally a chaka would send a blast toward those who were still in the cage. Most of the blasts hit the metal bars and scattered without doing any real damage to those inside, but an occasional howl of pain came from the daga and three of them fell to the ground.

As soon as Zinc pushed his way to the other side of the cage he transformed into a dragon and moved in front of Zoey to shield her from any further energy blasts. He sent dragonfire toward the next guard with the courage to pop out from behind the wall. The guard fell to the ground and another stepped out to take his place. Zinc sent a blast of dragonfire at that one too. Denzel held the cage away from the cement wall while Zinc helped Jachoo and Zoey through.

"Become human," Zinc said to Zoey. She did, but would have collapsed from the intense pain she experienced in her human form if Zinc hadn't been there to hold her up. He was pushing Zoey through the opening when an energy blast hit him in the back. He howled in pain and turned to let loose a blast of dragonfire which caused the chaka to jump back behind the wall. Like Zoey, Zinc could not get through the opening as a dragon. He needed to become human and when he did the pain would be unbearable. He cried out in pain and collapsed against the wall after he transformed, but Denzel reached out his arm and pulled him through the break he'd made. Denzel motioned for Jachoo to follow him, then picked up Zoey and Zinc and walked towards the portal and disappeared from sight. Jachoo hesitated for just a moment, but then set her jaw and stepped toward the portal.

Only Ben, in his dragon form, and Moses remained in the cage when they heard shouting from the rooftop above them.

"There are guards coming this way," Jeon shouted. "Hurry!"

Chaka guards surrounded Jeon and Samson and ordered them to put their hands behind their backs. They were about to tie them up when Ben and the brownie rose out of the hole in the prison roof. Ben transformed into a dragon and the guards fell back in alarm, their eyes wide and their mouths hanging open. Ben sent out a blast of dragonfire, which caused them to scatter and seek cover. Moses jumped off Ben's back and held the portal on the ground. He ran over to Jeon and Samson and grabbed their arms. He pulled them towards the portal that got larger as they approached and when they were close enough he pushed them through. Now only Ben and Moses were left. The guards came out of hiding, weapons held in shaking hands.

"Go," Moses yelled.

"Not without you," Ben yelled back.

CHAPTER FIFTY TWO

FIREHAVEN

"We go together," Ben yelled and grabbed Moses' hand. As they got close to the portal Moses reached out his hand and grabbed it so that it was not left behind. In no time at all they were back at Firehaven where they found chaos.

Samson was crying loudly with his arms around two young daga. Jeon was loudly sharing the day's adventure with his grandmother. Zinc and Zoey were arguing that the other one was more in need of Allison's gift as a healer. Some of the brownies were trying to take King Zane captive. Others were arguing that he was not their enemy in this new world. Sim and another daga were trying to stop the brownies who wanted to tie Zane up. Some daga were laughing, others were crying, and some just stood in silence staring at what was going on around them.

Zachery was laughing hysterically and dancing from one daga to another with his pendant in his hand. The daga did not understand why this strange looking creature was grabbing their hands and forcing them open. They were not cooperating. Some were bold enough to ask for food and water as they had missed both when Jeon overturned their food bucket.

Moses moved toward the brownies trying to tie up King Zane. "Stop," he ordered. "I rescue King. He is free. Get food and water now."

"We not slaves," one of the brownies replied. "Can't tell what to do."

"We help them," Moses said pointing to the daga. "They help us. Free Farneans help other free Farneans. Not willing, you return Zargon where no one helps brownies."

At those words, several of the brownies left to bring food and water for the newcomers. Moses went over to where Allison was to discover that she was in the process of healing Zoey, so Moses laid his hands on Zinc and healed the dragonborn Prince.

Zane walked over and took Zachery by the hand. "Zachery, I presume," he said.

"I am Zachery and you must be the reason for all this commotion. I presume you are the King they went to find."

"What are all these brownies doing here?"

"They were looking for a place where they could be free and I was looking for somebody to live on this world with me." Zachery crossed his arms and glared at the King.

"But they belong on Zargon," King Zane said.

"Not anymore they don't. I not only have company, but I have brownie Chosen. Did you know brownies could be Chosen?" Zachery giggled and slapped at his tail which was swishing back and forth.

The King just stared at Zachery with a look of shock on his face. Whether it was because of Zachery's bizarre behavior or the news that the Guardian had selected brownies as Chosen was not clear.

Zane closed his mouth, which had been hanging open, and shook his head.

"I didn't either," Zachery said. "But they can be. I want to know if any of the newcomers are Chosen."

"That can wait for later," Zane said. "Right now you need to welcome the daga and let them know you are their friend. They are frightened and need to know they will be okay. You will be a friend to them, won't you?"

"Of course. I am the Watcher of this world. I am a friend to all people on Farne. I am a righter of wrongs, a helper of the helpless and a trainer of the Chosen."

"Right now they are hungry and thirsty and need to know they are safe."

Zachery walked over to where the biggest group of daga stood. He raised his voice. "Welcome friends. You are welcome here whether you are a Chosen or not."

"What does he mean?" a voice asked.

"I will tell you about what it means to be Chosen after you have the food and drink the brownies have gone to get. Please sit and wait for their return."

The daga sat, but Jeon walked up to Zachery. "Zoey told me about Chosen and I want to know if I'm one. I certainly hope so." Jeon held out his hand and Zachery placed his pendant on it. It opened and the dials began to move.

"I now have four brownie and one chaka Chosen," Zachery hooted and then danced a jig.

After the newcomers were given food and water, Zachery tested them all. Both of Samson's children were Chosen, but they were the only ones among the daga.

The next morning Allison and Denzel took a ride on Ben's back. What they saw amazed them. Everywhere they looked the land was green with new growth. Off in the distance they saw healthy looking rain bearing clouds, but there were no toxic clouds to be seen.

"How far does it extend?" Allison wondered aloud.

"Let's find out." Ben rose into the air and flew in the direction they had gone the previous week. They flew far past the point where Allison, Moses and Zoey had used the gift of re-genesis and as far as they could see the land was green.

"Re-genesis has begun," Allison said, "and it will not be stopped until this whole world is once again fruitful and able to support life."

"You used that gift everywhere we stopped, didn't you?" Ben asked.

"Yes," Allison said.

"Even where the chaka live?" Ben asked.

"Yes, even there."

"I'm glad," Ben replied. "The world as they know it is ending, but a new one is beginning. I hope they learn to take better care of this world than their ancestors did."

CHAPTER FIFTY THREE

A SECOND QUEST

Ben got the impression that Zachery was going out of his way to avoid the Chosen from Earth and Zargon. Whenever one of them showed up where he was, he quickly left. Ben began to wonder if he was trying to keep them all on Farne. Finally, he cornered Zachery in the dining hall.

"You need to send us back," Ben said.

Zachery turned to leave, but Ben ran around and blocked him. Zachery giggled and fell onto a chair, but jumped right up again when he sat on his tail the wrong way.

"You need to send us back to our own worlds," Ben said again.

Zachery turned away from him, put his fingers in his ears and began to hum loudly. Ben moved in front of him and removed his fingers and said more loudly, "We have completed our work, now the Guardian expects you to send us back to our own worlds."

"I can't," Zachery said and giggled.

"Why can't you?" Ben asked loudly, dragonfire rising unbidden from his gut.

"There is no room of portals here," Zachery said.

"Where is it?" Ben asked.

"It would be somewhere around where your grandfather appeared on Farne."

"Then, I guess Moses will need to use the gateways he was given to send us back to our own worlds."

"If you do that your work on Farne will only be half done. You were sent not only to rescue the King, but you were sent to bring about re-genesis. Re-genesis will not be complete until the room of portals and the Guardian's chair are reunited with the Watcher, who is me." Zachery burst out laughing when he finished speaking.

"None of us were told that was part of what we were to do," Ben said when Zachery's laughter turned to giggling.

Zachery stood up straight and tall and glared at Ben. "I am the Watcher of Farne, Chosen by the Guardian and that means I just know things. This is what I just know. The room of portals needs to be restored to the Watcher, or the Watcher needs to be restored to the room of portals for re-genesis to be complete. It is not here, so we need to go find it."

Ben stared at Zachery. The Farnean Watcher was trying to maintain his composure, but every once in a while a giggle would escape and he would struggle to put a stern look back on his face.

"Okay," Ben said. "How can we restore the room of portals?"

"You start by finding them."

"What makes you think it still exists and wasn't destroyed by the war?"

"The Guardians portals and chair could never be destroyed, no matter how big the bomb. They would be in the one building still standing."

"There is only one building still standing where we found the king. We searched it and there was no room of portals of chair there."

"I tell you it is where you found the King. Maybe it is covered with dirt, or maybe it sunk underground, but it is still there and all you need to do is find it."

"Are you saying we need to go back to where the chaka turned us into slaves?"

A big smile appeared on Zachery's face and he giggled in joy. "I'm glad you understand. If I'd known you would understand this easily, I would have told you sooner. Now please tell the others so they will understand and agree to go. When we find the room of portals we will move everyone there."

"Who will move?"

"All of us except the wolves. They can stay here."

"The wolves will starve to death here," Ben said.

"Oh, all right, the wolves can come too."

"You're forgotten something important. We just escaped the chaka and they will still be there waiting for us."

"The chaka can join us if they wish. Or if they don't want to join us they can come here."

Ben sat down on a chair. He did not want to go back and risk being recaptured by the chaka and he doubted anyone else would want to either.

"I don't understand. Allison and I saw you standing by a door in the place between time and space. How could you do that if you didn't have access to a room of portals?"

"Yes, I was there. As the Watcher, I don't need to be near the portals to use them to go to the place between time and space, but I do need them to send Chosen to one of the Six Worlds."

"But when we stepped through the portals on our own worlds we came here. Are you sure we can't go back from here?"

"You must have been redirected here, but I know the Guardian wants you to restore the room of portals before you leave this world and I don't know how to send you back without them."

Ben stared at Zachery. His anxiety grew and he crossed his arms to hide the tremor in his hands. He did not want to return to the place of his captivity or risk wearing a chaka slave collar again.

Not long afterward Ben told the others what Zachery wanted from them.

"Are you telling me he expects us to go back to where the chaka are?" Allison asked, clearly horrified by the prospect.

Ben nodded his head.

"What's to stop us from using the gates Moses was given to go back to our own worlds?" Zoey asked.

"Need two gates. Zachery has one. Won't give back," Moses said indignantly.

"But he's got to give it back to you. It's not his. The Guardian gave them to you," Zoey said loudly.

Moses smiled at Zoey and nodded in agreement.

"I can get it back," Zinc said, as dragon smoke come from his nostrils.

Zoey smiled at Zinc and touched his arm. "Of course you can, my Prince," she said.

"We need to think about this," King Zane said, "We need to be sure the work the Guardian gave you is complete. If we leave here, we leave a world with Chosen that can't go anywhere, but worse, this world may not be able to receive help from the Chosen of other worlds when it is needed. I wouldn't want to leave the friends I have made here in that kind of situation."

"But surely we would have been told if restoring the room of portals was part of our mission here," Ben said. "Perhaps the Guardian has already chosen others to do the job."

"Perhaps, but I have heard of this happening before," King Zane said. "Chosen are given part of the mission when they leave their world, and the second part comes when they are on-site."

The Chosen and King Zane were silent as they thought through the implications.

"I think Zachery is right," King Zane finally said. "You were sent here, not just to rescue me, but to bring a new beginning to this world, and part of doing so involves restoring the room of portals."

"I agree," Ben said reluctantly.

"I agree," said everyone present.

"I hope we don't end up wearing slave collars again," Allison said.

Ben looked at Allison with concern in his eyes. "You could stay here. You weren't given the kinds of gifts that help in a battle."

"I've been given the gift of healing," Allison said. "If we go back to where the chaka are there is a possibility people will be hurt and the gift of healing will be needed."

"Moses can come with us," Ben said. "He also has the gift of healing."

"Allie best healer," Moses said, looking at Allison with adoring eyes.

Allison reached out and squeezed Ben's arm. "Don't worry about me Ben, I can be as brave as anyone here if I need to be," Allison said.

"Everyone who was sent should go," King Zane said, "partly because the Guardian had a good reason for choosing each one of you, and partly because you will be leaving to go to your own worlds from there."

"I just wish we knew where to look," Ben said.

"I think I know," King Zane said. "I arrived on Farne near a hill by a dry lake bed. I would have landed in water if there had been any in the lake. The room of portals is likely in a building buried under that hill."

Ben looked up and smiled. "I'm sure it is the same lake we stayed near and it is no longer dry."

CHAPTER FIFTY FOUR

BACK IN DANGER

After they had breakfast the next morning, Zachery met them in the yard outside his building. "Time for us to go," he said.

"You're coming with us?" Ben asked in surprise.

"Yes, of course," Zachery said.

"King go first. King think of place he arrive. Watcher next. I be last," Moses said, holding the gateway in his hand.

Within minutes they were all standing before the hill near where King Zane first arrived on Farne. It was the same hill the Chosen had camped near. The water in the lake was higher than the last time they had seen it.

"Hmmm," Zachery said, looking at the lake. "I must get one of the Watcher's to send me fish for this lake."

"There are nice fish on Earth," Ben said.

"Ben, Zinc, Zane, Denzel and I will look for the room of portals. Allison, Moses and Zoey will fly out as far as they can in every direction and use the re-genesis gift," Zachery instructed.

"I don't think it is a good idea for us to be separated," Ben said. "We should stay together."

"It's important that those who have the gift of re-genesis use it," Zachery said. "My people will need to grow food when they move here."

"I agree," Allison said. "If Zoey is willing, I want to fly to different spots and use the gift of re-genesis. Ben, I'll say it again. Stop worrying about me. The Guardian has given a gift and it must be used."

Zoey didn't say anything right away. She appeared hesitant to commit herself to a trip that took her away from the others.

"Of course Zoey will go," King Zane said. "She knows how important making this world habitable is, don't you Zoey?" The King smiled at Zoey, who glanced at Zinc before giving a brief nod. She transformed into a dragon so Allison and Moses could climb onto her back.

"Maybe, I should go with them," Zinc said. When everyone stared at him, he stumbled on. "You know, for extra protection."

Zoey turned and looked at Zinc, if a dragon could smile she would have. "That is sweet of you, my Prince, but we'll be okay."

Ben realized at that moment how much the relationship between Zinc and Zoey had changed. He just wished Allison looked at him the way Zoey looked at Zinc.

"Shoo, shoo," Zachery waved his hands at Zoey and her riders. "It is time for you to go and heal my land, and the rest of us must be off to find the room of portals."

"Don't worry, Ben," his grandfather said as the others flew away. "Your girlfriend is safe. She is in the company of one of my best dragonborn warriors."

"She's not my girlfriend," Ben said.

"No? Too bad, I like her," King Zane patted Ben's back and then followed Zachery toward the hill.

They found a cave and entered it. When they got to the end they cleared away dirt to discover a wall made of stones cemented together. There was a building hidden underneath the hill. If Zachery was right it was the historic school on Farne that contained the room of portals and the special chair the Chosen sat on to receive gifts from the

Guardian of the Six Worlds. They left the cave and went searching for the next one, hoping to find one that led to a door or a window instead of a wall. As the sun climbed overhead they went from one cave to another and dug away dirt until they found the outside wall of the building.

Ben lost track of how many caves they had gone into. He had dirt in his hair and his skin had turned black, dirt was in his ears and in the corner of his eyes. When he took a drink he washed the grit in his mouth down his throat.

They just finished clearing away the soil from the end of another cave to reveal a stone wall when disaster stuck. The earth overhead came crashing down burying Ben under it. Ben tried to push his way through the soil, but it was heavy and he couldn't move his arms and legs. In a few moments, he would have no choice, but to breathe in and all he would get was a nose full of dirt. In the seconds that remained to him, he wondered how many of the others had been buried with him. Was anyone still free? Was there anyone out there to rescue him? Ben was losing consciousness when a hand grabbed his arm and pulled him to the surface. Denzel was the first face he saw when he opened his eyes. Then he looked over and saw his grandfather covered in even more dirt than he was. His grandfather had been buried with him and been rescued just before he was.

Ben was trying to find enough saliva to spit out the dirt in his mouth when he noticed that Zachery and Denzel were staring at a point above his head. When he followed their gaze, he saw what they had spent more than half a day looking for. A window had been uncovered when the dirt caved in. He spit as much dirt as he could out of his mouth, then followed Denzel over the mound of fallen soil toward the window. Denzel stood on top of the mound and used his soil-covered sleeve to rub the glass. Ben looked over Denzel's shoulder and saw what looked like a dining hall with rows of tables and chairs.

"Here," Zachery passed Denzel up a fist sized rock. "Hit the window with this."

Denzel did and the window shattered. Zachery climbed onto the hill of dirt and through the broken window. The others followed him into the building.

While the others looked for a doorway into possible ruins under the hill, Zoey, Moses, and Allison flew in an ever-widening circle around the ruined city. They stopped many times and sent the re-genesis gift out in all directions. When they flew out from the city they had zigzagged to avoid toxic clouds, on their way back there was not a single toxic cloud in the sky. They could already see the difference their use of the re-genesis gift was making to the land around as they flew back toward the ruined city. Dormant seeds began to sprout and grow, particularly in places where good clean rain fell.

CHAPTER FIFTY FIVE

THE ROOM OF PORTALS

Ben was about to offer to lead the way since he had the gift of seeing in the dark, but Zachery called forth a ball of light and held it in the palm of his hand. The light revealed a broad set of steps at the end of the dining hall. Zachery headed straight for the staircase and started to climb. When they reached the fourth floor the Watcher led them to a door and opened it. As soon as Ben walked through he knew they had found the office of the previous Watcher of Farne. Sitting on the floor beside a desk was one of the Guardian's special chairs. It was identical to the one in Miss Templeton's office. The room of portals would be somewhere close by.

The ball of light Zachery carried in his hand exploded. The room became so bright everyone closed their eyes. They opened them to discover the chair alive with light flowing in and around the Celtic knots covering it. Light danced in the air above the chair and then reached out and completely enveloped Zachery.

Zachery felt as if the chair was a living creature, delighted that its centuries of sitting alone in the dark, was over. The light coming out of the chair reached out and touched each one of them. With the touch of light came laughter, which caused them to fall to their knees. And when the laughter was gone it left each of them filled with wellbeing and awe. They sat in silence for several minutes. It was King Zane who finally spoke in a whisper. "We need to find the room of portals for the day is ending. The others could be back already, waiting for us."

Ben was thinking about Allison and wishing she had been with him to share this experience. She would have loved what had just happened here. When his grandfather mentioned the others could have returned he wondered if she was safe. If the chaka found her, it wouldn't be long until they had a slave collar around her neck again. He wanted to be with her, so he could help keep her safe. But the truth be told, he also felt safer when Allison was nearby. He trusted her and knew that she would always watch his back, as he would hers.

A finger of light burst forth from the chair and pointed to one of the two doors in the room. Ben rose from the ground and quickly walked to the door the light had pointed to. When he opened it he found the Portal with its six doors – one for each wall of the hexagonal room, each one leading to a different world.

"It is time for us to find the others so they can go home," King Zane said from behind Ben.

CHAPTER FIFTY SIX

A MIGHTY WIND

A day spent in the hot sun using the re-genesis gift had drained the energy from Allison, who had to maintain the protective skin and eye transformation all day long. Zoey was tired after carrying the other two on her back as a dragon and then transforming into a human several times so she could use the re-genesis gift along with the other two. The only one who seemed to have any energy left was Moses. The two girls sat in the shade of a broken wall and watched for the others to return while Moses explored their surroundings.

"Do you think they found it?" Zoey asked.

"The Watcher is with them and Watchers sense things the rest of us don't," Allison said.

"Yes, but Farne's Watcher is not quite right in the head," Zoey replied.

"Yes, well—", Allison began, but fell silent as a wind came from nowhere to blow up from the ground between them and the hill. The wind raced to the top of the hill where it swirled around and around above it, gaining in speed and size with each revolution. Then it dropped down and began to strip the soil off the hill. Wind and dirt spun out in ever widening circles. At first it spun over their heads but then it dropped down and drove hundreds of tiny missiles into them.

Allison and Zoey screamed in pain. Zoey was about to transform into a dragon when Moses took her hand.

"Come with me," Moses yelled and pulled the girls behind him. They closed their eyes to keep out the dirt, and let Moses lead them to what had been the doorway of an impressive building. The building itself was gone, but the entryway was still intact. On the other side of the door were steps leading both upward and downward. The ones going upward led nowhere, the ones leading downward led to the remains of a hallway.

"We go down steps," Moses yelled.

Allison and Zoey cracked open their eyes and they flew down the steps to take shelter. The sound above them was deafening. Allison hoped Ben and the others had found a safe place to hide from the tornado. If not, they would be in desperate need of a healer and not have one with them. Dirt drifted down and coated them and everything around them as the wind howled above them. They heard walls crashing and hoped the remains of the building above them would not come down on their heads.

As suddenly as it started it was over. One moment it sounded like a hundred jet planes spooling up for takeoff, and in the next moment there was silence.

Allison, Zoey and Moses climbed up the stairs and looked around at the changed landscape. The wall they had leaned against was gone. Dirt covered everything as far as their eyes could see. The hill was no longer there and in its place stood a building.

"I guess this means they found the room of portals," Zoey said.

"Yes, definitely." Allison stared at the building in front of them and took a few steps toward it. "This was not a normal event. Finding the room of portals triggered the wind."

"It must be something the Guardian put in place," Zoey said, just before a blast of blue energy hit her in the back and she fell to the ground. Allison dropped to Zoey's side and just missed being hit by a blast of energy that went over her head. Moses jumped behind a large pile of stones to avoid being hit by the chaka weapon. He raised his hands and pulled air from every direction and sent it rushing towards them. The wind slammed into the chaka and sent them tumbling head over heels. Some lay on the ground unmoving. At least one would never move again as his neck was bent at an odd angle. Others pushed themselves up and sat on the ground dazed. One regained his feet and pointed his weapon at Moses. When he pulled the trigger he was knocked off his feet by an explosion from his damaged weapon.

Moses was astounded by what he had done. He didn't expect to have so much power go through his hands, and calling it forth left him drained of energy. If there were more chaka with weapons he was not sure he could protect his friends. He dropped onto his knees beside Allison, who sat on the ground beside Zoey.

"Moses, what have you done to my poor chaka," Zachery said and then strode on past to check on them.

Zinc was following Zachery and dropped to his knees on the other side of Zoey. "How is she?" he asked.

"She's dead." Tears streamed down Allison's face as she looked up at Zinc.

"She's not dead. She can't be. Do something," Zinc cried out, anguish clearly written on his face. He lifted Zoey up and cradled her in his arms.

"Try re-genesis," Moses said.

"Are you sure?" Allison asked. "I don't think it was meant to bring the dead back to life."

Moses shrugged. "She not dead long. Re-genesis bring dead world to life. I try re-genesis, you heal."

Allison and Moses placed their hands on Zoey. Moses sent a trickle of the re-genesis gift into the dragonborn girl. He stopped when Zoey's heart began to beat. Meanwhile, as soon as life returned, Allison sent her healing power into Zoey and restored what had been damaged by the blast. Zoey opened her eyes and looked up at her friends in confusion. Then she focused on Zinc and gave him a weak smile. "How are you, my Prince?" she asked in a whisper.

"I'm fine as long as you are," Zinc said and bent over to place his lips gently on Zoey's forehead.

Ben fell to his knees. "Are you okay?" he asked Allison quietly.

"I'm okay," she whispered weakly and leaned against him. "Did you find the room of portals?"

"We did. It was an incredible experience. I wish you could have been there because you would have loved it. I have a confession to make. It's not so much that I worry about you; I do, but I also feel safer knowing you are not far away. I like having my friend, the healer nearby when I'm going into dangerous situations." Ben smiled at Allison, a smile that conveyed how fond he was of her.

His smile sent warmth flowing through Allison's whole body and she sighed and closed her eyes. "I wish I'd been there too," she said quietly.

"I hope we will always be friends even if we can never be anything more," Ben said.

"I'm sure we'll always be friends." Allison's eyes were filled with warmth as she smiled at Ben.

"Moses, I need you here," Zachery called. Zachery was checking on the chaka. The two who were sitting on the ground appeared unhurt except for a few bumps and bruises. Three others needed a healer. The one who had used the broken weapon was beyond saving. As was the one whose neck was broken.

"I be looking after Zoey," Moses said.

"Zoey will be fine," Zachery said firmly. "I need you here."

"You be okay?" Moses asked Zoey.

She gave him a weak smile and a brief nod.

Denzel and King Zane followed Moses over to where Zachery waited for them. Denzel collected the chaka weapons. He broke any that looked like they could still be functional.

Moses began the work of healing those who were wounded. Zachery went along behind Moses, took the hand of a recently healed person and placed his pendant on their open palm.

Ben was incredulous as he watched Zachery. How could the Watcher think any of the chaka guards would be among the Chosen? He was not surprised when none of the guards were.

CHAPTER FIFTY SEVEN

DAWNING OF A NEW WORLD

"Go," Zachery said to the guards who had been healed. "Bring everyone, and I mean everyone up from underground."

"Our people will not be your slaves," the chaka said.

"I'm not looking for slaves," Zachery said impatiently. "But the chaka will not be allowed to stay in their underground home unless they agree to my conditions. One of which will be an end to slavery."

"Our leaders will never agree,"

"They will or your people will move away from here. Go," Zachery said again. "Bring your leaders here, I want to talk to them."

"They won't come," the chaka said.

Zachery turned in the direction of the underground caves and closed his eyes. A minute later the sound of a collapsing tunnel reached their ears.

"Tell them, if they do not come here at sunrise tomorrow my next target will be the utility corridor that provides water for your families."

The recently healed chaka looked at Zachery in shock and then looked at each other. The one who had spoken on behalf of them all, nodded. "We will tell them."

The chaka turned away and walked toward the entrance that would lead them underground.

"Oh, and tell them to bring any weapons they still have," Zachery called after them.

"Don't worry, they will bring every weapon we still have," one of the chaka soldiers said.

"If those weapons are fired, I might collapse all your tunnels," Zachery said. "Tell your leaders that and tell them to bring everyone with them so there is no chance of them being buried alive."

The next morning, when the sun came up, the chaka, young and old, came up out of their underground tunnels. For many of them, it was their first time seeing the outside world, but those who had been on the surface before looked around in surprise. The world was not as it was when they had last seen it. Patches of green were visible in what had previously been a dry and barren land.

Zachery knew without being told that the chaka who stood before him only carried broken weapons that no longer worked. The working ones were in the hands of thirty-two chaka soldiers who were circling around behind them. Zachery stopped to speak with King Zane. "Zane," he said. "You need to take all the dragonborn with you. There are guards over there who are hoping to launch a surprise attack on us. You have my permission to transform into dragons and scare the spit out of them, but please try not to seriously hurt them. Take their weapons away and burn them, and then bring them here."

Zane left with the dragonborn, while Zachery went to meet the six hundred and ten chaka who stood staring at the world around them.

Moses, Denzel, and Allison stood beside Zachery facing the crowd of chaka. The leaders were in the front, behind them were a few able-bodied men, and at the back were the women and children.

"There are a lot of guards missing," Denzel whispered to Zachery, who nodded. "I know, he said. "The dragonborn have gone to get them. We'll just wait for a moment until they bring them here."

Zachery turned and stared in the direction the dragonborn had gone. The chaka leaders followed his gaze and then looked at one another anxiously.

"We are here as you requested," the leader said.

"Not quite," Zachery responded. "But you soon will be. The dragonborn have gone to get your friends."

When the leader started to say something more, Zachery motioned for him to be silent. In a few moments flashes of light lit up the sky and cries of pain pierced the stillness of the morning.

"I hope your people will not be too badly hurt," Zachery said to the leader. "Denzel, please take these broken weapons away from them. I doubt the chaka can find a way to make these work again, but it is not good to leave things to chance."

Denzel moved to take the weapons away, but the chaka raised their weapons as if to shoot him. Denzel stopped and looked at Zachery, unsure of what to do.

"Go ahead Denzel," Zachery said. "These weapons are not functioning. They sent the good ones with guards who were supposed to attack us while they provided a distraction. It really isn't very smart to think you can pull a stunt like that on a Watcher. A Watcher always knows." Zachery put his hands over his mouth to stop himself from giggling.

Denzel stepped forward to take the weapon out of the leader's hands, while all around them chaka tightened their hold on their broken weapons. Denzel ignored them and yanked the weapon away. Then he took the weapon and broke it in half as if it were a pencil. The chaka leader stepped back in alarm.

The leader might still have given the order to resist, had the chaka guards he'd sent out earlier not walked out from behind a ruined building with their empty hands raised in the air. The fight went out of the chaka and they dropped their weapons.

"Please sit on the ground," Zachery commanded.

They sat and were soon joined by the ones the dragonborn had captured.

"If chaka want to be part of the new world we are building," Zachery said, "you can stay here and live as free people among other free people, but you must be able to live in peace with others who are not chaka. Later today I will start bringing daga and brownies here to live."

"There is not enough room under the city," the leader protested.

"They will not live under the city," Zachery said. "They will live and work on the surface."

"No one can live on the surface," the leader said.

"Yes they can and so can you, if you wish. Re-genesis has taken root. You can see the signs all around you. Soon the whole world will be filled with green and growing things, the sun will cease to be dangerous, and the rain that falls will be clean and refreshing."

The chaka stared at Zachery with skepticism written on their faces. Zachery went on undaunted. "My people will plant crops and harvest them and live in homes they build for themselves. As I said earlier, you are welcome to live on the surface with us. What you will not be allowed to do is capture any of my people and turn them into slaves or steal any of the food they grow. If you do, I will send you to another part of this world, a place where it will be much harder to live. A place where there might be dangerous animals, like wolves, that will think of you as food. Change is coming. I'd like you to be part of it, but I will not force you to be. You can live and die away from the light in your underground lair, or you can help build a new world with the rest of us, or I can send you far away from here."

The chaka stared at Zachery, saying nothing. The grim look on most of their faces said it all. They did not trust him or believe life was going to change for the better. However, the occasional chaka was looking around in awe and seemed to be imagining new possibilities.

"Now, stay where you are. I'm going to come around and lay my pendant in the hand of those who are grown or almost grown." With those words Zachery giggled for the first time since the chaka had come out of their lair, but it was no longer the giggle of a half mad lizard man, but the joy of a man who was very happy with his lot in life.

Zachery went from one chai to another with disappointing results.

"Why is he wasting his time?" Zoey asked Zinc.

"He is crazy," Zinc replied. "He can't really expect to find more Chosen among the chaka."

A moment later Zachery shouted. "I have another Chosen."

When he was done, he had found two more Chosen among the chaka.

"Truly the Guardian's ways are different than the ways of the peoples of the Six Worlds," Zinc said.

"Maybe that is a good thing," Zoey replied.

CHAPTER FIFTY EIGHT

THE KING'S DECISION

Later that day, King Zane came to where Zinc sat with Zoey. "Zinc," he said. "I need to talk to you."

Zoey looked from father to son. "I'm going to go and see what Allison is up to," she said as she stood and walked away.

Zane sat down beside his son. "I have decided not to go back to Zargon at this time."

"But you have to come back," Zinc said. "That is the whole reason we came to Farne."

"Was it? I don't think so, besides you did rescue me from being a slave to the chaka. You are a true hero and I am so proud of you."

"But the people of Zargon expect you to come back and be their King."

"I am sure your sister is doing a good job leading the dragonborn."

"The dragonborn need you. I need you."

"You have proved you can get along without me, but my friends the daga may not be so lucky. They are a gentle peace-loving people who are easily taken advantage of by the wicked. I'm going to stay here to help protect them from the chaka. If I leave it to Zachery I'm afraid they may end up back in slave collars. I want to stay to protect the daga and help Zachery establish a school for the Chosen. You can't argue that Zachery doesn't need my help. I think it's clear he does. He is getting better, but he is still not fully functional. I will be the first teacher at Firehaven. Maybe, once things are established here and the school has other teachers, I will return to Zargon, but I don't think I'll want to be the King again."

"Somebody else can stay and help Zachery do what needs to be done."

"No, the Guardian's rules say every Chosen who comes through the portals to a world not their own must go back when their quest is done. I'm the only one who can stay, because, I didn't come to this world as a Chosen, so the rules do not apply to me. I'm thinking the rules may not apply to Moses either since it seems the Guardian of the Six Worlds intends Farne to be the new home of the brownies. It is a change that is going to be hard for the dragonborn, because we have become quite dependent on the work of brownie servants."

"Brownies should return to Zargon," Zinc mumbled. Not sure as he said those words that he actually still believed them.

"I would agree with you if I hadn't worn a collar and been forced to work as a slave. If I was going back, I would advise my people to treat the brownies well, and some of them might choose to stay on Zargon and continue to serve the dragonborn rather than risk coming to a world they know little about. That is what I would advise them to do if I was going to return and be their King. I would like it if you would do that for me when you go back."

"But to walk away from being King…" Zinc's voice trailed off.

"You know as well as I do that being a King of the Dragonborn is not easy. They must be the most cantankerous people on any of the Six Worlds. I was ready to let go of the throne in frustration a long time ago. The thought of going back does not fill my heart with joy, but staying here to help rebuild this world does. Can I have your blessing, my son? Will you forgive me if I stay here?"

Tears came into Zinc's eyes, but he nodded his head and threw his arms around his father to hug him.

"Zachery has asked me to tell you he is sending the Chosen back to their own worlds tomorrow," Zane said.

Zinc simply nodded his head, not trusting himself to speak.

CHAPTER FIFTY NINE

RETURN TO ZARGON

Mack sat in the great hall surrounded by angry dragonborn. A thick cloud of smoke hung in the air. Sitting beside Mack was Zinc's half-sister, Zanderella, who was acting as Queen of the dragonborn until her father's return.

"It is not just the brownies that are disappearing," a clan leader said. "Other things have gone missing as well. What do either of you know about it?"

Mack and Zanderella stared at each other, each hoping the other had an answer. They were spared finding one when there was a commotion at the back of the room. The cause of the commotion became clear when Zinc and Zoey walked through the crowd to stand in front of them.

"I see you were unable to find the King," Zander, the clan leader standing closest said.

"We rescued him from captivity on Farne, but he chose to stay there and help that world rebuild," Zinc said. "It is my father's will that Zanderella remain the Queen of Zargon for the time being."

A loud voice Zinc recognized as Zilbert, his mother's cousin, broke in. "What! That can't be true. If you couldn't find the King, you should just say so."

Zinc felt the dragonfire within him come to life. Smoke rose above his head to join the cloud that already hung in the air. "I am not a liar," he said loudly.

"He is telling the truth," Zoey said. "We did rescue the King, but he chose to stay. I heard him confirm that Zanderella should continue to lead the dragonborn." With those words Zoey sank down on her knees and bowed her head to Zanderella. Zinc sank down on his knees beside her. The two of them bowed their heads and then rose to stand before Mack and Zanderella.

"I'm glad you've returned," said Zanderella. "I only wish father had come back with you to take back his throne."

"He trusts you to lead the dragonborn, and so do I," Zinc said.

"Thank you," Zanderella said surprise. "It means a lot to me to hear you say that."

"I overheard what was being said. You want to know about the disappearing brownies and I can tell you that those who are missing have gone to Farne," Zinc said loudly.

"How did they get there? Did you send them?" Zilbert asked Mack with a tone that dripped of accusation.

"I have no idea how they got to Farne, I didn't send them through the portal. Can you tell us how brownies ended up on Farne?" Mack asked Zinc.

"The brownie sent to Earth to learn to be a healer," Zinc began, but was shouted down.

"Impossible! Brownies can't be healers."

"This brownie is a healer which is why I sent him to Earth," Mack said.

Again there were shouts of disbelief.

"Quiet, let's hear what my brother has to say," said Queen Zanderella.

"The brownie sent to Earth was chosen by the Guardian to go to Farne," Zinc said.

"Ridiculous, why would a brownie be sent there," said the closest clan leader.

Zinc ignored him and continued on. "Before the brownie left Earth he was given gateways, those gateways were used to move brownies from Zargon to Farne. Some of those brownies ended up being selected by the Guardian to be Chosen."

A roar broke out among the gathered dragonborn. When it quieted down Zilbert spoke. "I have no doubt someone is making up stories about brownies being selected as Chosen, perhaps as an excuse to steal them from their owners. What I want to know is what you can do to get them back." Zilbert directed his final question to Mack.

"The first thing I'll do, is find out whether the Guardian of the Six Worlds was at work," Mack said. "If this is the Guardian's work, then there is nothing I can do. There may be little I could do anyway, if the Watcher of Farne insists on keeping the brownies there."

"Brownies don't belong on Farne. They belong here," Zander said. "You've got to put a stop to this."

"It will stop for now," Zinc said. "The portable gateways were sent back to Earth and returned to the Watcher there."

"So no more brownies will disappear?" Zander asked.

Zinc turned to face the dragonborn leaders. "There will be no more brownies disappearing in the immediate future. However, we need to treat them better or the Guardian may decide to rescue them by making another portable gateway available."

"So, what my brother is saying is this," Zanderella said. "you are the only ones who can stop this from happening again by changing the way you treat the brownies who serve you. You need to stop treating them as slaves who have no rights. I am going to develop a policy statement related to the freedom and protection of Zargon's brownies to be discussed the next time we meet."

All around the room the clan leaders muttered to one another.

Mack stood. "The Chosen and I are leaving. It is time for me to hear about their quest and test them to see when they will next go off world. They will share their story with the rest of you after the evening meal tomorrow."

"When you are finished reporting to the Watcher, come see me, both of you," Zanderella said. "We have much to catch up on and I want to hear how father is."

"Nothing would please me more," Zinc said. As he said the words, Zinc was surprised at how true they were. He really did want to repair his broken relationship with his half-sister.

CHAPTER SIXTY

RETURN TO EARTH

When Ben, Allison and Denzel arrived back on Earth they were taken directly to Miss Templeton's office. Allison gave Miss Templeton the portable gateways she held in her hand.

"So the brownie was sent back to Zargon," Miss Templeton said.

"No, Moses stayed on Farne," Allison said.

"That's not right," Miss Templeton said. "The Chosen should go back to their own worlds."

"It appears the Guardian is doing something new," Allison said, and proceeded to tell Miss Templeton how Moses had brought brownies from Zargon to live on Farne.

"What I don't understand is how brownies, chaka or daga can go to worlds where the people look so very different than they do," Denzel said when Allison finished speaking.

"What makes you think the people on the other worlds look like you?" Miss Templeton asked.

"Are you telling me there are chaka or daga on other worlds?" Denzel asked.

"There are no chaka or daga on other worlds."

"Then how can they actually go to other worlds? They'll stand out like sore thumbs no matter what world they go to."

"The Guardian can do as the Guardian chooses," Miss Templeton said. "Just because Chosen come to Earth and look like us, it doesn't mean they really do. Their true appearance may be something entirely different.

"What do the people look like on non-human worlds?" Denzel asked.

"Perhaps one day you will find out for yourself," Miss Templeton said.

"Are you going to test us today?" Ben asked, wondering what world he would go to next.

"Yes, I always test my Chosen when they have been away on other worlds." Miss Templeton pulled the chain that held her pendant from over her neck and held it over Denzel's hand. The dial spun around and around without coming to a stop.

"It looks like you are going somewhere, sometime," Miss Templeton said, "but at this moment there is no clarity as to when and where.

The same thing happened when Miss Templeton tested Ben and Allison. The dials spun, but did not stop.

"It looks like we are all going off world again," Allison said. "When we do, I hope it is together."

"Me too," Ben said.

"And I hope it will be sooner rather than later," Denzel puts his arms around Ben and Allison's shoulders and drew them close.

"There is one more thing Allison should tell you before we go," Ben said.

"What's that?" Miss Templeton asked.

"I had some unusual experiences," Allison said. "I often just knew things without being told and once I spoke words that were not my own. I am certain the words I spoke were the Guardian's."

Miss Templeton's eyes got large and she sat up straight in her chair. "Could it be…?" she started, and then stopped and stared at Allison. They sat in silence until Ben spoke.

"What does it mean?" Ben asked, with a troubled look on his face. "Is Allison going to be a Watcher?"

"It is too early to say for sure," Miss Templeton said, "but I think we should explore that possibility."

The three friends left Miss Templeton's office and walked to the dining hall where a line up had already formed for the noon meal. They stood at the end of the line and waited. The boy in front of them left to pick up a tray he'd forgotten. When he moved, Allison saw her roommate Crystal standing next to Trevor Robson. Before she'd left for Farne, Trevor had been trying to convince Allison to be his girlfriend again. Now he stood with his arm around Crystal's waist and his mouth close to her ear. Allison didn't know if he was nibbling on her ear or whispering in it. Crystal was leaning against Trevor and stroking his neck.

"Hello Trevor," Allison said. "Have you missed me?"

Trevor jumped like a daga on the hot sands of Farne. One moment he was standing next to Crystal and the next he was three feet away and she was sprawled on the floor.

"Allison, this isn't what it looks like," Trevor said.

"Well this is." Allison grabbed Ben by his shirt and pulled him toward her and kissed him on the lips. When she let go, Ben fell. At first he stared at Allison with a shocked look on his face, but then he smiled and put out his hand so she could help him up.

ABOUT THE AUTHOR

Dianne was once asked what kind of animal she would be, if she could be an animal. The person who asked the question was shocked when Dianne said she'd like to be a dragon. There are times in everyone's life when being able to fly high and breathe fire sound very appealing. However, if you can't be a dragon, or have a dragon as a pet, then the next best thing is to write books with dragons in them and get a dog. Dianne lives in the Pacific Northwest with her husband Doug, his three cats and her beloved dog Thomas. Thomas gets Dianne out walking almost every day, which is the next best thing to flying on dragon wing. Dianne rescued Thomas, but he is rescuing her one walk at a time.